# THE GATHERING OF THE ASPECTS

*Paul-Michel Ratté*

CORMORANT BOOKS

The publisher gratefully acknowledges the support
of the Canada Council and the Ontario Arts Council.

Edited by Gena K. Gorrell.

Cover from William Blake's illustration
for *Macbeth*, entitled 'Pity'.
Cover design by Thom Pritchard, Artcetera Graphics.

Author photo by Jim Quirk.

Printed and bound in Canada.

Cormorant Books Inc.
RR 1
Dunvegan, Ontario
Canada K0C 1J0

Canadian Cataloguing in Publication Data

Ratté, Paul-Michel, 1962-

The gathering of the aspects

ISBN 0-920953-97-2

I. Title.

PS8585.A844G38 1996      C813'.54      C96-900636-5
PR9199.3.R32G38 1996

*To Michelle, Courtney, and Melissa*

# CHAPTER 1

Sophia Dépardieu should never have accepted the call to set up a rendezvous this late in the night, but the offer of twice her usual rate would have been a foolish one to pass up. Nonetheless, she was still apprehensive. Usually street freaks and psychotics phoned at this hour, in the hope of isolating her for a freebie. She imagined her ad in the back pages of *Fleshworks* magazine:

TRIXIE

All fantasies. Heads or tails.

Role-playing. S&M Toys.

Heterosexual only. No multiples.

555-1791

Bordered in bold lines of black and pink, it was the most eye-catching of all the ads in the magazine. It attracted a lot of business. The early years of risk and street soliciting had been very costly to her, physically and emotionally, but with careful money management she had saved her earnings and turned to soliciting through classified ads, getting off the street and exercising a little more control and personal safety in a dangerous lifestyle. Her broad range of sexual services and her use of an answering machine provided both a steady income and a means of screening her clients — to a degree.

So Sophia had returned the call to a Mr. Joseph Langley. On the message he had claimed to be residing at suite 1115 of the Chelsea Excelsior, downtown. This address set her mind somewhat more at ease. The Excelsior was an expensive hotel and catered to the upper echelon. Furthermore, Langley's voice had a calm, intelligent tone that instilled a sense of reassurance. She left a message that she would meet him in the foyer of the Blue Orchid at three a.m.

Sophia paid a monthly rate to keep a one-room apartment on the seventh floor of the Blue Orchid. Nothing fancy, minimally furnished with a queen-sized bed, a television set, and a card table with two chairs. The bathroom was scarcely more than a hole in the wall, with a tub, a rust-stained sink, a medicine cabinet stocked with condoms and mouthwash, a noisy toilet. She never spent the night there.

The small apartment, however, was kept clean. Cleaner than the dump deserved: the room always aired and dusted, and crisp linens (always smelling faintly of Javex) placed on the mattress and pillows. It served well for business, and preserved the sanctuary of her real home.

Sophia glanced at her bare wrist and cursed herself for forgetting her watch. She pushed open the hand-painted glass door, stepping out of the warm foyer to check the street for Mr. Langley's approach. No one. The wind was cold and swirled up beneath her short skirt, forcing her knees to clamp tightly together.

Why the hell did I bother to accept, Sophia asked herself. She wasn't dressed for this kind of weather, but Mr. Langley's message had requested "a cheap, dirty look". Her own fucking fault. The more variety offered, the greater the personal sacrifice; it was a downside to the life, and one she hated.

She stepped back inside the foyer to wait. Fifteen minutes, she promised herself, standing above the warm-air register. The forced air rubbed against her calves and up her thighs. Sophia closed her eyes and enjoyed this tiny luxury. Leaning her head against the graffiti'd and knife-etched wall, she could easily fall asleep standing up. Fatigue was trickling down her muscles, weighing them down. Her shoulder drooped slightly, allowing her purse to fall with a thud at her feet, startling her awake. As she bent over to pick it up, her eye caught a dusting of snow falling from a disturbance outside and above the door.

Curiosity and boredom drew her back out into the cold morning darkness. She looked up.

"Oh, there you are —" A smile spread across her painted mouth. "Come on. Come on down," she called gently, as she reached into her purse. She made soft, inviting, kissing sounds. In her hand was a small white paper bag that she shook in a coaxing manner; its contents made a light, dry, shuffling noise. "Come on. It's me. Come on come on come on."

The sound of approaching feet distracted her from her interests above the doorway. "Finally," she whispered. She quickly placed the paper bag back into her purse and snapped it shut. A man was quickly walking towards her.

The man was hatless and had his face buried for warmth inside the collar of his long overcoat. As he drew nearer, Sophia observed that the coat was not of the sort businessmen wore, and that he was younger than Langley's voice had sounded; this man was in his late twenties, early thirties, with a shock of mousy brown hair. She had expected Langley to be in his mid-forties, at the very least.

This man's gait was quick-paced; he was anxious to reach his destination. This wasn't Langley. This guy's going right on by, Sophia thought to herself. Damn it all.

As the man crossed in front of her, she called out to him, asking if he knew the time. Judging from his expression, she must have startled him. He stopped abruptly and took in her statuesque form, squinting slightly through his wire-rimmed glasses, trying to make out her face in the poor light. He apologized and said he didn't know exactly what time it was, but figured it was some time after three.

There was a moment of awkwardness, and Sophia noticed that the man was jostling the weight of something in his hand. A couple of books.

He proceeded down the darkened street, the sound of his shoes diminishing, fading further as he passed each streetlamp.

7

She felt lonesome suddenly — in a stupid sort of way — when she could no longer hear the only human indication that had been audible in this empty street.

Shit, where the hell was Langley? She strained her ears to pick up a sound, any sound. Except for the deep and distant gurgle of sewer water somewhere under the street, she could hear nothing.

Her teeth were beginning to chatter but, try as she might to persuade herself to go home, the lure of double her usual rate kept her firmly rooted. Tonight had been very slow — one call. A full-body oil massage with a hand job.

All evening a fine, dry snow had been falling intermittently. Once again it had begun falling from the black above, like flecks of platinum in the glow of the streetlamp. She took a step away from the glass doors to see if the man with the books was still in sight. From the middle of the sidewalk, she thought she could make out the silhouette of a man in front of a store window; but the streetlamp there was burnt out and only a dull grey light from the storefront illuminated that section of the pavement. She moved her head slightly to focus properly, but the distance, the absence of light, and the talc-like snow made it hard to tell if anyone was really there.

Sophia shook her head and wrapped her arms around herself in a warming embrace — Where are you, Langley? Turning back to the warmth of the Blue Orchid's foyer, she saw the huddled source of the fallen snow she had come out to investigate, perched above the door. Again she reached into her purse and extracted the small paper bag, and poured its contents onto the sidewalk.

In a silence infinitely more beautiful to her than the arid snow, a small flock of street pigeons fluttered to her feet to peck at a handful of stale pink popcorn.

Through the hazy film of finger smudges and other human contacts with the glass door of the Blue Orchid, Sophia watched the pigeons feed. The throaty cooing of their contentment could be heard in the foyer.

She recognized these birds. They were part of a larger flock that lived in the crevices, ledges, chimneys, and gutters of this street. She wondered where the rest of the flock was, and why these particular strays were still about. It was unusual to see pigeons active at this hour of the morning. Wasn't it?

Regardless, Sophia was pleased to see them. They reminded her of the pigeons that had congregated around the grain-bins on her papa's farm in north-western Quebec when she was a little girl. With her baby sister, Joelle, in tow, she would steal away to walk the fence-lines and follow the pigeons through the fields to engage in mutual play, a sort of ritual. Chasing the flock into the wind just to watch them rise, again and again, against the summer skies. Out past the reedy green pond and then all the way back to the grain-bins, where she and Joelle would sit on a haywagon, breathless, to watch their pigeons feed on scattered bits of corn, soybean, and barley.

Of all the birds around the farm, the pigeons were her favourites. They held the bounty of God's glory in their mottled plumage. So regal in tones of gun-metal grey, white, and copper. Wings and tails banded and speckled — no two alike — when fanned in flight. And their smooth heads reflected the tiniest particles of light with iridescences of gold, green, purple, and bronze. No other bird could match their grandeur.

The white chickens, ugly with bald patches, were noisy and stupid, incapable of translating wind and space into flight as they nervously passed their days scratching in the dust of the barnyard, while the brown hawks that patrolled Papa's fields with killing yellow eyes were too distant and remote to be God-like. And the barn swallows living in their tiny mud cups in the beams of the barn were beautiful, all sleek metallic blue, but despite their proximity they appeared too self-absorbed in their aerial acrobatics to want any part of the human world.

Sophia found herself smiling as she watched this small

gathering of street pigeons plump themselves on her offering of popcorn. Even now, as an adult, so far removed from the dreamy poetry of her youth, she felt a genuine love for these pigeons on the other side of the dirty glass. They were still beautiful to her. Although they were stripped of all the divinity bestowed upon them by the grace of a child's imagination, there still remained a stain of piety; for she wanted it to be so. She needed it to be so.

# CHAPTER 2

After the polite rapping, the dressing-room door swung open slowly. And a voice seeped in through the space: "The singers have almost finished their number . . . you're on in one minute, Reverend."

No sound came from within. The stagehand sent to summon Lucius Del Roberts back on stage peered into the dressing-room. "Reverend . . . ?"

The evangelist's back was hunched over his dressing-table and his shirt was plastered to his back. On the floor were scattered pages of lined paper covered in erratic scrawl. The stagehand removed his headset and took two steps to stand almost beside the reverend.

Roberts stopped writing and clenched his pen with a whitening fist; his head snapped around, eyes burning. "Another set," he hissed.

"What?"

"Another set! Have the choir do another set!"

"But, Reverend," said the stagehand, recoiling. "They aren't — we aren't — prepared! What hymns will they do?"

Roberts rose from his chair. "Improvise, you stupid shit!"

The stagehand backed into the edge of the partially opened door, giving way to a flash of panic. "But . . . what about the format . . . ? The script . . . ?"

Through clenched teeth, Roberts repeated, "Improvise!"

As he exited, the stagehand put the headset back on with fumbling hands. "Jimmy! Jimmy! Cut to a station break! Hurry! Cue up the conductor, orchestra, and choir! We gotta stretch it!"

The reverend stood alone in his dressing-room. He could vaguely hear the commotion down the hall, as he turned back to the dressing-table and the piece of paper. He looked at the mess on the floor, at all those crazily marked papers, and sat himself down hard and closed his eyes.

Blackness, blackness, blackness. Even this tiny peace seemed forbidden; his memory suddenly twitched. I wonder if maintenance swept up today's birds, he asked himself. Jesus, did they check the eavestroughs? The gutters?

All at once he began to shake. With a gesture like reluctant obedience, he felt for his pen again and centred the paper. His grip upon the pen tightened, causing his hand to quiver. His eyes burst open and his hand once more produced the spastic penmanship. He gasped.

The orchestra began to play the first strains of "The Old Rugged Cross", as Roberts sniffed back a tiny trickle of blood running from his nose.

There was just enough time to rinse off in the shower, put on a fresh shirt, and comb his hair. He raced to the edge of the vast white stage, panting.

Roberts stood waiting to be cued while assistants hastily made up his face, adjusted the knot in his tie, and placed a tiny earphone that curled around his ear. He checked his heavy Rolex. Almost two a.m. In six more hours the campaign would be over. It would all be over. Everything he had worked for.

After this telecast, Lucius Del Roberts was walking away from the multimillion-dollar ministry he had built. Just dropping the whole thing, praying he could escape unscarred.

Another assistant attached a tiny cordless mike to Roberts' shirt as the choir finished the last hymn of the impromptu set. She smoothed his shirtfront and tie and looked into his face. "Are you okay?" she asked.

Roberts half-nodded. There was a long silence out there . . . out in the sanctity past the stage exit. It crouched low, as if waiting to pounce.

What now, the reverend wondered. What will it be now?

The assistant put her hand to her earphone, listening. She peered out quickly to catch the director's frantic hand signals. "Reverend, please! We're rolling dead air . . . !"

Roberts stood frozen.

The entire technical crew waited breathlessly. Sound men, lighting crew, camera men, stagehands, and directors, all had their hands poised on their respective back-ups. Waiting.

The assistant, standing with Roberts, was just shrugging her shoulders at the director, gesturing I don't know, when the reverend finally stepped out into the light of the white stage.

Roberts walked past the columns of white marble to the golden pulpit at centre stage. All cameras followed his every move, waiting. He stood at the pulpit and gingerly fingered the worn leather cover of the Bible resting there. He opened the old book. The sound of the flittering pages came through his chest mike, filling the Cathedral of Light. It was that silent. The audience of over twelve thousand sat motionless, perfectly hushed.

The reverend closed the Bible with a slam that echoed throughout. He gazed up through the domed ceiling of glass into the dark morning sky, raised his hands, and said, "What have I done?" Some of the audience nodded with their own interpretations of his utterance.

He walked out from behind the pulpit to the edge of the stage with his head bowed. Hands on his hips, he looked up and scanned the sea of faces staring back at him. "WHAT HAVE I DONE?"

Silence.

Then a single voice spoke from the congregation: "You've spread th' Word." The voice was small, wherever it came from. Many more heads nodded emphatically.

Roberts covered his face with his hands and stood silent. When he lowered his hands, his face registered blankness.

"Lower a boom mike," he instructed. "Right here in front of the stage. I want the people to speak this morning. I want to hear from them."

The director signalled for a boom to be plugged in and wheeled to the foot of the centre aisle. He transmitted into Roberts' hidden earphone: "What the hell are you doing?"

Roberts paced the stage while everything was being set up. "The format," he could hear the director urge into his ear, "follow the goddamn format!" Ignoring the plea, Roberts extended his arm in the general direction of the voice in the congregation. "You," he called out. "Come down here and speak with me." His tone clearly betrayed urgency. "Please," he persisted. "I feel . . ." The reverend closed his eyes. "I feel so alone up here."

After a few moments, a man stood up. Two cameras swung around and followed his way down to the boom. Roberts watched the man approach. As the man neared the stage, the reverend recognized his type — knew what he was: the "targeted audience". He watched this simple man look up at the synthetic glory of God with awe.

Roberts came to the edge of the stage. "Thank you for coming down, sir. What, may I ask, is your name?"

The man beneath the boom mike pushed up his crooked glasses and opened his mouth, but some sound way back in the cathedral distorted his response. Roberts cleared his throat and apologized, asking the man to repeat his name. As the man did so, the sound happened again — only louder. Roberts shielded his eyes from the powerful stage lights and looked up, trying to see into the darkened recesses of the cathedral.

The director stood confused, gesturing towards Roberts on stage. "What the fuck is he doing now? This fellow is trying to tell him his name and Roberts is ignoring him!"

The man beneath the boom waved his hand meekly, trying to get the reverend's attention. But Roberts kept looking towards the back of the cathedral.

The director held his small headset mike close to his mouth.

14

"Roberts!" he whispered angrily. "What is the matter with you?"

Roberts couldn't hear the director's comments in his earphone; in fact, he couldn't hear anything except the sound that was intensifying in the back of the cathedral. The sound, which initially had been more of an abrupt disturbance, like something moving about, suddenly took on a rhythm, the recognizable cadence of a horse in step. Roberts' eyes grew wide. From the deep shadows of the back rows, a black horse trotted down the centre aisle, led by a small child.

The great black beast came down the aisle pounding its large hoofs, tossing its mane impatiently. The child, a young girl wearing a simple white dress, walked casually to stop just behind the man at the boom. The horse raised its black head, ears back, and snorted angrily.

Roberts, who had been standing in growing horror as the two spectres approached, reeled back a few feet on stage. He cried, "WHO ARE YOU?"

"I bin tryin' t'tell ya. Th' name's Wendyl," said the man beneath the boom. "You awright, Rev'r'nd?"

Roberts swallowed. In his ear he heard the director say that they were going to stop broadcasting and feign technical difficulties. "No! I'm fine! I'm fine!" Roberts shouted.

The horse and child stared at him.

"Well, y'sure look spook'd t'me," replied Wendyl.

They still don't see them, thought Roberts. Never do. Each time . . . during each broadcast . . . coming on stronger. Wilder. Closer. More threatening.

"Y'want I should sit back down?" asked Wendyl.

Roberts' gaze remained fixed past Wendyl's head, staring back at the two apparitions.

Wendyl looked directly behind himself, then into the confused faces of the nearby audience members. He cast one last glance at Roberts and made for his seat.

Without taking his eyes off the black beast and child, the reverend said, "Don't leave me!" Wendyl stopped and turned,

15

startled by his tone. "I . . . I . . . Don't go, sir," said Roberts with forced control, his eyes finally locking onto Wendyl's. "Come on back to the mike. Speak your mind."

Wendyl sheepishly walked back under the boom and adjusted his glasses. "I dunno," he said, shrugging his shoulders.

Roberts cleared his throat. Smiled. "Big chance here . . . um . . . Wendyl, right? Well, Wendyl, what would you like to say to me? The floor is all yours, sir."

Wendyl looked down at his feet and mumbled something.

"What was that, Wendyl? The congregation couldn't hear you. Speak up. Don't be shy. Go on."

Raising his head slightly, Wendyl spoke flatly: "Wanna say, great thing yer doin' here, Rev'r'nd. Fer alla us."

There it was. The Hook: "Fer alla us." Roberts drew it in like oxygen. It was the hearing of it. The reminder of it. The knowledge of it. Their vulnerability. Their need. His power.

Roberts came alive like a wind-kissed spark. Something within him put on dark armour and took up arms. His face creased with a smile and he shot a glance over Wendyl's shoulder that made the horse paw the aisle and shake its head. The little girl lowered her eyes.

They won't have it, he thought. I won't let them. Whatever the fuck these things are, they can't take me. Can't take my empire. Can't take my followers. I'll stand.

"Yer fightin' th' good fight, Rev'r'nd," continued Wendyl.

"The good fight?" Roberts' eyebrow arched.

"'Ginst evil, a'course."

The reverend nodded. He gestured with a wide sweep of his hand. "Tell the people, Wendyl. Tell them all why you think so."

Wendyl snorted goofily. Shook his head, then spoke matter-of-factly: "Look round ya, Rev'r'nd. Would ya have all this goin' fer ya, if ya weren't?"

Stupid fool, thought Roberts. "Tell me, Wendyl," he said. "Could you tell evil if you saw it?"

The horse bared its teeth and snorted wildly. The small girl stood quietly.

Wendyl pushed up his glasses and shrugged again. "Sure. Sure I could."

Roberts looked out into the congregation, scanning them. Then, turning his gaze back to Wendyl, he asked, "What's it look like? Where's it come from? We all know it's out there, don't we? Live with it every day. Read about it in our morning paper with a cup of coffee. Maybe even exercise a little bit of it ourselves, in our thoughts and our deeds, but it's so small we hardly notice, do we? Or do we? For the most part, we think evil lives elsewhere. Away from us. It lives in the dope deals; in the drive-by shootings; in the war-torn villages of places we've never heard of before. Evil lives . . . OUT THERE. . . ."

The congregation sat silent.

The director began to feel a little more at ease, thinking: It's falling back in line. Roberts is rolling.

Roberts began to stalk the length of the stage. "You know, evil lies much closer to home than we often want to accept. It's in our pores. It's in the air we breathe, people. IT IS WITHIN, IT IS WITHOUT!"

The congregation stirred.

"In our fallen state," Roberts pressed on, fist clenched, "evil is woven into the very tapestry of our souls. Many of you good people — and I see you out there! I know who you are, how you live! — TRY to remove this irregularity from your tapestries, to improve the depth and texture of the design! But it can't be cut out. It can't be unravelled. It is a permanent stitch in the design, good people. IT CANNOT BE REMOVED!" Roberts continued to pace. Removed a white handkerchief from his pocket; dabbed his shining brow and wiped his mouth before going on. "All we can do," he said in a cautionary tone, "is try and weave around it with a better stitch."

Wendyl half-raised his hand. "Rev'r'nd?"

"Yes, Wendyl . . ."

"What if ya can't remember th' pattern fer th' design?"

Pretty pointed for a fucking hick, thought Roberts, dabbing his wet face again. Smiling warmly, he answered, "That's what I'm here for, Wendyl."

"Amen, Rev'r'nd."

## CHAPTER 3

It was as if the blackness were pressing against the glass. The night trying to force itself in. He placed his hand on the wall, beside the window-frame, almost expecting the wall to swell with the threat of implosion. It could have been like any other night. Should have been. But tonight, the taking notice of it, gnawed like a cancer.

He smiled nervously in spite of himself. Just fatigue, he reminded himself. It's just fatigue. But as he removed his hand from the wall, it trembled. "God Almighty. . . ."

Still snowing. Falling gently, silently. Deceptively. There is nothing peaceful about snow. Winter is a season not of rest but of spiritual ague. Snow comes first, and with it anxiety, as the planet slowly succumbs and sleeps the deeper sleep.

Thomas Gorgon rubbed his burning eyes in defeat. There is no point in romanticizing that which isn't romantic, he thought, returning his gaze to the book in his lap. For the past seven hours, Thomas had been trying to glean some measure of inspiration from the snow that fell beyond the thin pane of glass that separated him from the night.

He continued to thumb through the dog-eared copy of T.S. Eliot's Selected Poems. In less than forty-eight hours a complete syllabus was expected on the dean's desk, outlining Thomas's intentions for a new college course he called "THE BALD CRY — Postmodernism and Poetics"; it was slated for next spring semester. He had barely chosen the poets to be analysed, let alone the poems; something made the task at hand less than pressing, despite the impending deadline.

For weeks Thomas had been distracted, irritable, and utterly without focus with regard to his work. This change in his personal and professional demeanour seemed to have occurred at about the same time the dreams began.

The dreams. Night after night, bizarre images and scenarios flashed in his mind. Just recently, in the past week, there had been the trek through a desert where swarming insects churned sand into the hot air, swelling the tongue to choking; then there had been the figure of a corpse buried beneath a pile of wet, black leaves on endless train-tracks, beneath a dark sky; and the Down's syndrome child running on a treadmill, whipped with a riding crop by a pretty girl in a party dress. . . .

And so it was for Thomas Gorgon, night after night. Crazy images, more curious than frightening; awakening him, making the balance of his sleep restless. A sleeping pill could have probably remedied this annoyance, except that the dreams had stopped being dreams and had become something else. This thing was different from the dreams. This thing was building in layers within his mind — sharpening, intensifying, with each recurrence. It was something in the process of becoming. But the truly terrifying part was that Thomas Gorgon's mind was becoming saturated with something that carried the weight of the revelatory. It was as if his mind were trying to reveal itself *to itself*. Thomas clearly remembered how the horror had begun with the sound of their cries. . . .

He riffled the cool pages beneath the pad of his thumb, read the familiar verse — *hollow men, stuffed men* — and felt nothing. He reached across the desk and turned off the desk light, enveloping the room in darkness. He cocked his head back and plopped the ratty Faber & Faber on his face, drawing the rich, musty smell of shelf dust and old pages into his nostrils. He rocked gently in his chair, listening to it creak. His chest swelled as he drew deeper and deeper breaths. Slowly he began to lull himself into much-needed sleep. He stretched his arms out wide and curled them into a delicious warming flex — and he was startled by a sound. He sat bolt upright in his chair, sending the book flying off his face. "Holy shit!" he gasped.

Immediately he shielded his eyes from an excruciatingly painful whiteness that had altered the entire room. He rose from his chair, still covering his eyes with the backs of his hands; staggered for a couple of steps and warily eased his hands from his face. As his eyes adjusted, he realized that the whiteness was not emanating from a light source of any kind. The entire room had simply become white. And furthermore, gone were the usual trappings of his study; completely vanished were his desk and chair, his bookshelves, and all the effects on the walls. Thomas suddenly found himself in a contained white void.

Dumbfounded, he moved in tight concentric circles, taking in the metamorphosis that had negated his study, all the while trying to control his frantic gasps for breath. He moved cautiously to the nearest wall and with great trepidation placed his palm on the pristine surface. His hand recoiled, but unnecessarily; the wall was cool and smooth. He then placed both hands on the whiteness and scanned the surface. The built-up protective lining of his study was gone — the once safe, familiar sanctuary was now threatening him with perfectly seamless entrapment. He backed towards the centre of the room again and ran his fingers through his hair. His hairline was matted and cold with sweat.

What the fuck gives, he was asking himself, when again he heard the sound. It came from behind him.

Thomas stopped breathing. His heart was thundering in his ears when he turned to face the source of the sound. And there on the floor were five naked infants. Two boys and three girls; all pink and blue-eyed with dimpled elbows and knees, happily gurgling and moving their arms and legs about with newness.

Thomas stepped back from the infants in fear. He abruptly hit the wall and slid himself down into a corner, bringing his knees to his chin. "Jesus, not again. . . ." He squeezed shut his eyes and screamed into his kneecaps, shaking with horror.

When he reopened his eyes, Thomas saw that his outburst had not alarmed the babies. In fact, they appeared to be perfectly content and unaware of his presence. Just like all the other times.

Back again. What is with these fucking babies, he asked himself. Where the hell do they come from? What do they want from me? And what's happened to my house? His mind was frenzied as he tried to make sense of these events. Each visitation became more intimate, more confrontational; but this was the first time all the different babies had appeared together.

He continued to stare at the five infants from where he sat on the floor, rocking. They continued to appear unaware of him, staring about themselves in awe.

Unlocking his fingers from his knees, he abruptly clapped his hands, hoping that the sound might prompt the babies to some normal reaction: crying or head-turning or anything remotely human. But they still showed no reaction. He then decided that direct physical contact might evoke an acknowledgement.

Slowly he crept towards the child closest to him, a little girl. She had her legs up and was amusing herself watching her toes wiggle. Thomas was within inches of the baby girl when he noticed the expression on her tiny face change. Her blue eyes blinked sharply, as if she was startled, and her mouth opened in a silent cry. He got off his hands and sat back on his heels. The four other babies were also beginning to show a negative reaction to something. All of them had stopped smiling and were starting to cry, wrinkling their faces as little tears welled in their eyes.

Initially, Thomas thought his encroachment was the cause of the babies crying — until he witnessed, in absolute horror, their tiny limbs ignite in flame. The infants thrashed wildly on the white floor, screaming in anguish as their soft bodies burned. Thomas tried to lunge forward to save them, but his body would not respond; his muscles had seized. He was paralysed. He watched as the babies' skins peeled away, exposing twitching muscle; watched their silky fine hair burn; watched their eyes roll back in their sockets; watched hot black blood trickle from their ears and noses.

With all the strength he could muster, Thomas jerked back his head and screamed in despair, causing the volume of *Selected Poems* to slide off his face and tumble down his chest onto the floor. He winced from the pain in his neck as he straightened his head forward. "Shit. . . !"

Thomas gasped as he looked out his window into the night. Beads of sweat became heavy and trickled down his forehead and temples. None of the previous nightmares had suggested the arrival of these visions. These babies were more than just dreams, more than just shocking images — the questions that plagued his waking hours were: How? And why?

It was still snowing. Thomas turned the desk light back on, filling his study with warm soft light. He bent over and picked up the book that had fallen under his desk; it had landed on its pages, like a weak tent. Inserting his thumb into the open pages, he flipped the book over to read the last verse of "The Hollow Men", and muttered nervously, "Some whimper."

He closed the book and placed it on his desk. He gazed at the snow trying to penetrate the pane of glass, and thought to himself: No point in romanticizing. . . .

## Chapter 4

A wind meandered up the street gathering candy wrappers, cigarette butts, and a couple of full-length newspaper pages that seemed to dance and twirl together in a spastic pas de deux. The wind paused momentarily in front of the Blue Orchid, causing the pigeons gathered there to puff their breast feathers as it whipped the street garbage into a wintry cyclone.

The stale, warm air had been lulling Sophia into deep, nodding periods of sleep. Exactly how long she had been drifting off she could not tell, but her mouth was gummy with an off-taste, and her tired eyes tended to slip out of focus — when they were open. She ran her red nails through her hair, sighing with finality, "This is bullshit."

She took a single step towards the door and noticed that the pigeons were huddled together tightly, heads bobbing in all directions. Spooked. Her eyes darted up to see the shadowy silhouette of a man. Langley? Had to be.

The man stood motionless. She wondered how long he had been standing there. Was he watching her? He cut a large and striking form in the darkness. She backed away from the doorway and awaited his approach.

When he finally drew closer, the light from within the foyer revealed a stout, well-groomed man in his mid to late forties. He was clad in a heavy, dark trench-style coat of fine wool and on his head was a black wide-brimmed hat. In his hand was a leather briefcase.

As he approached the glass door, the pigeons exploded into flight with a loud drumming of wings and the empty street was filled, suddenly, with the sound of escape.

The large man entered the foyer accompanied by a swirling cloak of frozen air. He removed his hat and stomped his western-style boots. "Trixie, I assume?" His voice was deep and strong.

Sophia nodded. "You're very late, Mr. Langley."

He smiled warmly. His face was inviting and intelligent. "I'm sorry. I am fully prepared to compensate you with . . . shall we say, a bonus, on top of your promised double rate." Langley put his briefcase down and placed his hat on it, then proceeded to undo the buttons of his long coat. He glanced about the walls and ceiling of the foyer.

She was annoyed that Langley hadn't offered any kind of excuse for his tardiness, but her annoyance and fatigue were quickly fading. After all, he had finally shown up; he was, if not outright handsome, attractive in his confident carriage; and further, he radiated a conspicuous aura suggesting that he could make good on the double rate.

Sophia gestured towards the staircase. "Shall we, then?"

He picked up his hat and briefcase and nodded his approval, and gestured for her to lead.

She began mounting the staircase with her back to him. "There's no elevator in this building, so you're gonna have to tough it up seven flights." She smiled jokingly as she added, "Hope this won't wear you out."

If Sophia Dépardieu had turned around, she would have noticed the nervous tic developing on Langley's face.

**You've chosen well, Azrael.**

For three flights of stairs there were no words spoken. On the landing of the fourth floor, she asked Langley if he had the time.

He stretched his arm out to expose a heavy gold watch. "Seven minutes after four. Tuesday the twenty-sixth."

"The twenty-sixth!" she gasped. "Mon Dieu . . . I almost forgot . . . chère Joelle." She stood frozen on the landing.

25

"Are you all right?" asked Langley, trying to catch her eye.

She continued to stare in rumination. "Yes. . . ."

"You're French. Québécoise?"

She blinked hard. She turned to face his smile. "What did you say? I'm sorry. . . . I . . ."

"There's very little trace of an accent," he said.

"Excuse me?"

"I was just commenting on how well you speak English. I couldn't help but notice that you speak with a French lilt." He gently touched her arm. "Are you all right? You look a little disturbed."

"No. I'm fine."

Langley nodded politely. "Couple more flights, then?"

"Yes," she said distantly. "Not much farther."

As they proceeded up the staircase, the sounds of a rumbling farm tractor, Bébé Joelle's carefree squeals, and a father's reminder filled her innermost ear, saturating her mind with gloom.

Her memory tumbled end over end through a vacuum and landed at that dark, familiar moment in time thirty-three years ago, when a soft summer breeze was blowing, carrying the sweet smell of alfalfa, timothy, and red clover, and the threat of rain.

The sky was pale, marred only by a couple of distant clouds that looked like horse's manes.

Her father, Ezra Dépardieu, a tall, leathered man with wide, dark eyes, had pulled his ageing tractor and hay-bailer into the barnyard. The rebuilt iron workhorse coughed violently as it sat parked in front of the Quonset. The chickens flapped their useless wings at this noisy intrusion and regathered a few feet away.

Ezra jumped off the tractor, looking around for his two daughters. Forever impatient and agitated, he called out in a voice entangled with barbed wire, "Sophia! Sophia!"

The two sisters were picking the wildflowers that grew between the Quonset and the grain-bins. Upon hearing her name,

26

the eldest daughter grabbed her baby sister's hand and spoke in a guardian tone: "Joelle, Papa's calling me. You wait here. I'll be right back. Don't move from here, okay?" The two-year-old looked up, smiling, hands full of daisies, flax, and buttercups. "Understand, Joelle? Stay here."

Sophia ran to the mouth of the steel Quonset. Her heart was pounding. Papa was angry again.

The battered tractor convulsed. Ezra stood cursing, looking to the skies.

"Yes, Papa?" asked Sophia.

"Where the hell were you?" Ezra snapped. "And where's your little sister?"

"Just back there," said Sophia meekly, gesturing behind the Quonset.

Ezra's eyes blazed. The lines in his brown face were deep and menacing. "Rain's coming. Soon. I can smell it in the air." He removed his greasy cap and wiped his brow with a handkerchief. "I've got to try and fix this piece of junk and finish off the west field."

A cooler breeze brushed Sophia's arm, and stirred the dust in the barnyard.

"Feed your sister some lunch. I won't be coming up," Ezra said, turning away into the Quonset. From deep within the structure, a cavernous order bellowed out to the young girl: "AND BE SURE TO HAVE SUPPER READY FOR TONIGHT!"

"Yes, Papa," she replied sadly.


It seemed longer than two years since her father had changed. Ezra Dépardieu had always been a stern man — made hard and tired from spending his life chasing the season, living on a shoestring budget, working the land of his ancestors alone, without sons. But the bitterness that now blackened his heart had been brought on by the death of his beloved wife, Medora.

She had died in bloody premature labour, bringing Joelle into the world. The child, Medora had told Ezra, she prayed to

God would be a strong son. For she knew her husband needed this pragmatic miracle.

"It'll be a boy. A fine boy, Ezra," she would whisper, placing his thick hand upon her stomach. "I speak to God every night and I tell Him how badly we need a son. I know He hears me, Ezra. I know He will bless us with a beautiful baby boy."

Ezra loved his wife. She was the finest woman he had ever known. And all he had ever wanted out of life was to put a smile on her face through the good work of his hands. To work his fields and cows for the singular glory of Medora's happiness.

However, it was not to be. Ezra's dreams began to wither on the day his father, Émile, died in his sleep. That day marked the beginning of Ezra's living death, as his dying hopes cast dark seeds into his heart and mind.

From then on, with Émile dwelling in a brighter Eden, Ezra's vision of paradise here on earth gradually became distorted. His first baby girl, Sophia, was no longer a blessing to his eclipsed mind; she was a misfortune. A liability.

In his subconscious, a maddening clock had begun to tick. Fear and uncertainty made the whole of Ezra's world into cogs and wheels. The universe became a vast mechanism measuring and anticipating the expiration of his tenure. Ezra saw it everywhere. It was in the rise and fall of the day's sun, the birth and death of the livestock, the seeding and harvesting of the crops, the changing of the seasons. Ezra perceived it all spilling out at an incredible rate. The passing of time became a foe, each elapsed second taunting him with the inevitability of his failure as a farmer. Each passing day saw him withdraw deeper and deeper into some kind of darkness, avoiding the loving faces of his wife and daughter, afraid to see the futility of his efforts mirrored in their eyes.

Ezra's pride forbade him to admit that he could not single-handedly run the entire farm. Slowly, the once neat and picturesque little property became shoddy: the buildings and roofs needed mending and painting; the cattle were forever filthy; the dung was piled high; sowing and harvesting were always running late; the equipment became worn from lack of diligent maintenance.

In a few short months Ezra became gaunt and sickly, working from four in the morning until ten or eleven at night. His failing health made it necessary to downscale the operation. He rented out the fields he and his father had once worked to the neighbouring farmers. He sold off over half his herd.

La Ferme Dépardieu & Fils had been reduced to a skeleton operation, barely subsisting. This ate away at Ezra's soul. But the morning Medora finally convinced Ezra that she had to do her share of the work wounded his pride and buckled his self-esteem.

Ghostly with exhaustion, Ezra slept too deeply that day to be awakened. Medora kissed his pale face and walked to the barn, cleaned out the manure, then fed and milked the thirty-five cows. She returned to the house at six-thirty, as the sun was starting to rise. She perked a pot of strong coffee and began to prepare some breakfast.

The sounds from the kitchen stirred Ezra, startling him from his stupor. In all the years he had lived with Medora, he had never been in the house to hear the sounds of breakfast being prepared.

He arose abruptly, his head reeling, and slowly made his way downstairs to confront his wife.

And she was waiting for him.

Ezra's eyes were wild. "Goddamnit, Medora! The fucking sun is up! Why didn't you get me up?"

He had never spoken to her that way before.

Medora set her jaw and stepped up to him, and her hand connected with his face. "Don't you blaspheme in this house, Ezra Dépardieu," she hissed. "And don't you ever use that tone of voice with me."

She could see the anger melting from his face.

"But Medora..."

29

"You're no good to me or Sophia if you're dead."

It was then that he noticed the smell of cattle on her person, and saw the cuffs of her sleeves soiled and covered in cow-hairs.

"What have you done, Medora?" he asked, his hands spreading in an empty gesture.

"Only what needed to be done," she replied firmly. "You can't go on this way, Ezra. From now on we share the work around here." And with that she returned to the stove to tend the eggs snapping and popping in the skillet.

Ezra stood in the kitchen, stunned. His eyes began to well up and burn with his sense of defeat, and with the warmth of love that radiated from his beautiful wife.

From then on things were different. Medora would work in the barn, milking and feeding, while Ezra worked the fields. And slowly he regained his physical health.

But there were other changes too.

Medora became pregnant in the grey days of February. She continued to rise before the sun and do her chores in the barn, even as her womb began to round out. She remained happy with her lot in life.

But at the same time something black was growing inside Ezra. Something he hated, something he kept hidden from Medora. Something spawned in his own soul, and fed by self-loathing.

All day he would work the soil or repair machinery and buildings, hiding his ugliness. Eventually the small farm was restored to a level of respectability. But the restoration was just a veneer. It was a thin coating that contained something seething — something sad and dark, that Medora had never imagined could be a consequence of unconditional love.

In late November, when Medora was full and awkward in her ninth month, tragedy struck.

It began on a morning like any other. Ezra had risen even earlier than usual to finish combining the last of the corn that stood dry and brown in the frozen fields. Medora rose at four-thirty. She got dressed and checked on Sophia sleeping peacefully under a heavy layer of blankets and quilts. She locked the house and pocketed the key. The walk to the barn was black and cold, and the earth felt hard beneath her boots. Her chores were carried out in a happily mundane fashion. She could no longer rush the job, in her condition; everything had to be done with subservience to nature's transformation of her body. But she didn't see this as an inconvenience. Bowing to nature was a farmer's lifestyle, a farmer's wisdom.

Medora strapped the milking stool uncomfortably beneath her womb, fired up the vacuum pump, and waddled, with two milkers and a washpail in hand, to her first pair of cows. She watched the milk being drawn into the clear plastic reservoir bowls hanging beneath the udders. When the steel and rubber fingers had finished drawing milk, she proceeded to the next pair of cows, to wash their teats in preparation for the milker.

Gently she squatted between the two cows, easing her weight onto her milking stool. She dipped a paper towel in the warm water and began to wash and massage the next cow's udder and teats.

She didn't notice the painful swelling of mastitis that had inflamed the back of the udder she was washing. As she tugged on the teat of the inflamed area, expelling a thick, yoghurty discharge, the cow swung out sharply with its hind hoof, connecting with Medora's belly.

Medora was hurled backwards onto the cement aisle, landing in a puddle of urine. The cow pawed her stall in agitation, shaking her large head.

Medora unstrapped the milking stool and painfully crawled to a pile of clean straw against the wall. She pulled up her skirt and tore away the crotch of her heavy leggings, which were already wet and bloody.

"Mon Seigneur . . . !" she cried. She placed a hand between her legs and felt the warm flow of fluid. A sharp pain surged through her body, forcing her to bear down.

"Oh, Mon Seigneur . . . ," she repeated in agony, over and over. To give birth all alone in a filthy barn — she was terrified.

She pulled off her heavy cardigan and spread it between her legs. Another wave of pain flooded her mind. She screamed and clamped her teeth tightly, and she pushed.

As the first rays of sun seeped into the barn, her agonizing labour continued. All the while, she was crying out for her husband and praying to her God, whom she could not understand at this time, but still turned to.

In the final pushes, as the tiny, wet head emerged, Medora grabbed handfuls of straw and screamed to the cobwebbed rafters. As the shoulders presented the final obstacle, she gathered up her last bit of strength and leaned forward to turn the tiny pale body into position to slip out. Another stab of pain and a baby girl fell from her body onto the sweater. Medora leaned back onto her elbows and tried to control her rapid breathing.

She looked down between her bloodied knees and saw the pale newborn lying wet and steaming, limp and silent. She struggled to pull herself up and raised the little girl by the ankles, striking the child firmly on her wrinkled bottom.

Nothing. Not a sound.

Another blow to the tiny buttocks.

There was a moment of silence that hung in the barn like a hovering swallow; then a slight spasm and a loud cry, followed by a string of mucus. The baby girl wailed and shook, and the new flesh turned pink.

Medora cradled the baby in her arms and whispered her thanks to God. She reached into a pocket of her skirt, pulled out a piece of binder twine, and tied off the cord; then, with her pocket knife, she severed it. She opened her dress and put the baby's mouth to her nipple.

Exhausted, she put the heavy sweater over herself and the baby; it was wet, but it would still keep them warm.

The baby hadn't taken to her nipple. Her breast was hard and was beginning to trickle milk.

But she was so tired.

Medora propped straw under her cradling arm for support, and positioned the baby's mouth directly on her breast. Ezra or Sophia would find her soon enough. In the meantime she just wanted to sleep. She closed he eyes and felt the welcome rush of warmth that accompanies overdue slumber. The sound of the vacuum pump in the milk-house was fading away, as were the remaining smells of the barn.

Yes, she thought dreamily, someone will soon be here. . . .

In fact, it was hours before Sophia wandered to the barn in search of her mother. By that time Medora had lost a great deal of blood. She lay in the bed of straw, pale and cool to the touch, with only an occasional wisp of steam escaping her lips.

Sophia ran to a neighbouring farmhouse to cry that her mother was in the barn, covered in blood. An ambulance was called.

Sophia rode with her mother and newborn sister to the hospital. Medora died before the ambulance pulled into the hospital grounds; but before she passed away she regained consciousness for a few moments, took Sophia's hand, and whispered these final words: "Remember, Mommy will always love you. I'll be waiting for you and your sister. Be a good girl." And with that she attempted a smile, turned her head, and exhaled for the last time.

When Ezra finally made it to the hospital, he was shaking with fear and guilt. The details of his wife's death and the visit to the morgue for identification had a numbing effect on his mind. But it was at the hospital nursery — as her father stared at his nameless daughter in an incubator, just three weeks shy of full term — that Sophia first noticed the change. The cruelty.

She approached her father. He stood in a trance, staring at the tiny baby in the plastic clamshell; he didn't acknowledge Sophia at all.

She tugged at his pantleg to show him her tear-stained face, to show him her pain; to be held.

Her plea for comfort was answered with a haphazard backswing that struck her in the face. He never took his eyes off the newborn baby.

Sophia slowly walked back to where she had left her baby sister waist-deep in wildflowers. She rounded the corner of the Quonset to find Joelle not there.

"Joelle . . . ?"

She ran down to the grain-bins. The baby wasn't there either. She went out farther, to the fence-line, to see if Joelle was chasing the pigeons — she wasn't.

Sophia hurried back to the flowerpatch and noticed that the tall grass was bent towards the opposite side of the Quonset. "Joelle!"

She scrambled the length of the Quonset, following the trail of disturbed grasses and weeds. At the corner, near the shadowy entrance, she looked past the ailing tractor to see Bébé Joelle wandering in the barnyard. In her tiny hand was a sparse bouquet of daisies and dandelions.

Sophia could not see her father. He was probably deep inside the Quonset, searching for tools or parts. She sighed in relief. With any luck she could scoop Joelle up and rush her home before Papa saw the baby unattended.

Joelle was ambling towards the sputtering tractor, calling out for her father. "P'pa . . . ? P'pa . . . ?"

And before Sophia could take a single step, there was that sound. That distinctive metallic sound. A click, followed by an explosion that jack-knifed the tractor and bailer four feet in the air.

The shock waves knocked Sophia back into the cool, long grass. The corner of the Quonset absorbed the brunt of the blast.

Ezra ran out of the Quonset, weak in the knees, to see his old tractor and hay-bailer in the middle of the yard, twisted, black, and burning. A heavy column of blue-grey smoke rose in billowing clouds.

Sophia staggered over to her father, who looked as if he had turned to stone. She slipped her hand tentatively into his as the stench of scorched diesel and oil filled their nostrils.

Ezra looked down at his little girl — at the small bleeding cut just below her hairline, the silent plea in her wide eyes. And he wrenched his coarse hand free, almost knocking her to the ground. He stared at her with wild eyes. "WHERE'S THE BABY?"

Sophia couldn't answer. Hot tears ran down her face.

He clamped a hard hand around her thin arm, shaking her. "WHERE IS SHE? YOU WERE SUPPOSED TO WATCH HER." The child shook her head in mute fear.

Ezra dropped his daughter and scanned the barnyard frantically. Through the smoke of the wreckage he saw Joelle lying in the dust, thrashing.

Bébé Joelle's eyes were wide in fear and pain. Her small features were charred raw from the burning diesel that had splashed in her face, and her tiny mouth formed a silent O as she tried to draw breath into lungs that were still on fire from the diesel she had inhaled. Ezra held her tiny body close to his, gently rocking her.

Sophia watched her little sister die in pain from a distance — and then watched her father's wide back shake with sobs. She approached the pair of them with cautious steps, and stood there holding herself, shaking. She wanted to be close.

When Ezra sensed her presence behind him, he spun around. His lips curled back and his voice was a snarl. "You, Sophia," he said. "You killed your sister. You killed the last bit of my wife — of your mother — that was left." He buried his face in Joelle's limp body and cried.

Sophia just walked away, back to the house. Halfway up the dirt lane, she heard her father screaming, "HOW DOES THAT MAKE YOU FEEL, SOPHIA? HOW DOES THAT MAKE YOU FEEL?"

Ezra's screams still rang in Sophia's ears as she and Langley reached the seventh floor. "Here we are," she said. "It's the last door down the hall. On the left."

They walked quietly down the long, dimly lit hallway and stopped at a door numbered 710.

The tic on Langley's face was becoming worse, causing the corner of his mouth to twitch.

As the key slipped into the lock, a fluttering shadow along the doorframe caught Sophia's eye. She looked up and saw a large moth beating its bronze wings against the light cover. The large night-flyer scanned the entire curved surface, trying frantically to get at the hot wires of the lightbulb within.

It paused momentarily and stretched out its wings, revealing dark stains on the extremities.

"Beautiful, isn't it?" she asked Langley.

There was no response. She turned and faced him.

A stone-like expression had set on his features. He nodded slightly. "Very nice," he said flatly.

The look on Langley's face made her a little uneasy; it was such a stark contrast to the warmer, more congenial impression he had created in the foyer. She shook off her doubt as she turned the key, releasing the deadbolt. The door swung open.

Langley gestured for her to enter first. "Pearls before swine."

## CHAPTER 5

After about a half-hour of unstructured Q & A, scriptural readings, and hands-on blessings, Roberts received direction in his earpiece. The tone was one of hushed frenzy. "Reverend, let's return to format," urged the director. "Intro your 'baby' and we'll roll it, c'mon."

The "baby" the director referred to was the SOS Sunshine Project — an immense inner-city park where street youth could escape the pressures of gangs, drugs, and violence. The proposed project, still largely a dream in blueprint, was ambitious: converting an old railway yard into a green refuge for troubled and underprivileged kids. Projected to take three years to complete at a cost of over $400 million, it was designed by Roberts to be his earthly legacy: a walled Eden of trees, fountains, and biking trails. Also planned for within the walls were a counselling and rehab centre, a library, a museum, a movie theatre, a state-of-the-art playground, and, in the centre of the park, a ten-thousand-seat agora for live entertainment.

A young woman was now standing beneath the boom; running off at the mouth, she spoke in a constant stream that required no oxygen.

Roberts nodded vaguely, at both the director's suggestion and the young woman's babble.

There was still a considerable line-up behind the boom, and the reverend's nod didn't mollify the director. "All right, enough already with the free-form," he said, clearly irritated. "Reverend, we need to get back on track! We'll roll the film while you take another breather." He turned off the transmitter on his headset. "Asshole," he muttered.

Before the young woman under the mike could complete her say, Roberts raised his hands, interrupting her. "Ladies and gentlemen, we have a treat for you all. A preview of the future. Our ministry's future. YOUR invested future. . . ." He turned and gestured high above. The church quickly darkened as a large 70mm screen drifted down and a prerecorded narration began describing the images as they splashed upon the screen.

The young woman stood silently in the dark, her mouth still open in mid-sentence, while the members of the audience who were in line to speak filtered back to their places.

Abrupt, thought the director. But it'll do. He shook his head. This whole damn thing was going to hell in a handbasket. Just a few more hours. Thank God.

Roberts retreated quietly to the pulpit to pick up his old Bible. Before heading for the light of the stage exit, he squinted in the darkness. Still visible was the darker line of the horse's ears, and the child's white dress glowing like a patch of cloud-filtered moonlight.

They won't ever touch me, he thought. They can't touch me. Like all the other weird visitations. Worried what they were . . . why they were. They're vapour. Fuck'em. . . . I don't give a shit any more. And I don't let them move me . . . not from the house that Lucius built. . . .

As he passed into the light of the stage exit, Roberts paused, then back-stepped to speak with the assistant who had helped him with his chest mike. "Tell the director to cancel the running footer about this being the last twenty-four-hour campaign."

The assistant shot Roberts a look of confusion. She remembered the suddenness of all the hushed speculation, the memos, the crew meetings, leading to the final assembly of all employees of the SOS ministry — right here in the cathedral — to view a video presentation made by Reverend Roberts himself: a briefing of about fifteen curt minutes confirming the dissolution of the ministry, without any explanation. Or even an apology. That had been only two weeks ago.

"What was that . . . ?" she asked.

"Just give the director my instructions," said Roberts. Walking down the corridor, he could hear his order being carried out with jumbled incredulity. He smiled and raised the Bible in his hand, kissing its leather cover — it was the kiss with which a selfish lover insults his latest conquest, when he's through.

Just then the lights pulsed, flickering like strobes in a nightclub, and then dying. Roberts gasped. He was engulfed in blackness. Quickly he turned to face the stage exit, but the assistant was gone. He took a step towards the sharp rectangle of light that led to the stage, then stopped abruptly. Something was wrong. Through the exit he could make out the jumping silvery light off the big screen . . . but . . . the sound was missing. And not only the audio from the film; there was absolutely no sound out there. Just the profound stillness that screams: Vacuum.

The silence was overwhelming. It was a thing so complete that it seemed to consume all, leaving nothingness. And because it had this horrific perfection, when a small sound finally did pierce Roberts' ear, it sent him against the wall. He turned in the darkness to face the tiny noise. His mouth was open but he couldn't breathe. Where was it? What was it?

*jingjingjing*

Small. Metallic. Musical. Low and in front.

*jingjingjing*
*jingjingjing*
*jingjingjing*

It had a pattern. Sort of. And it was drawing away.

The lights in the corridor flickered for an instant and Roberts saw something in front of him. He couldn't be sure, but there was motion and . . . long, loose, wavy hair or fur . . . something. . . .

*jingjingjing*

The lights came back on. And there in the middle of the corridor, up ahead, was a long-haired goat with a bell around its neck. It stared back at Roberts for a moment, trotted forward for a few feet, then stopped; again it turned to watch him. After another few moments it trotted on a bit farther, jingling the small bell. Stopped. Turned and stared.

What in the hell, thought Roberts. He stood and watched this peculiar ritual until the animal was nearly at his dressing-room door. He rubbed his eyes and laughed. When he reopened his eyes the goat was gone — and behind him again was the large, blunted sound of the audience as they obediently watched the film presentation.

Is it over now?

They're weakening, thought Roberts. They know they can't take me. And their taunts have been reduced to this: stupid farm animals and phantom children. And to think I almost threw it all away. I'm not going mad. Jesus, I'm probably more firmly rooted than I've ever been. . . .

As he reached his dressing-room door, he paused before turning the knob. Then he smiled and entered. Still strewn over the floor were his frantic writings. He knelt down and gathered them up into a dishevelled pile that he dumped onto his mirrored table. He stared at the papers; he wasn't going to bother putting these with the others.

These writings — which he had once feared to be the product of budding dementia — had to be some sort of nervous, guilt-driven behaviour. A venting, a release. It happens. Choices are made. Often cruel ones, deliberately. There are choices of profit and gain to protect; it's instinctive. Hunters and prey. Victors and victims. The urge to preserve and to avoid pain is a powerful motivator — primal in sustaining life. With human-kind, the pulse in the brain and the throb in the will is *fuck or be fucked*. There's no denying it.

So — deliberate, cruel choices are made. And there are ventings for these choices.

It just happens.

Reverend Roberts sat down at his dressing-table and stared

at his own image in the mirror, then down at the top page of the pile resting on the table. His eyes glided across these last lines he had written:

> What is the world, people?
>    It is I —
> I, this trader of love,
>    This source of salvation;
> People, this sorrow
>    through which we go
> Is I.
>    I am I.
>    I am I.

The weight of the book on the reverend's lap diverted his attention from the pile of writings. The leather-bound Bible had been given to him by his mother, Eleanor Roberts, as a graduation present upon his completion of Bible College. The book had been, at that time, one hundred and forty-seven years old — a Roberts family heirloom. Brought across the Atlantic by Lucius's great-grandfather, Upton Malcolm Roberts, when he emigrated from Lincolnshire in 1801.

The words HOLY BIBLE, embossed on matured leather, begged Roberts' fingers to scan their form. He did so. Tiny flakes of gold stuck to his fingertips. After examining the particles, he brought his fingers to his mouth and licked them clean.

Reverend Roberts reached over the pile of writings to an intercom at the far corner of his dressing-table and issued an order — an abrupt summons for refreshments. Shortly there was a knocking at his dressing-room door.

"Enter," he said in a low voice.

A young girl entered the darkened room and spoke hesitantly to his back: "What would you like, Reverend?"

The sound of the girl's voice had a sweetness that instantly stirred something in his lap and mind. He closed his eyes and drew in a long, slow breath. Without turning around to face the girl, he said, "A fruit plate. Some cheese. And a bottle of Evian . . . make sure it's room temperature!" He emphasized this tacked-on proviso. "I don't want it cold!"

"Yes, Reverend."

The girl began to withdraw from the room, but stopped to address his back again: "Reverend?"

Roberts moved the Bible over his crotch. "Yes, child?"

"I almost forgot. . . . I was given this for you." Her long white arm was extended. In her hand was a folded piece of blue paper. "It's a note."

"Just put it on my dressing-table, darling."

With his eyes closed, all he knew of her proximity was the slight displacement of air scented by her skin and hair. His nostrils flared. Floral soap. He heard the tiny dry scrape of the note touching his piled writings.

"Thank you," he said.

"Welcome."

The girl exited silently. He cleared his tightening throat with an anxious cough.

The reverend opened his eyes and saw the folded blue paper. The message was handwritten; Roberts recognized the writing as belonging to the director. It read:

> After film, Williams & Pratz reps doing their thing for your "baby". Then we'll go with that tenor soloist and the choir. Should eat up a half-hour. Compose yourself. I'll have you cued for the phone-ins.
>
> P.S. What's this about cancelling the running footer?

Reverend Roberts crumpled the message and tossed it over his shoulder. He slipped his hand beneath the Bible and adjusted himself, smiling at his response to the scent of the opposite sex — the "animal-wild in men", his mother used to call it.

His smile withered as he pulled his hand from beneath the volume; not from a sense of shame at the obvious vulgarity of his actions, but from something else.

He flipped the cover and read an inscription, written in an elegant script:

> May, 1961
> Do for the glory of God.
> You are now His engine of goodness
>     and righteousness —
> Help rid the wickedness.
> Love always,
> Mom

Rid the wickedness.

Roberts closed the book. His mind darkened. Wickedness? Rid it? I think not. We have both been driven by your pain, Mother.

You to your wits' end. And me to . . . this. Rid the wickedness? I wouldn't even if I could. I almost wish I could feel sorrow for your suffering, but I can't.

The evil men do is part of a natural process, Mother. A process particular to our species, but proper. Evil is the means by which the human animal tests its mettle — some crumble while others soar.

I would never attempt to make this idea tolerable. Because it is not tolerable. It is harsh. It is hurtful. But it is the way of our species.

Mother, your secret shame that spread . . . has done me a world of good. I thank you. Sincerely. The obsession that bloomed from your pain turned me into what I am. Mother, you never should have asked God to come into your life. And He never should have accepted — the union became ugly. His mark on your mind was little more than a territorial pissing. I am God's stain.

Mother, I have come to understand that, in this life, any good is educed from evil. There is no basic goodness in this world — only spoiled evil. And we choose to call that spoiled evil "good".

Eleanor Roberts had been made into a dark woman. Two misfortunes in her life had caused this: an affliction she kept hidden, until it became impossible to hide; and an intolerance, bred of confusion over her secrecy, that took her baby boy away for ever.

The latter blow occurred sometime during the night of April 11, 1947. The following morning, Eleanor awoke before six a.m. to find the other side of the bed cold. She propped herself up and called out into the darkness of the hallway for her husband: "Clayt?" She put on her housecoat and walked to the bathroom to see if he was ill. He wasn't there. She went downstairs into the kitchen — not there, either. She unlocked the front door and stepped out onto the porch, and pulled her housecoat tightly around herself. "Clayt?" she called out.

Buick was still in the driveway.

No sound coming from his workshed.

Eleanor shook her head and went back inside. She walked upstairs and peeked into the room of her two boys. The curtains were drawn, so she reached for the switch to illuminate the hallway. A narrow strip of light divided the dark room. As she opened the door the strip widened, revealing a floor littered with a catcher's mitt, some marbles and jacks, a Captain Marvel comic book, and a couple of toy six-shooters.

The bed on the left had little Lucius, just two years of age, curled up with his yellow bear. The door opened a few more inches with a faint creak and Eleanor curved her neck around it to look into the bed of her older son, Joey. She blinked and took two fast steps into the boys' room. Joey's bed was empty. Eleanor's throat tightened, her heart skipped a beat.

She stood, glacial, thinking: It's happened.

She went back downstairs and out onto the porch again. Her breath was fogging. The car's still here, she thought to herself again. The car's still here. It was feeble reassurance.

Calm.

Calm.

Calm.

They could be anywhere, she reasoned. It doesn't have to be because of —

Coffee. She decided to brew a pot and see if — if what? Eleanor's blood was racing and her heart thrashed inside her chest like a snared animal.

That morning passed outside the realm of time — as happens whenever human events are stretched taut by the denial of inevitability.

When the kitchen clock had stretched to noon, the police were notified. An APB was issued — not for a kidnapping but for a missing person. Later that afternoon, she and Lucius drove to the police station and filled out a report detailing the odd particulars of the disappearance: no note, no missing luggage or clothing, no money withdrawn from their bank account.

"Were there domestic troubles? Did you and your husband have a fight recently?" asked the officer, typing away.

Eleanor shook her head vigorously.

The police officer stopped typing. He hadn't seen her response, as he'd been watching his fingers pound the keys. "I said: Were there dom —" he began to repeat.

"No," Eleanor replied. Perhaps too forcefully.

The officer looked up.

"No," she said. "No fight recently."

The report was completed and she was assured that all measures would be taken to find her husband and son. "Go home. We'll keep you informed."

The APB failed to locate Clayton and Joey within twenty-four hours. Searches were then organized, including a manhunt with a pack of six bloodhounds that covered a ten-mile radius through farmers' fields and woodlands. But all efforts were fruitless. After the third day passed, the enthusiasm of local authorities, and of the neighbouring counties, waned. Eleanor was repeatedly informed that police and volunteer resources were being employed to the fullest, but that unfortunately those resources did have limitations.

It was then that the suggestion arose to inform the RCMP of the abduction (what the disappearance was now "officially" tagged). With poorly hid reluctance, Eleanor agreed to employ their help in finding her husband and child.

She filled out all the necessary paperwork, answered all the necessary questions and in general appeared to be fully co-operative with the RCMP — until she deliberately lied.

"Now, Mrs. Roberts, do you have a recent photograph of your husband and your son?" asked the officer.

Eleanor swallowed painfully. "No, I do not."

The officer was taken aback. "Mrs. Roberts, we need the photographs to print up posters and distribute them across the country."

"I have none," she replied, fighting back tears.

The officer handed Eleanor his handkerchief. "All right, any photograph is better than none. But please — the more recent, the better our chances of having somebody recognize your missing family."

She nodded and hid her face in the white handkerchief.

When Eleanor returned to RCMP headquarters later that afternoon, she had only one photograph — of Joey as a toddler, dressed in a sailor suit.

"Mrs. Roberts, this isn't very recent. According to your report, Joey is seven years old." The officer was clearly agitated by Eleanor's lack of co-operation. "And where," he asked, in an escalating tone, "is the photo of your husband?"

Eleanor began to cry again. "As I told you this morning . . .

I have none." She kept her eyes to the floor, as she knew she was a terrible liar. "My husband hated having his picture taken. Would always flat-out refuse. We don't even own a camera."

The officer's suspicion was rising. He asked, "What about a wedding photo? Surely your husband conceded —"

"They were lost," blurted Eleanor. "Years ago."

"You lost your wedding photos?"

"Yes."

"All of them?"

"The whole album."

Eleanor could sense his rapid breathing from across the desk; could feel his eyes on her. There was a long silence that forbade her to breathe or move.

Finally he said, "Fine." But to Eleanor's ears it sounded like a low growl, or a distant roll of thunder. "I guess we'll just have to go with this," he added, flapping the photo of Joey.

"May I go?" asked Eleanor.

"For now," said the officer flatly.

For now. For now. For now. He knows I'm lying, thought Eleanor as she got into her car. He's suspicious. It all sounded too fabricated. He knows I'm covering something up.

On the way home, she continuously tugged at her white cuffs and fidgeted to ensure that her top collar-button was securely fastened — all completely unconsciously.

As that spring of 1947 matured into summer, with its shades of green and gold — the days turning into months, punctuated by regular follow-up phone calls, letters, and visitations with the RCMP — Eleanor felt that their focus was gradually shifting to her. Paranoia? Or maybe it was just the frequency of the contact . . . maybe she was misinterpreting their policies and procedures?

They'll never know, thought Eleanor. They'd have to get under my skin to find out what sent Clayt scampering off into the dark, and what it is that keeps me from helping them find him. Nothing matters any more between us. Neither of us cares

47

to build a bridge. I choose to hide what I cannot help; and he chooses to run from what he cannot know. We have built walls.

After they had been gone a hundred and twenty-eight days without a single lead to their whereabouts, interest in the case of Clayton and Joey seemed to dwindle. Eleanor noticed a drastic decrease in RCMP contacts. The "intensive push" phase of the investigation was over; it was all reduced to a file remaining "open", an assurance of keeping in touch, and courteous empathy for her grief.

Her lies about the photographs having been swallowed, Eleanor Roberts could get on with grieving for her loss. There was no way she could have allowed Clayt to be captured and returned; that would have meant a trial, and a trial would have meant probing, and probing would have led to. . . .

No — she couldn't bear it. Or even the thought of it! The cost — possibly never seeing her first-born son again — would have to be borne. Such, she felt, was the price she had to pay for accepting what God's will had done to her.

For years, since it had begun to spread over her, Eleanor had searched for a reason why God allowed such a particular suffering — a suffering that was bound, and perhaps even designed, to beget suffering in others.

If You are truly all goodness, dear Lord, she would pray, what kind of goodness can come of this affliction? What have I done to deserve such torment? Until You bless me with an answer, I shall keep Your enacted will hidden.

But her prayers, she feared, floated mutely through dead space, never reaching God's ear. Her prayers were somehow wrong to ask; they lacked wings. And that was why she now had to endure the weight of suffering on top of suffering.

For those first months of mourning, there had been an emptiness in her core. Eleanor existed in a state of gesturing that hovered between the living and the dead. The rest of that summer was spent learning how to translate her pain into indifference; it was the quickest way of managing the overload.

Near the end of August, she began to receive correspondence. The first missive was postmarked Roseton, Manitoba. Eleanor held the small yellow envelope in her trembling hand, afraid to open it. She read the address marked in pencil, recognizing the letters produced by Clayton's hand. She carried that envelope for a good part of the day, in the pocket of her apron, feeling its flat weight gently bump her thigh as she tried to do her daily housework. When she had put Lucius down for a nap, she sat at the kitchen table with a cup of tea and took out the envelope. She smelled it; ran her fingers gently over it; pressed it to her chest; tried to extract something — anything — of her estranged husband and her son from the envelope's surface.

When she finally slipped a knife along the top edge, she saw two hundred-dollar bills and a "letter" — just a few lines on a blank card — that read like a progress report about her Joey:

> Joey's learning with a tutor.
> Good grades, too.
> His health is good. Getting tall.
> All is well.
> Love to Lucius.
> C.

Eleanor Roberts never showed the authorities this first communication — or any of the others that followed. The envelopes arrived every three to four weeks, with varying sums of cash and always a brief card about her Joey. The postmarks detailed a gradual move westward, which she charted on an atlas with red ink. The temptation to bring these letters to the RCMP was at times overwhelming; she wanted her baby boy back. But she never did. She couldn't.

She first had to wait for God's explanation.

# Chapter 6

A small digital clock that lay buried under a heap of papers and books on Thomas's desk read 2:47 a.m.; it was at this time that he gathered up a few overdue library books and decided to take a walk.

Upon leaving his study, he stopped in the doorway and gave one last look over his shoulder to reassure himself. A cursory glance set his still jarred nerves a little more at ease: desk, chair, bookshelves, usual miasmic ambiance . . . all there. He pursed his lips and nodded. "Too strange," he whispered as he headed down the stairs.

By the front door he put on his coat and scarf, and checked himself in the mirror. His face was stern and pale and strands of mousy brown hair were plastered against his brow; he unglued them with a brisk fanning of his fingers. As he peered into the mirror he saw the reflection of the bare mantel above his fireplace in the next room. The sight of it gave rise to a sudden pang of anguish and an accompanying memory. It was the type of memory forgotten not gracefully, with the passage of time, but by an abrupt act of will. He cast down his eyes and felt a deep, strange sadness well up inside him.

Compelled by this sadness, Thomas went into the room and stood before the cold fireplace, and ran his hand along the empty mantel. He stood fixed, wondering why tonight the memory of such an obscure moment in his life should be triggered by the image of his fireplace. He hadn't thought of her or of that moment in . . . years. What had it been, he asked himself . . . five, maybe six years ago? Right after the incident had happened, it had bothered Thomas profoundly. Gnawed at him from within. Probably because the look on her face when he exploded irrationally had seared a brand on his mind that represented his experiences with all women. His stomach knotted at the self-deception — women? How about people in general? He had never been able to develop a relationship with either sex with any real degree of success. There was always a barrier. Always an element of alienation. Of emotional detachment so profound that it felt . . . physical. His whole life, Thomas had felt like an outsider. He rubbed the mantel dust from his palm with his thumb and watched it fall through his fingers. Like dry snow.

Feeling the weight of the books in his hand, he turned and headed for the front door.

The early morning air was much colder than he had anticipated, and he was not half a block from his house when he wished he had put on a sweater under his coat. He pulled his collar tighter around his neck and quickened his pace to ward off the swirling eddies of autumn night air. As he walked, he randomly recited lines of Eliot's poetry to himself, to ease and distract his mind. He kept his eyes fixed on the rhythmic passing of the sidewalk cracks, never looking up. The cold was making his hands and face sting, and cold tears filled his eyes, making him blink hard. He continued to walk briskly past black doorways and alleys, but slowed to a complete stop at a single lit storefront; it was an electronics and appliance store. The front window was lit by a feeble low-wattage source; the eye-catching brightness came from a single TV, a harsh splash of colour that, to Thomas, seemed unwelcome, almost intrusive. Nonetheless, despite the chill temperature, he stood and stared at the screen. This singular set was framed by five others of the same model all around it, but they were all dark.

Thomas recognized the figure on the screen, in its shirt-sleeves and tie, meticulously coiffed and glistening with perspiration; it was Reverend Lucius Del Roberts, a television evangelist who claimed to be the true and only liaison between humanity and the divine. The reverend's ministry was called the Source of Salvation Network — the SOS Network.

Thomas thought Roberts was a shit-sucking leech like all TV evangelists, preying upon the lonely, the desolate, and the simpletons of this planet; asking for money in exchange for grace and a seat in heaven's dominion. But the reverend's inexhaustible passion had quickly won him an ardent and equally passionate following. In the three short years since the SOS Network had stormed popular culture and the airwaves, he had become the undisputed champion of the Lost Tribes of God, as he put it, and had grossed $730 million in worldwide contributions.

Thomas placed the library books between his knees and cupped his hands in front of his mouth to blow warmth into them. There was no mistaking the reverend's appeal and drawing power. Even without the benefit of sound, Thomas was enthralled by his muscular delivery of "The Great Message" — the man was a pumping engine of sweat and fiery dicta. It was freakish the way Roberts never seemed to tire, or so Thomas thought. A bright yellow line of words suddenly raced across the bottom of the screen:

THE SOS NETWORK'S LAST 24-HOUR
SALVATION OF SOULS CAMPAIGN!!
PHONE NOW! OPERATORS STANDING BY!!

Last campaign, thought Thomas, smirking. Too good to be true. He picked up the books from between his knees and continued on his way to the night depository slot at the library.

As he crossed in front of the Blue Orchid Hotel, Thomas was startled by a voice from behind him; it came from a woman standing in the dark recess of a doorway, outlined by the yellow light of the foyer.

"Excuse me," she asked, "do you know what time it is?"

Thomas couldn't make out the woman's face for the shadows. But she was dressed in a short dark skirt and blue hosiery; her shoes were red, and scuffed at the pointed toes. Her perfume was heavy and musty.

"No," he said, "I . . . um . . . don't really know. Sometime after three, I should think." The woman did not respond, but shifted her red-shod feet with apparent agitation and impatience. Thomas stood in awkward silence for a few seconds, then turned away to continue down the street. He looked back over his shoulder, but the woman was gone.

The library was at the end of this next block, just around the corner. He again quickened his pace, so that he could dump the overdue books into the slot in the door and get home out of this biting cold.

Approaching the large steps of the library, he broke into a canter, took the steps three at a time, and rammed the books through the slot, hearing them land on the other side of the door with muffled thuds. He then stood at the top of the stairs and shoved both hands deep into his coat pockets, feeling relieved to be rid of the schoolboy guilt of harbouring overdue books, and a little chicken-shit for not returning them in broad daylight.

At the bottom of the stairs he patted a stone lion on the head as he left, whispering in its cold ear, "Bill me."

It was with mute panic that Thomas reeled backwards at the sound of a baby's cry as he walked back home from the library; he froze where he stood. The baby again cried out; the noise came from an apartment window above one of the stores. Another cry isolated the location to across the street, above a dry cleaner's. Thomas gasped in relief. A real child.

Through red sheers that hung in a window, the form of a mother comforting a child was plainly visible; she was cradling the infant and gently swaying her arms to soothe it. Thomas stood there a little while trying to imagine the warmth and tenderness of a mother's arms and bosom, but only felt a pain in his heart. The pain of emptiness, like hunger. A sunken hollow in the soul that becomes the complete definition of the self, as it flourishes, erasing all trace of hope or love or esteem or beauty. A darkness that becomes all that is knowable with any certainty. An emptiness so complete that it is like death.

Thomas bowed his head. At his feet was a puddle that contained a swirling meander of mauve and green from spilt gasoline; he gently toed the liquid paisley, watching it slowly change until the blackness in his heart and mind became tolerable, manageable again. It never disappeared.

Dirty dirty water. He imagined that the ugliness that filled his soul was trickling within him, down his leg and out of his big toe, polluting this small puddle. It was a childish way of handling the pain, but futility is often the last resort of those made languid from loneliness.

Thomas filled his lungs with cold night air and willed his feet to take him to the end of the street and around the corner.

When he did reach the corner, he quickly passed the old stone Catholic church, a tiny Gothic edifice that bore the horrific name "Saint Peter in Chains". The church was surrounded by black wrought iron, and on the gate was a plaque that dedicated the place of worship to "OUR LORD in the year 1843". On the steeple was a dark crucifix with a Christ whose gaze seemed to follow you, like eyes peering out from behind a painting. Despite the smallness of the crucifix, it always appeared to loom menacingly, like a bird of prey. Thomas hated this little church. So dank and venerated. The sensation of being followed by Jesus' whipping-post caused him to look back sulkingly over his shoulder. His eyes remained fixed upon the tiny black cross; he was almost expecting it to swoop down on his bare head, when his foot struck something soft and unyielding, causing him to trip. His hands pitched forward to break his fall, and he scraped the palms of both hands.

"Damn it," he hissed, as he stared at his raw palms peppered with sidewalk grit. He wiped the dirt and blood droplets onto his pants. The cause of his fall was a large mound of newspapers. Oddly, the papers were not bound by any twine or wire; they should have scattered. Thomas picked himself up and stood over the pile, shaking his hands to get rid of the sting. Angrily he swung back his foot to kick at the pile, when a firm, gruff voice rose from underneath the newspapers: "Don't do that again."

Thomas jumped back. "I . . . I'm sorry," he gasped. "I didn't see you."

At one end of the mound there was a rustling. First a hand emerged, an old weathered thing with coarse, enlarged knuckles; then, as the papers were tossed aside, a face. It was the most pitifully wretched face Thomas had ever seen.

The old man's face was deeply lined with hardships. His skin was brown from exposure and the tips of his ears were black and peeling. But what held Thomas's attention was the old man's eyes — the left one was milky white with a cataract, and the right one was dark brown with a purple oblong pupil, like that of a goat; the eye moved rudimentally in the socket, as if scanning for input.

Thomas stared, caught in the perverse fascination of the grotesque, savouring, watching that primitive eye trying to focus. He thought the old man must be blind.

"What do you see?" asked the old man slowly. Thomas was startled by the initiation of conversation, and couldn't answer right away. After a clumsy pause he answered, "Nothing," and was about to turn away.

"Wait. Talk to me," said the old man.

Despite his revulsion, Thomas was drawn to the ragged old man lying on the cold pavement. "What do you want?"

"Just talk to me. Please. My name is Gabby."

"I'm Thomas. Thomas Gorgon."

A long silence ensued. The two men just looked at each other. Finally Thomas asked, "Are you all right?" He was taken aback by the tenderness of his own enquiry.

"Been worse."

"Do you live here?"

"For now."

There was again a deep silence. The old man was smiling gently, revealing an ugly broken mouth and a thick yellowed tongue.

A cold gust swirled. Thomas clenched his bloody palms into fists and dug them into his pockets. "Aren't you scared?"

Gabby stopped grinning and said softly, "Aren't you?" — a simple retort that carried the weight of the world to Thomas's ears. The old man's dark eye continued to rotate jerkily, like a chameleon's.

"Tell me," said Gabby, "what brings you out tonight at this godless hour?"

"Overdue library books," replied Thomas. "I was working late and" — he paused; don't get into it, he thought — "and I needed a breath of fresh air. You know, clear the head."

Gabby shifted his weight and propped his head on his hand, then asked playfully, "Library books? You don't look like a schoolboy to me."

"I'm a teacher," said Thomas. "I teach literature at the community college."

"So . . . you teach books."

"I teach ideas. Feelings. The thoughts of passion in great men and women."

"Towards what end?" enquired Gabby, as his roving goat-eye suddenly locked dead onto Thomas's face. Thomas could feel his heart pounding in his chest; he was startled by the riveting look of the dark eye.

"End . . . ?" he asked, almost in a whisper; he was caught off guard by the philosophical nature of this simple question. "What do you mean?"

"Why do you do it?"

"I still don't follow. . . ."

Gabby smiled warmly. "Just what is it you're looking for?"

"I'm not looking for anything," said Thomas, with an edge. "It's a job."

"Shovelling shit is a job," replied Gabby, "and you don't shovel shit."

"So therefore I've got to be looking for something?"

"It kind of follows, doesn't it? I mean, think about it. Why else does a man spend his life with his nose in books? And why does he share what he knows?"

Thomas shook his head, smiling. "You ask strange questions, buddy."

"Answer me just one thing, will you?" asked Gabby, still smiling in a fatherly manner. "Have you been happy doing what you do? Learning books and sharing what you know?"

"Yeah. Sure, I guess. It beats shovelling shit."

"So you learned books to get out of doing something else for a lifetime."

Thomas furrowed his brow slightly. "Well, not exactly. I mean, I . . . I love books. I love reading. So it seemed natural for me to become a teacher. Might as well do something you love and get paid for it, while you're down here. I do what I do for love; not out of avoidance."

A sly smile creased Gabby's face. "I don't believe you."

Thomas was instantly annoyed by this impertinent toying. "Excuse me?" he said sharply. "What seems to be your fucking problem? You seem to be the one looking for something. Is something lost? What are you after?"

Gabby closed his eyes and rolled onto his back; his old face became solemn. "Don't get upset, son. Nothing's lost. All I wanted to know was, what did you really want to do? What were your dreams, your hopes for yourself?"

The warm earnesty of the last question drew Thomas back in and softened the tone of his voice. "I always wanted to be a writer. A novelist."

"Why aren't you?"

Thomas cast his eyes upward into the black morning sky. "I tried a couple of times, but . . . I . . . never completed anything I started."

"Run out of things to say?" asked Gabby.

"No. I always had plenty to say, it's just that I'd become so consumed by fear and self-doubt that I'd eventually quit."

"What were you so afraid of that it could kill a dream?"

Thomas felt his hands becoming sticky with blood; the linings of his pockets were slightly cold and wet with it. "That no one would care what I had to say; that my thoughts were mine and only mine and of no interest to anyone else."

"Were your thoughts and words that ugly?" asked Gabby.

Thomas shook his head. "No — I thought they were beautiful. Realer than real. Truly. My imaginative flights were reinventive, striving to make the ugly beautiful. My story-lines restructured the commonplace, made it noble and dignified. There was something so exhilarating about the notion of filling another person's mind with my visions. I really loved to write. I just felt scared. The deeper I delved into things, the greater my fear of rejection."

Gabby continued to lie on the cold, hard pavement with his arms crossed. A gust of cold air caught a few more pages of newsprint and sent them waltzing down the street. He reopened one of his eyes, the dark one; its curious oblong pupil was still able to fix on Thomas's face. "If you truly love writing, why not just do it for yourself?"

Thomas could feel the still goat-eye boring through his skull, probing. "Because writing for yourself is pointless," he explained. "I just don't see the value in it, you know?" He sighed. "I know a lot of writers believe that not anticipating an audience creates a 'truer' artistic voice . . . but to me that's egotistical bullshit. Good literature and writing are just story-telling . . . and story-telling has always been a communal thing, since primitive man; that's its beauty. It's about participation, about belonging. To me, that's what a true artist strives for . . . am I making any sense to you? Gabby? Hello?"

The old man lay quietly. The black wind played in his sparse hair, whipping the strands about like hoar-flame. For that brief moment, Thomas thought Gabby looked almost like a character from a Blake etching.

"Are you an artist, Thomas?" asked Gabby. Thomas stared down at the wretched old man at his feet. Although he had never produced a single volume or even published a line of poetry, in his heart of hearts he could only answer in a soft sad whisper, "Yes. . . ."

"Why do you think so?"

"Because I am afraid of being forgotten."

A cold gust of wind tossed about his head, so Thomas pulled his collar up and hunched his shoulders, pulling his coat tight across his back. "Doesn't that thought scare the hell out of you?"

"Take a good look at who you're talking to, son," said Gabby. "I am the Forgotten."

"I'm sorry," said Thomas remorsefully.

"Don't be. You weren't responsible," Gabby reassured him. "But tell me about this thing you have about being forgotten. I don't get it."

Thomas cast a quick glance skyward at the gentle fall of snow, and shivered involuntarily.

"Want to go home, Thomas?"

His initial reaction was to tell the old man, yes; but despite the cold, the snow, the annoying throb of his hands, he made no motion to leave. His mind was too alive, firing grapnels into his memory bank, hooking onto seemingly random memories, triggering emotions — first the barren mantel in his house . . . and now something even earlier, from his childhood.

"Can I tell you about Sister Frances?" he asked suddenly. He didn't understand why he wanted to continue this strange meeting, but he felt compelled to, and he waited anxiously for Gabby's response.

"Who is she?"

"The first real woman in my life as a boy. The first real constant in a life of emptiness and mysteries."

"Mysteries . . . ?" asked Gabby.

Thomas let his heart heave painfully; he swallowed. He gestured a wave of futility with empty hands as his eyes became moist. "I have no real roots, Gabby. No family. No ties. I have almost no identity except for my name."

"What happened? Where are your parents?"

Thomas shook his head sadly. "I don't really know. I didn't start asking questions until I was twelve or thirteen. I was raised by nuns in a secluded convent. I was placed there as a newborn infant by some government agency. From what I was told by the Mother Superior — as I grew older — this agency subsidized my food and clothing, and financed all the materials for my education, which was carried out by the nuns."

"Who were these government people?" asked Gabby.

"I'm not entirely sure," replied Thomas. "Whenever I enquired, I was given some bullshit line about my benefactors wanting to remain anonymous, and all benefits being cut off if I found out the source of my good fortune."

"And you bought that?"

"I was a boy, Gabby. Just a lost kid . . . Jesus, when you have a Mother Superior and a government agency for parents, you grow up pretty fucking intimidated."

"Yeah, I guess you would," said Gabby. "Well, what about now?"

"You mean now that I'm an adult?"

"Yeah."

The snow continued to fall softly but steadily over the two men. The old man's hair, which shortly before had caught the wind like a ragged lion's mane, was now limp and threadbare with the melted snow. Thomas felt a pang of affection for the poor old creature lying there, forgetting his own discomfort as he looked down at a broken face hungry for human warmth.

"Well, one afternoon when I was about seventeen, Sister

Frances and I snuck into the Mother Superior's office when she was out on business to look through her files."

"And . . . ?" urged Gabby.

"We found my file, all right. Practically empty. No birth certificate, no hospital records of any kind, no official release forms, nothing."

"You said the file was 'practically empty'," corrected the old man.

"Yes," said Thomas slowly as he reminisced. "Except for two items. A small black and white photograph of an infant — I presume it was myself — and a very brief typewritten letter, no more than three paragraphs, that provided basic information about the child in the photograph. My name. My age and birthdate. Weight, eye colour, race, religion. . . ." Here Thomas hesitated, staring beyond Gabby with burning eyes as he pieced the memory back together.

"What is it, son?"

"There was no mention of my parents' names in the letter. All I know of them is that they were 'DECEASED' — in a fire." Despite the removed angle of Thomas's face, Gabby could plainly make out the course of one angry tear.

"Anyhow," said Thomas quickly, "the Mother Superior returned unexpectedly and caught us snooping."

"What happened?"

"Naturally, she was pissed off. Tore a strip off Sister Frances and myself. Separated us. A couple of weeks later, she had Sister Frances transferred to another convent. I never saw or heard from her again."

Gabby looked up into Thomas's face; watched as he continued to speak at length of emptiness, of severance; watched him blink away rising tears; heard him strain to control his voice.

Gabby closed his eyes and had to remind himself: Nothing's lost.

# CHAPTER 7

Eleanor Roberts' white dress swept with the afternoon breeze to join with the billow of the white bed linens. The snowy crispness of the dress became invisible within the greater wave of the laundry; were it not for Eleanor's head, hands, and calves, she would have disappeared entirely.

The smell of the sun coming off the laundry and his mother's dress was wafting over Reverend Roberts' mind when a knock on the door startled him.

"Yes?"

"Your food, Reverend," said the girl's voice through the door.

Roberts shook his head to clear it and ran his fingers through his hair. "Enter, child."

The door opened eventually, after the young girl fumbled with the knob and the tray of food. As she entered the darkened room, Roberts could feel her approach through the floor.

He spun in his chair to see her.

His eyes scanned the girl. Her long hair was in transition from its original youthful blonde — her maturing tresses radiated a darker burnt gold. Her angular limbs and straight hips were like a closed crocus, concealing their impending glory. And through her blouse, the budding of breasts pushed her nipples to small coned points.

Roberts could feel his heart in his chest. She's probably thirteen . . . maybe fourteen, he guessed. Hired part-time. Probably the daughter of one of the employees.

As she laid the tray of fruit and cheese on the table, Roberts drew in her smell again. His mouth felt wet. Animal-wild. He imagined taking her, right there in his dressing-room. Flipping her over. His mind whirled, he felt his penis engorge.

"There," she said, smiling. Eyes like light.

Roberts was reeling. To feel something so beautiful, so pure; to know what was lost, forbidden, denied . . . all his life.

The sound of his dressing-room door closing brought him out of his daze. He pulled a Kleenex from a box on his table and dabbed his brow and upper lip. He gazed at the fruit plate: grapes, kiwis, pineapple wedges, cantaloupe, strawberries, a wedge of hard white cheese, and a small round Brie. He put his hand around the bottle of water to check the temperature of it — tepid, good — then drew a long pull, gulping until he began to feel the tepidness pool in his stomach.

He placed the Bible beside the fruit plate and headed for the bathroom. Standing over the toilet, he undid his fly and extracted himself. He stared at his member and his memory harked back to the beginning of the animal-wild; it had all begun with an innocent question. He had asked his mother who the man and the other boy were, in an old photograph he had found in the attic.

His mother was in the backyard, hanging bed linens on the line to dry.

"Mommy?"

"Yes, Lucius?"

"Who's with me and you, here?"

Eleanor pegged a pillowcase to the line and turned to face her son. "Where?"

"Here, Mommy," said Lucius, holding up the photograph.

Eleanor's face went ashen. "Where did you get this?" she asked sternly.

The small boy took a step back.

"What were you doing in the attic?"

"Just looking at stuff."

She snapped the photograph from his hand and looked

deeply into it. Her face contorted and tears began to fall. She pressed the image to her bosom and eased her shaking legs down as she sat beneath the flapping laundry.

Lucius began to cry too. The first sight of vulnerability in a parent is terrifying to a child; he wanted to run. But before he could, Eleanor composed herself just enough to wave him closer. He approached this thing transformed — to his tender eyes this was no longer Mommy, but something else. He stood above this big trembling hurt sitting in the yard. She looked up at him with swollen eyes.

Lucius reached down and stroked his mother's hair. At her son's touch, Eleanor went limp and her wet face fell against his stomach, almost knocking him over. Her wails intensified. Lucius wrapped his arms around her head and held her, mother and son melting into a statue of grief.

A neighbour hearing the commotion approached the fence and looked into the Roberts' yard. She just stood there, watching. When Lucius became aware of her presence, he was piqued by a sense of violation. He raised his arms to shield his mother and screamed, "GO 'WAY! GO 'WAY!" Until the intruder withdrew.

Reverend Roberts clenched his teeth to control his trembling jaw. He finished urinating, flushed the toilet, and returned to his dressing-table. He could remember his mother trying to control her sorrow; could still feel the cool of the backyard grass against his bare legs as he sat down beside her.

Eleanor slipped the photograph into a pocket of her apron and wiped away her tears. She looked down at her son and tried to smile, but the words she spoke kept her features grave: "They are people who left us a long time ago, Lucius."

"Who are they, Mommy?"

"Your daddy and your brother."

Lucius continued to stare into his mother's eyes, eager and

curious to hear more.

"They left us four years ago," continued Eleanor. "You wouldn't remember it at all. You were just a baby."

"Where are they, Mommy?"

She shook her head. "Out west. Last I heard, a place called Trochu, north of Red Deer."

"Where's that?"

"Far away."

"Are they coming back?"

"No, Lucius. They're not."

"But how come?"

Eleanor's eyebrows came together and her lips drew tight. She pulled at the cuffs of her sleeves and twisted her neck to feel if her collar was still fastened. "Your daddy felt he couldn't live with me any more." She turned away slightly, her eyes distant.

Never taking his eyes off his mother's face, Lucius slowly dipped his hand into her apron pocket and removed the photograph. He stared at the image; especially at the likeness of himself and the other boy, who stood a good head taller, with a swashbuckler grin. Lucius pointed to him. "My brother?"

Eleanor nodded. "That's Joey."

"Will I ever see him?"

"Probably not, Lucius. Your daddy moves around a lot. Takes Joey all over. I haven't seen or spoken to either of them since they left us."

Mother and son sat together quietly beneath the flapping sheets. Lucius stared at his red canvas Keds.

Eleanor looked at her son, wrapped her arms around the little boy, and squeezed. Hard. "Don't leave me, Lucius. It would kill me." Her voice rang dead, like the toll of a stone bell. "Promise me, Lucius . . . promise me you won't ever let it take you over. Like it did your father, like it will your brother. Promise me you won't let it get you. . . ."

Lucius was frightened. "What, Mommy?"

"The animal-wild."

"The what?"

Eleanor closed her eyes. "Nothing. Just promise me."

Lucius couldn't answer for confusion.

"Promise me," she repeated, tightening her hold.

"I promise, Mommy."

Eleanor turned her son's chin up. She searched long into that little face, until she caught a shadow-glimpse of what she thought would be the man this child had promised her. That was the beginning of the animal-wild. A frightening promise.

Alone in her bedroom that evening, Eleanor stood before a large cheval-mirror and untied the ribbon that fastened the collar of her nightgown. She undid the buttons and let the gown slip off her shoulders and onto the floor.

Standing naked, she scanned her reflection and said to it, "Is this what it's all about? Is this shame I keep hidden a sign? Am I Your agent in banishing the animal-wild?"

Her words evoked only a deeper silence. She stood looking at her skin in the mirror, forcing her mind to decipher God's will as it pertained to her private agony.

It was at that very moment that Eleanor Roberts believed she had cracked God's code, interpreting His great silence as an acquiescence.

She wrapped her arms around herself and wept tears of joy. She now understood. It was all crystal-clear to her, no more confusion or pain. No contradiction existed within the omnipotence of God — at least, not in the mind of Eleanor Roberts. She closed her eyes; "I am Your agent, Lord . . . ," she whispered. "And our son, Lucius, shall be Your instrument in ridding the animal-wild."

A terrible anxiety was drying the reverend's mouth and dampening his hairline. He paced in a small circle, his mouth moving silently.

Has the clean-up been done, he asked himself. Somebody

had better have bagged and dumped today's birds. I know there were birds. Always are. Dropping like flies around this place. Could it be a gas leak? No. Some sort of bird disease? I don't . . . Jesus, something's got to be done.

He walked over to the window and tied the curtain back. It was snowing, and flakes were accumulating along the fine-lipped edges of the lead that criss-crossed the pane. He looked out onto the grounds and tried to see under the shrubbery. No dead birds. Filthy fucking things, he thought.

Roberts returned to his desk and leaned back in his chair, testing the limits of the swivel. He dangled a bunch of red grapes about his mouth and plucked them with his teeth.

He gazed out the window at the snow and felt a deep gratitude for being on the warmer side of the pane. This tiny thought of gratitude caused him an involuntary spasm. He hated the cold. Completely. Obsessively. He hated the sensation of coldness touching his skin — an autumn breeze, an air-conditioned room, snow, and, most horrific of all, cold water. He never swam in a pool or lake; never took a cool shower on a humid summer afternoon; a stethoscope placed on his chest would make him gasp aloud. Even the stage of the Cathedral of Light was equipped with fans to keep the air-conditioned air off the stage and over the audience. Roberts would sooner put up with the stickiness of his own sweat than feel even a gentle gust of cooler air. Just the thought of anything cold touching him made him quiver. This profound abhorrence of cold was linked to the animal-wild.

The young Lucius Del Roberts had grown up not knowing that he was a detonator and that his mother's swelling psychosis was a bomb, set to go off at the onset of his puberty. The explosion took place one evening when Lucius was twelve years old. Eleanor had mounted the carpeted staircase like a jaguar. Silently. At the top of the landing, she paused and turned towards her son's bedroom door. She placed her ear to the door and listened; hearing nothing, she gently turned the knob. The door swung open without a sound.

In the moonlit room, Eleanor could see the bedsheet propped up by her son's head, like a tepee. She walked softly to stand beside the bed. In one swift motion, she whipped the sheet back to reveal Lucius hunched over, eyes wide with surprise and shock. The boy's pyjama bottoms were at his ankles, and in his hand was his rigid penis.

Lucius mutely shook his head.

Eleanor grabbed the wrist of his offending hand, wrenching him out of bed. She dragged him across the floor to the bathroom, tugging his pyjama bottoms off his feet.

"GET IN THE TUB!" she screamed.

Lucius did so, shivering with fright.

Eleanor's eyes were hooded with intent and purpose as she pulled a scrub-brush from the vanity. Returning to the tub, she turned on the cold-water tap, letting it run. She knelt by the edge of the tub and looked up at her son. "Grab the shower-curtain rod! Both hands! Face me!" she ordered. She placed the bristles beneath the icy water. "Now, not a sound from you, Lucius," she warned.

Lucius turned his head away and clamped his teeth onto his bicep, as his mother took him in her hand and scrubbed away his sin.

"Lucius?"

The room was dark and she heard no response.

"Baby? It's Mom. . . ." Eleanor walked into the room and stood beside the bed. Her son was curled tightly into a ball and his face was buried in the pillow. Gently, Eleanor sat on the edge of the bed. She placed her hands deep in the thick terrycloth pockets of her housecoat — her fingers were still numb with cold.

"Understand, sweetheart," she said softly. "This was necessary. We have to kill this thing before it gets the better of you

. . . before it takes control." She placed a cold hand on her son's curved back. "Don't think of this as a punishment, Lucius . . . it's not. Think of it as . . . a baptism." She paused, gripping the pile of the carpet with her toes, then said, "You know how a newborn has its sin of exposure to this world washed away . . . ? Well, that's what this is like: another baptism. Our little baptism. Tonight we washed away your sin before the eyes of God. Your exposure to the sin particular to manhood, Lucius. It has come alive in you, as it does in all men . . . but you are fortunate, Lucius; you have me to help you through this." She stroked her boy's hair and whispered, "I have vowed to protect you, to keep you pure. And I will do whatever it takes to wipe out any traces of ugliness that stain you, my little son of God. And I will do so for as long as it takes."

She kissed the back of his head and left, deaf to the screams that had been filling the room since she first entered.

For as long as it takes . . . that was the promise Eleanor Roberts had made to her son; it was the centre around which her growing derangement spun; and it was what turned the entirety of Lucius Del Roberts' adolescence into a forced denial.

The years of secrets, lies, manipulation, depravity, and madness put him through all manner of penance and absolution: bare-kneed prayer on cracked walnut shells, genital beatings for spied nocturnal erections, and the continual "baptismal" scrubbings with ice-water — all done before the eyes of God.

Eleanor believed: like Christ, her baby boy was destined to send ripples that would kiss ten thousand shores.

It was not until his fingernail lifted that he stopped writing. The force with which he held the pen had pried back the index nail, to hinge at the quick. He let out a sharp cry and threw the pen at the wall. He raced to the bathroom and held his bloodied finger under a feeble ribbon of warm water; watched the blood swirl around the silver ring of the drain. From the mirrored vanity he took out a few bandages and wrapped them around his finger, after folding forward the loose nail. His mouth felt dry, his molars ached from being clenched. His arm and neck hurt with muscle fatigue from the writing, from the strain.

The reverend returned to his dressing-table, stunned by the disarray he had obviously caused but could not remember creating. Fruit and cheese were scattered all about, the bottled water rested in a patch of wet carpet, and once again the writings were strewn everywhere.

Wearily he knelt down and regathered the pages of crazed script, content to let them sit on the floor. He righted the bottle of water and retrieved the tossed tray, placing it before his bent knees. As he collected the fruit and cheese, his fingers came upon something else littering the floor — the crumpled blue note he had tossed over his shoulder. He peeled open the paper ball and reread the director's postscript: "What's this about cancelling the running footer?" As he did so, a question of his own — one of intent — loomed like a shadow across a private horizon. Roberts could only shake his head. He had no answers.

As he picked up the last of the food from the carpet, Roberts was suddenly struck by an odour. It was so thick and oily that it seemed to coat his tongue as it passed through his nose into his mouth. The taste was musky, warm, and moist. He rubbed his tongue against the roof of his mouth to get rid of it. It was strong. Nauseating. And then something else . . . unmistakable . . . the smell of fish! — blended with the musky odour, causing the reverend to open his mouth and gasp.

He rose with the tray and returned to his dressing-table, setting the tray down. Fresh air, he decided, was definitely in order. He turned to his dressing-room door but was sent staggering back by the sight and sound of a large monkey that gave a sharp, simian bark.

Roberts' knees buckled at the abrupt ferocity and gaping jaws. He collapsed into his swivel chair and stared at this latest apparition.

The monkey was a thick-shouldered brute covered in coarse

black hair; its eyes were wide and dark, shiny with rage. And when its thin lips were pulled back, revealing yellow incisors, the creature was formidable. It sat down on a wingback chair of red leather, close to the door. Roberts observed, in the monkey's hands, a large silver-backed fish. The fish was long and muscular and gasped with useless gills, thrashing its great tail.

The monkey tilted its ugly, sloped head and gazed with a probing intelligence that made Roberts shift his eyes away. The monkey then looked down at the fish struggling in its grasp and pursed its lips, seemingly contemplating its next course of action; then, in a swift, arching motion, it raised the fish above its head and cried out in a clear, cultured tongue, "Ecce! Corpus Christi!" The reverend stared in horror as the monkey lowered the great fish and sank its fangs deep into the silvery back, severing the spine. The large fish was dropped to the floor, paralysed, fanning desperate gills until it died.

Roberts stared at the dead fish, into its flat jellied eye and at the bite wound, ragged flesh and sharp bone. The shock of seeing an apparition this close — mere feet away — was beginning to subside; never before had one appeared within the sanctity of his dressing-room. Never this close, never with such ferocity. In the very beginning, it had all been so subtle — in fact, Roberts hadn't even realized that the little oddities were aimed at him. The things he happened upon were curious or, at worst, mildly annoying. Then his uncertainty had cleared as the apparitions slowly intensified, both in frequency and in semblance. They altered from being unexpected (yet rational) events that merged with the commonplace, to being violently illogical visitations that no one else could see or hear.

The chasm between reality and dark reverie had then dwindled to a mere crack; it had been just a casual step from one realm to the other. The closing of this gap now pushed Roberts to question his sanity, to contemplate escaping the cloistered world of privilege he had created; just dropping it all, walking away. He had planned to do it after this broadcast . . . after this

71

broadca . . . but. . . .

The reverend summoned his composure and cautiously straightened himself in his chair. The monkey continued to watch with unblinking eyes. Frightened though he was, Roberts attempted to communicate with it: "Wha . . . who . . . are you . . . ?"

The monkey sat motionless for a moment, its face registering no inclination of understanding; then, with lips curled back, it announced, "Ego sum ego."

"I am I?" Roberts grabbed fistfuls of his hair. "Jesus Christ!" All previous apparitions had been mere presences — some shocking, but nothing more. This monkey was definitely more. It was not only dangerously aggressive, but intelligent and confrontational.

Could this creature lash out at me, wondered Roberts. Could it make contact? Touch me? Hurt . . . even kill me?

He doubled over, clutching his head, but twisted his neck up to peer at the monkey still staring him down. Those eyes. Unblinking. Round black shiny marbles, bald of expression yet burning with emotion. Roberts wanted to hide, to cry.

The monkey shifted its weight and hoisted itself up slightly onto gnarly knuckles, to rub its naked buttocks on the arm of the chair. It grunted with satisfaction. Roberts watched, unable to avert his gaze from the heavy sway of the animal's testes and the emergence of a glistening pink spike through the dark hair. He was transfixed by the easy rawness of the gesture.

"Reverend!" It was the director's voice over the intercom. The sound of it jolted Roberts bolt upright. "The tenor's just about to start his last number, then we're cutting to a commercial break. You've got seven to make it to stage. The panels lit up this morning for the phone-ins. Hope you're up to it . . . Reverend . . . ?"

Roberts was petrified. He finally allowed himself to swallow when he realized that the monkey was neither startled nor going to attack.

Again the intercom blared: "Reverend? Are you there? You

72

all right?"

Roberts caught his breath. Slowly he reached behind to the transmit button, then replied, "Be right there." He looked into the monkey's eyes and felt a flood of relief as he read its nod of dismissal. He felt around the table until he found his Bible, then cautiously rose from his chair. Even standing above the seated monkey, he felt small. He made an arching side-step over the dead fish and opened the door. The rush of hall smells usually unnoticed — carpet, mechanically moved air, dust — was welcome.

Roberts stood in the doorframe, feeling a little safer to be behind the monkey with a clear path of escape; his legs were tight, ready to bolt at the first sign of movement.

But the monkey sat motionless, keeping its back to him. The confrontation seemed to be over. Roberts stepped back, out of the doorframe and into the hall, and quickly walked its length; at the corner he turned to look back.

The monkey was now in the hall, facing in the opposite direction. Slung over one shoulder was the carcass of the dead fish. The primate's gait seemed weary, its back curved, as it lumbered down the hall.

## CHAPTER 8

"We can work out the particulars as you make yourself comfortable," Sophia said, inviting Langley in.

Langley walked slowly to the centre of the small room. He placed his briefcase on the card-table and hung his heavy coat over the back of one of the chairs. He kept his wide-brimmed hat on but undid the button of his suit jacket.

Then he walked over to the window and peered down into the empty street below.

**Azrael . . . ?**

"So, Mr. Langley . . . what exactly did you have in mind?" Her voice resonated with a slight echo.

**Azrael, can you hear me?**

In the bathroom, thought Langley. He had not heard her walk in there. He shook his head.

**Keep it clear.**
**Stay in focus.**
**Pay attention, Azrael.**

He turned away from the window as she came out of the bathroom.

"So, what'll it be . . . ?"

"Um . . . the usual, you know. . . ."

She smiled. "Mr. Langley, there is no usual."

"You know, a straight lay. . . ."

"Full hour?"

This was choking him. "Sure. . . ."

"Are you all right, Mr. Langley?" she asked. "You're

74

sweating."

"Yes, I'm fine."

"Why don't you take off your jacket?" She walked behind him and slipped it off. "There, is that better?" She noticed the line of perspiration that ran from between his shoulderblades, darkening the cotton.

"And relax," she said, tossing his jacket onto the table with the coat and briefcase. "This won't hurt a bit."

Langley's heart was thundering.

"Let me loosen your tie." The musky perfume in her hair made him shiver.

As she undid his Windsor knot, she looked down and admired his belt buckle. "Are you some sort of cowboy?" It was a heavy silver buckle, with large turquoise stones in the corners and a gold cowboy riding a bucking bronc. Below it was a date and inscription: 1958 SUMMER FAIR CHAMPION.

"No, it was my daddy's."

"He was a cowboy?"

"A ranch hand." He could feel the sweat trickling from his hairline. Itchy under his hat.

She went slowly to her knees. "Why don't we loosen it, as well . . . ?"

Langley's hands shot out, seizing her wrists. "DON'T TOUCH IT!"

"You're hurting me! Let me go!"

He was shaking. Squeezing her wrists. He was out of sync . . . this was taking too long.

**Relax, Azrael!**
**You'll lose her.**

His hands opened like the jaws of a steel trap. "I'm so sorry," he said, covering his face.

**You stupid motherfucker!**
**Coax her back.**

She sat on the floor, looking up at him. Scared.

**Azrael, you asshole! Say something!**

"I'm sorry. I . . . I'm just nervous. I've never done this type of thing before," said Langley, through his hands.

**She ain't biting. Look at her face.**

"Please," he insisted. "Could we just carry on and forget my outburst?"

She picked herself up and stood behind the curved iron footboard of the bed. "Listen." Her voice was shaky. She swallowed. "Maybe this sort of thing isn't right for you."

"No . . . no . . . please. . . ."

**Keep talking.**
**Reassure her.**
**Compose yourself.**

"It's just that . . . I haven't been with a woman for a long time. Seeing you down there on your knees . . . you know . . . sort of panicked me, that's all."

She stood there quietly. Unsure.

"Please . . . Trixie, right? . . . I promised you double your usual rate, plus a bonus." Langley reached out behind, to his suit jacket, and pulled out an eelskin billfold. "Here, now . . . what do I owe you? . . . Please . . . I just wanted some company tonight." The open billfold was full of credit cards.

She cleared her throat. She felt reluctant to proceed with this trick, but the sight of all those credit cards re-created his aura of respectability. Maybe he really had only panicked. Maybe it would be all right.

"Too long out of the saddle?" she said jokingly.

A smile spread across Langley's face. "Yeah. . . ."

**Got her.**

"My usual rate is a hundred and fifty an hour."

Langley fanned the bills in the billfold and extracted three hundred and fifty dollars. Crisp bills.

"Will this do?" he asked.

She took the money and folded the bills neatly in half, sharpening the crease with a blood-red nail. A done deal. "Why don't you come over to the bathroom and we'll get down to business."

"In the bathroom?" asked Langley.

She took him by the hand. "I always prep my clients."

Langley leaned against the doorframe of the bathroom as he watched her undress.

She laid her short skirt and blouse, neatly folded, on the tank of the toilet. He admired the length and smoothness of her back and legs. She was a tall woman. He estimated that she must be close to six feet, even without her heels on.

She turned to face him.

She was a beautiful woman. Almost too beautiful, he thought, to be doing this kind of work. Her hair was dark, nearly black, and fell in thick, luxurious locks. And her eyes were a warm shade of hazel-green. Her red mouth was well shaped.

Contained within the black lace of her bra and panties were full thick breasts with dark nipples and an inviting patch of black, downy hair.

This was not a young woman, thought Langley. Late thirties to early forties. But well preserved. Fit.

She noticed him admiring her and smiled.

She sat on the lid of the toilet, put the stopper into the drain of the sink, and ran some warm water.

She beckoned with her finger for him to come closer. To stand in front of her.

He did so. His face was carved in stone again.

She dipped a facecloth into the warm water and began to soap it up. "Why don't you drop your pants?"

Langley placed his hands on the large buckle, then paused. "What's your name?" he asked in a low voice.

"What?"

"You heard me," said Langley, his voice taking on an edge "Your name. What is it?"

"Trixie."

She could see he was growing impatient. His breathing was rapid and shallow.

"Your real name." His face began to twitch.

"Trixie," she repeated.

"You're pissing me off, bitch. I asked you a simple fucking question. Now answer it."

She sat there on the toilet, mute with fear and confusion. In her hands the facecloth was dripping with soapy suds. She felt completely trapped, cornered by this large man. Her throat constricted as she uttered a feeble plea for mercy: "Please. . . ."

Langley's fist shot straight out and connected with Sophia's face, sending her head snapping back. Blood gushed from her nose and her eyes rolled back.

Before she could fall forwards, he grabbed her by the back of her hair and slammed her head forcefully against the porcelain sink, splitting her forehead open.

Her body went limp.

Langley loosened his grip on her hair. He savoured the sound of her flesh slapping against the cold tiled floor, and smiled; it was a smile of pride. A craftsman's pride.

The first lash struck with a sickening thud. It connected as she began to stir.

The shock of this new pain stimulated her primal survival instinct, accelerating her return to the light of consciousness. She jolted and her knees slid out from beneath her. She tried to scramble to her feet, but something other than her disorientation kept her from righting herself.

She thrashed. She hurt. She couldn't bring down her arms. It took what felt like an eternity in chaos for her to work out that she was tied to the footboard of the bed. This sudden realization made her freeze — to stop and get her bearings, to re-evaluate.

She blinked hard to clear her vision of the blood and blur; vaguely she could make out something bright and colourful binding her wrists. But her mind was clearing more quickly from her sight. She quickly took a mental inventory of her situation, based upon these immediate sensorial certainties: she could not break free, she was naked, and she hadn't been sexually violated — yet.

All the while, her vision was slowly coming back into focus. But where was Langley? She couldn't see or hear him. Once again the impulse to panic surged through her. She wanted to scream.

Stay calm, she told herself.

Then suddenly a small sound came to her awareness. From behind, over her shoulder. A curious little sound; it was mechanical, sort of, and manual . . . metal on metal . . . rubbing . . . it sounded like a file! The sound drew closer. She remained frozen. Holding her breath.

"There, that's much better." She twisted her head around painfully to see Langley standing over her, talking to himself. In his hand was indeed a file. He was rubbing its ridged edge along the prong on the underside of the large silver belt buckle, sharpening it. He stood admiring the shiny prong, testing its needle-sharp point with his finger. "Yes, much much better." He placed the file back into his briefcase and took out a small book — it looked like a diary. A tiny latch was popped and Langley began to read:

> . . . he doesn't understand. That I must kill it. For the glory of God. The torment I put him through is for the greater good. The wounds will heal. The damage of love I inflict is small compared to the damage the animal-wild would do. . . .

Langley shut his eyes momentarily. He closed the book and placed it in his briefcase beside the file. *Joey's coming.*

**AZRAEL!!**

The voice just wouldn't let him alone.

"Yes, yes! I know!" said Langley, swiping at invisible hornets. *I will save you.*

**WHO WILL?**

"All right! You will . . . ! I will. . . ." *Mommy can't hurt you any more.*

". . . the darkest angel has lit . . . ," whispered Joseph Langley.

Absolute horror flooded Sophia's mind. She closed her eyes and began to pray softly to Our Lady of Sorrow — a childhood habit acquired from her mother. "Je vous salue, Marie, pleine de grâce; le Seigneur est avec vous . . ."

Langley's eyes were wet, but he laughed wildly. "What's that you're doing? Are you praying? Now?" He knelt down beside her cringing nakedness, smiling. "That was a Hail Mary, wasn't it? I recognized the rhythm." His breath was hot and moist in her ear. "Believe it or not," he continued, laughing, "I'm an old altar boy. It's true."

She paid no attention to his mockery. In earnest she continued to pray.

Langley placed a finger under her chin, drawing her face to his. She opened her eyes and stared unflinchingly at him.

"Do you really expect God to charge to your rescue like the fucking cavalry?" he hissed. "Do you?" He looked into her face; at the long tracks of blood running from her split brow. "Take stock of your situation. You can't get any farther away from God than you are right now."

She closed her eyes. "Mère de Dieu, priez pour nous, pauvres pécheurs, maintenant et à l'heure de notre mort . . ."

Langley examined the deep, indented bruise on her back; it was already changing from scarlet red to purplish black. At the touch of his probing finger, she flinched.

He smiled and shook his head. "Jesus, I bet that fucking smarts."

She began to cry noisily in frightened bursts, but fought back her sobs and squeezed her eyes tight to stop the flow of tears. Her wrists, bound above her head, were beginning to throb; she could no longer feel her hands.

Langley stood up and kicked her in the buttocks. "Get up, bitch."

She achingly rolled onto her knees and pulled herself up, using her bindings for leverage. The sudden surge of blood made her see colour bursts and buckled her knees. A surge of nausea and the acidic taste of bile followed.

She heard Langley undressing, and shivered.

The wave of nausea mercifully passed. She looked slowly over her shoulder at Langley standing behind her. In his hands was the belt. He was naked except for his hat and his western boots. Under any other circumstances, with any other trick, she would have smiled to herself and feigned a turn-on. But this large, muscular man was a frightening sight in his sick and dangerous fetish.

She saw that, between his legs, he was swollen but not erect. Her stomach turned again. She swallowed before asking her captor, "Why are you doing this?" She rested her head on her extended arms.

He walked up to her and ran a finger over the bony nubs of her arched spine. "Just what is it you're asking? Do you even know?" he asked.

She didn't respond.

He squatted on his naked haunches beside her, looking up into her bloodied face and distant eyes. He tipped the brim of his hat upwards slightly. "Have you any idea of the scale and magnitude of your question?"

She shook her head — more in utter disgust than in response to his question.

"What is it you want to know?" Langley reached out and gently slapped her dangling breast, watching its soft heaviness sway to and fro. "Is it the rhyme and reason of your predicament? Is it the colossally huge WHY of this violence against you?" He continued to toy with her breasts, as a cat does with a mouse before devouring it. "Your question is laughably common and stupid."

He stood up and walked behind her, placing his hand on her rump, feeling its smoothness. As he began to speak again, his voice took on a pontifical air. "Don't try to find a design or order to all this — because you haven't the time." He was pacing now. "But I'll tell you this, what I've learned to be true: there are only two orderly universes on this planet. Both are complexly structured entities. One is a physical cavity that transforms into a heaven, the other a random, pointless magnetic catalogue, expanding incessantly till it becomes a hell. Do you follow me? You see, our severed lives, as humans, unfold between these two poles, these two entities — the womb and the mind."

Langley was becoming increasingly agitated as he spoke. She could hear his voice rising. But — even more unsettling — he had begun to swing the belt around like a lariat. The dangerous buckle flashed in the light as it swung. "Do you follow me?" he asked again.

Sophia shook her head mutely. Tears of despair were forming in her eyes; she had resolved in her own mind that she was going to die at the hands of a lunatic. A lonely smallness was seeping into her soul. "No, I don't follow . . . I don't understand."

Langley stopped swinging the heavy buckle and stepped up behind Sophia, roughly grabbing her vulnerable genitals. The sudden pain drew the wind out of her, making her gasp for air.

"We emerge," he said angrily, "from *here* — this Eden between your legs — into fucking chaos. Cast out innocent! Alone! Spending our whole lives trying to soften the shock of exposure!" He let loose his grip between her legs and resumed pacing.

The pain made Sophia feel nauseated again.

Langley continued to pace silently. He had gathered the length of the belt strap between his hands and folded the leather.

With each second step he jerked his hands out sharply, snapping the belt, punctuating his thoughts.

Sophia jumped with each loud crack of the leather. She closed her eyes and began to pray again, in silence.

After quite some time of pacing and belt-cracking, she could hear, once again, the whirring sound of the silver buckle slicing the air behind her; but it was the sound of Langley's voice that made her jump in fright, as he recommenced his oration.

"We're such fragile creatures," he said softly, and the forlorn tone in his voice made Sophia turn to look at him. Just then he erupted with tears and an inhuman wail: "THERE'S NO BLAME, MOTHER! I DON'T HATE YOU! I DON'T . . . NOT EVEN FOR WHAT YOU'VE DONE TO MY BROTHER! BUT IT HAS TO BE FIXED, MOTHER! IT HAS TO BE WIPED AWAY!"

**Easy, Azrael.**

Langley had fallen to his knees, weeping. Grinding his face into the floor. Eventually he composed himself and stood up. He wiped his eyes and took in a cleansing breath before proceeding: "You know, it's a fucking miracle that what is happening right here . . . right now . . . isn't more commonplace . . . a fucking miracle. . . ." Once again, the buckle could be heard swinging overhead.

Sophia tried desperately to move her hands. She had never known that numbness could be so painful.

"Such a barrage of input . . . ," continued Langley in a lost voice. "Without coherency . . . we're expected to sort it all out . . . all the pain, all the suffering and misery . . . expected to rise above the confusion and contradiction. . . ."

A sudden sound of glass breaking overhead made Sophia cry in a sound that was half scream, half whimper. The swirling buckle had connected with the light over the bed. Shards of glass fell on the mattress and pillows. The small room became shadowy, illuminated only by the light from the bathroom. Sophia could hardly catch her breath.

Langley stopped twirling the belt and the heavy buckle hit the floor with a thud. He walked up alongside his trussed victim, dragging the buckle behind him, and sat on the bed. Some of the jagged pieces of glass could be heard breaking beneath the weight of his naked buttocks and thighs. His face registered no pain.

He removed his black hat and leaned forward, wedging his face between two iron spindles of the hooped footboard. "People react in one of two ways . . . hey, pay attention, bitch. . . . " Sophia opened her eyes and lifted her head. Langley's blank face was only a foot away. A grotesque smile slowly creased his face. "I'll only be saying this once." The smile just as slowly faded. "You and I are prime examples of the two types. Both of us trying to adapt to all this shit. But, as our situation so blatantly reveals, one of us succeeded and one of us failed."

Sophia could see that his erection was starting to grow. He reached through the spindles of the footboard and cupped her bloodied face. "You did what you could, didn't you? But, like most, you yielded; fell apart; submitted to the pain this life brings, accepted it." He began to stroke her hair. "Have you any idea of the price you paid for your submission?"

Like the cold darkness that now filled the room, Sophia felt an eclipse in her soul that shadowed her will, making it unrecognizable as her own. Maybe Langley was right. Maybe, she thought, I really have become a habitual victim. Weakened over the years by fear.

"You paid with your identity," explained Langley. "You became a follower. What was it that divorced you from yourself?" His eyes were like dark wells in this poor light. Sophia avoided looking too deeply into them for fear of falling in. Such close proximity to madness has its seductive qualities. "Was it a religion? A philosophy? Or maybe something even more dangerous, say . . . like love? Do you even know?" He pulled his face away from the iron footboard and shook his head doubtfully. "Probably not. . . ." He picked his hat up off the bed and placed it squarely on his head. As he rose from the bed, Sophia stared in horror at the bloody shards of glass still stuck in the flesh of his buttocks and thighs. The once crisp, white sheets were spotted with widening bloodstains.

Langley stood directly behind her, running the length of the belt through his hand. "The type of fear that consumed your mind tends to blind as well . . . so I would doubt if you could actually pinpoint the exact moment when you were duped. . . ."

Sophia looked behind to see that Langley's member was fully engorged with blood, and his eyes were fixed in empty space. "Like most who are blinded, you were eager to find a path . . . a scent trail to follow; so you put your nose to the dust and sniffed a spoor" — he had begun to swing the buckle around again; it whirred more rapidly and forcefully in the darkness — "and the saddest thing is that your submission actually contributed to the great dissolution of the human race. . . ."

The heavy silver buckle was now whistling above them. "You see . . . the whole body of human knowledge . . . intended to bring us closer together through understanding and enlightenment . . . did just the opposite . . ."

Sophia sensed a culminating tone in his dirge. Her muscles were tightening with anticipation of the first blow.

". . . for the only consistent trend in human history has been the collapse of the communal . . . of the tribal . . . the fabric of unity has been unravelling for centuries. Accelerated by human intellection and probing, to the present condition of total isolationism . . ."

His steady ravings did not betray the fact that his eyes were slowly filling with tears of madness and desperation, or that his lip was quivering with a fear perhaps even more profound than Sophia's; for his was the fear of the dispossessed, of the very type he himself was raging against.

". . . we can only come to know ourselves through communion with others. When we fail to do so . . . we become so strange to ourselves" — his tears were falling steadily as he

strained to pull his thoughts into jagged coherency — "because
. . . self-knowledge is really knowledge of God. Lose touch with
each other . . . and . . . we lose touch with God . . . we lose touch
with the Divine within us . . . and . . ."

Sophia could now plainly hear him beginning to sob like a
baby as he lamented, ". . . and we become animals. . . ."

The depth of genuine sorrow in his last comment — as genuine as his distorted vision of reality could muster — forced upon
Sophia a curious burden, a burden that came in the form of an
unexpected emotion. A perverse feeling rushed over her from
some unimagined source.

Somehow, she felt pity for her captor.

She struggled to repress this feeling, but something powerful within her resisted. Her pity for Langley welled up, and it
terrified her. She would have felt less frightened if this pity had
sprung from another source, but it hadn't. It was her own —
and that was what was most alarming.

Where did such generosity of spirit come from?

Where had it been hibernating?

Sophia scanned the deepest alcoves of her mind for the
source of such unreasonable behaviour. But even as she searched,
her heart became fuller and fuller, and to her own astonishment
she felt this rise of pity turn into love. She had never experienced anything like this before. Such purity of feeling, of emotion.

Why now?

And why for this son of a bitch?

Just watching this perverse emotion grow and flourish, being unable to control it, once again made Sophia feel victimized.
But the harder she tried to suppress this loving tenderness for
Langley, the stronger it became — she could actually feel it surge,
like a tide swell.

She finally succumbed. Allowed her mind to merge with
emotion, to become one with it. And when she did, something
happened — something like a chemical reaction, spontaneous

and new, filling her whole body with ecstasy. A rapturous awareness of herself, so unspoiled that it could only be described as
virginal.

Sophia had, in that singular moment of personal glory,
achieved the paragon condition of her own being: experiencing
the most perfect incarnation of herself. Never before had she
felt such wondrous potential and ability. Oddly, she no longer
felt human. However, this rapture was interrupted by Langley's
psyche tipping into the dark realm of violent release.

Sophia was startled by the sound of duct tape being peeled
from a roll, and the hard slap of Langley's hand applying it to
her mouth. The wide silvery tape held fast, making any type of
utterance impossible.

She could hear him stalking about behind her. His boots
made clomping sounds against the floor that Sophia could feel
through her bent knees. Then, suddenly, there was the electronic
pop and static crackle of the small television coming to life. The
screen forced a blue glow into the darkness as it warmed. Langley
spun the channel dial rapidly, as far as his wrist could turn, then
back again. He did this three times before stopping on a channel. Then he raised the volume, filling the room with the sound
of a large choir singing a hymn.

He jacked up the volume again, pleased with what was being transmitted. The sound from the tiny speaker in the TV became distorted as the music was frayed by a hum of reverbera-
tion from the chassis of the set. Like birds trapped in a house,
the music and voices rose to the shadowy corners of the room
and flapped against the ceiling, trying to escape. The gathering
of confined sounds made the room smaller. Sophia could feel
the loudness of the trapped music flocking above her. She
couldn't breathe. Her skin burned and itched with impedance
as she prepared to die.

## CHAPTER 9

The snow had tapered off to a very fine grey dust that hung in the air instead of falling. By now, both Thomas and Gabby were chilled to the marrow. Some of the remaining newspapers that covered Gabby's legs were damp, turned into a solid clump. Thomas noticed that the old man was starting to fidget uncomfortably under the weight of the cold, wet mass on top of him, and suggested that they move somewhere else.

"Where do you have in mind?" asked Gabby.

Thomas nodded his head up the street. "How about those stairs beneath the awning?"

"Sure," said Gabby. He propped himself upright and pulled off the dampened mass of newspapers. The wet papers, now cast aside like a discarded tortoise-shell, revealed two stumps where legs ought to have been; this took Thomas by surprise, and his response caught Gabby's dark eye, making him snicker and say, "Clipped wings, son."

"Jesus, Gabby, how do you get around?" asked Thomas.

"Like this. Come on." With a grunt, he righted himself onto his knuckles and ambled off on his fists in a herky-jerky manner, his long grey hair swaying and his breath puffing in tiny clouds from the effort.

At the foot of the stairs, beneath the awning, Gabby paused and looked to the landing six steps up.

"Need a hand?" asked Thomas.

"Shit, no — a pair of legs," said Gabby, starting to laugh in spite of himself. Thomas shook his head ruefully, and watched the old man raise himself muscularly up the stairs to the landing;

he turned on his hands to face Thomas and sat himself down on the edge of the top stair.

Thomas took the stairs two at a time and sat down beside Gabby. "Show-off," grumbled the old man. This was the closest Thomas had been to Gabby, and he had expected to be overwhelmed by some sort of bodily stench, so he sniffed carefully; but he found nothing unpleasant. Both men smiled at each other in friendship, and sat silently absorbing this new setting for a few minutes, staring at the street shiny with wetness.

Gabby turned to Thomas, closing his milky eye and allowing his goat-eye to rotate randomly in its socket again. "So, tell me more about this nun," said Gabby.

Thomas ran his fingers through his wet hair, slicking it back. "She was one of my tutors. She was responsible for my lessons in English and literature. I had many tutors for various subjects, but Sister Frances was my favourite."

"Why was that?" asked Gabby.

"Oh, I don't know," replied Thomas. "She treated me different from the other nuns. With the others I was just another chore . . . another responsibility; but Sister Frances wanted to be friends." Thomas smiled to himself as he spoke. "She asked me questions about myself and wanted to know what I thought about things. She cared."

"She sounds real nice."

"She was great," said Thomas. "Although when I first met her she really scared the shit out of me. I was just a little kid at the time, maybe four or five, and I remember sitting in a large bare room with white walls, no windows, just a fluorescent light overhead and this modest gold crucifix on the west wall. . . . I really hated that fucking room for some reason" — Thomas swallowed hard — "felt really uncomfortable in that room, waiting for my tutors to come in. . . ." His voice trailed off.

"You okay, Thomas?"

"Yeah. I'm fine. What was I saying?"

"The nun scaring the shit out of you."

"Right," said Thomas, rubbing his forehead in mild agitation. "She was the very first tutor I had when my education formally began. She walked in and just kind of stood there like this massive black monolith with wire-rimmed glasses. She was fucking huge. So I started to cry."

Gabby smirked. "Tough guy, eh?"

Thomas couldn't help but grin too. "But to make matters worse, she charged! Wrapped her arms around me and tried to console me. I can still remember so vividly being smothered by a soft black tent. At first I screamed, but then I suddenly stopped. All I knew at that moment were two large warm arms that cradled me in a thick warm bosom. I cannot, to this day, remember ever feeling safer than I did in that embrace. I had never been held like that . . . ever. I can remember her smell, and the feel of her cheek on top of my head as she rocked me."

Gabby just sat there and faced Thomas, taking it all in, while his dark eye continued to roam.

While all the other nuns would routinely come into the study room and teach young Thomas only their respective academic disciplines, Sister Frances embellished her lessons with some unusual, subjective pieces of wisdom. Thomas felt a peculiar obligation to apologize on her behalf. "I guess isolation of any kind breeds distortion," he said; as a footnote, he added, "We're curious animals, aren't we?"

"We sure are," agreed Gabby.

Here Thomas paused and toed the wet grit on the step, listening to it scrape beneath his sole. "But I don't believe she ever meant to do me harm."

"What do you mean?"

"Some of the things she told me — they were . . ."

"Odd?"

Thomas half nodded. "Yeah — odd, but not hurtful," he stressed.

"Like what?" asked Gabby.

Thomas became very restless and hesitant to proceed. He

avoided eye contact with Gabby and stared at his knees.

"Listen," said Gabby. "If you don't want to talk about it . . . that's fine. You just seemed so keyed up about talking about this nun. . . ."

"I just don't want you thinking badly of her," said Thomas to his knees. "She meant a lot to me."

"Sure, sure."

There was a long silence. "She meant no harm. . . ."

"Of course she didn't," agreed Gabby. "So — what kind of things would she say to you?"

Thomas cleared his throat loudly. "Lots of things. Stuff that wasn't on the curriculum." He cleared his throat again. "Stuff that was . . ."

"What?"

". . . unorthodox. . . ."

Gabby shifted his weight and wiggled his stumps before asking, "So, can you give me a 'fer instance'?"

Thomas looked into Gabby's dark eye. The old man beamed invitingly. Thomas cleared his throat and licked his lips. "Um. . . . She . . ."

"It's all right, son," said Gabby softly. "Don't bother. This seems hard for you. Talking like this."

"No!" replied Thomas quickly. "There was this one thing she used to harp on. Over and over it used to come up. She told me never to repeat it to the other nuns or the Mother Superior. . . ."

The old man leaned forward, turning an ear slightly to Thomas's face.

"It was . . . um . . . this thing she called . . . 'God-envy'."

"God-envy?"

"That was just one of the strange notions she passed on to me during our lessons," said Thomas, slightly ashamed.

Gabby leaned forward even farther, to catch Thomas's eye. "Wanna tell me about it?"

A wind raced down the slick asphalt and swirled around

them, stirring a discarded candy wrapper and a few flattened cigarette butts on the sidewalk in front of them.

Thomas had just parted his lips to speak when he was distracted by a not so distant flurry of wings thrashing for space and distance. The noise came from up the street, close to the corner where he crossed to head home. He couldn't see where it came from, exactly, but he caught a fleeting glimpse of beating wingtips and fanned tails soaring beyond the hazy glow of the streetlight to disappear into the blackness above.

Gabby cleared his throat loudly. "Thomas — you distract easily. I think this evening is taking its toll on you."

"No shit," said Thomas, still turned away.

"Wanna call it a night?"

Like some strange incantation, Gabby's simple question rekindled Thomas's urge to speak to this lonely old man.

"Sister Frances told me that men have always feared women. That they spend their entire lives suppressing thoughts and feelings of anger and anxiety over them. That the predominant motivator in men's behaviour is not sex or hunger or political ambition, but fear."

Gabby sat still, listening. The tone in Thomas's voice was one of grave assurance, as if what he was relating were received truth. Gabby's dark eye was once again still, fixed upon Thomas as he continued to speak. "Men, as a sex, do indeed lead lives of quiet desperation. Desperate to play catch-up. To duplicate. To become like The Source. . . ."

"The Source?"

"Yes. The Source. Chosen of all earth's creatures to emulate God's greatest power, the ability to create. Women are the chosen ones. The preferred ones. God's vessels of divinity on earth. And we know it and hate it. It blackens men's hearts and souls with envy."

"God-envy is really envy of womanhood?" questioned Gabby, raising a bushy eyebrow. "And you believe this . . . ?"

Thomas wrestled with intuitive belief. "I don't know. But

these thoughts and feelings are in there, you know. Locked in. Whenever I think about it, I struggle with it myself. Struggle with convention, and unorthodox ideas that I can't uproot. Sometimes I look at women and think of their ability to bear children, and I'm so fucking awestruck by the sheer majesty of the task that I'm almost completely convinced that Sister Frances was right. That women walk this planet — have always walked the planet — as . . ." He choked on his next word. Choked on conventional ideology and wisdom, but eventually finished his thought: ". . . as Jesuses."

Thomas slowly looked at Gabby, who was silent after absorbing these words. Both men stared at each other.

"I . . . I know how twisted that sounds," said Thomas.

Gabby hunched his shoulders. "Do you?"

"Yes, I do. But there's a sort of logic to Sister Frances's ideas. A sort of mystical logic that transcends linear reasoning, a logic of instinct and blood."

Gabby raised his dark eye, and spoke in a deep, resonant tone that shocked Thomas. "Equating Christhood with corporeal logistics is a curious business for a nun, don't you think?"

Thomas sat stunned and couldn't answer. "Corporeal logistics," he repeated to himself; the words sounded strange coming from this street person, they didn't fit his image. He was becoming unnerved as he watched the old man's mouth work, echoing his last remark.

"'A logic of instinct and blood,'" marvelled Gabby. "Where would a nun take a young man with these ideas?"

Thomas shook his head, feeling ashamed again; having said too much.

"She . . . ," began Gabby.

"She meant me no harm!" Thomas yelled.

"So you've said. . . ."

"SHE LOVED ME! SHE LOVED ME!" Thomas was now screaming. His voice filled the empty street and, like the violent whirring of wings that had distracted him earlier, disappeared into the black heavens.

Gabby could see that Thomas was on the verge of tears. He placed his hand firmly on Thomas's quivering shoulder and said, "Tell me the rest."

Thomas looked into Gabby's goat-eye; looked deep into the purple oblong pupil; and again, something beyond his own will urged him to continue.

"She told me that a woman's monthly bleeding was a communion with God. A reminder of her blessing and duty. A truer bond than the empty symbolic gesture of wafer and wine performed at the altar by men."

"Empty . . . symbolic . . . gesture . . . ," whispered Gabby to himself.

"And . . . and that, like Jesus, women and only women can achieve rapture through the pain and bloodshed of creation. Creation of new life, new hope, new order — Christ on the cross and womankind in laborious childbirth — through blood to rapturous agony. You know, Sister Frances even had this wild crucifix that was like no other in the entire convent."

"How so?" enquired Gabby.

"Well, all the other crucifixes had a dead Christ on them. Hanging limp with His passion all used up."

"Yes . . . ?"

"But Sister Frances's Christ was still alive. Thrashing in pain. The whole crucifix was hand-carved out of wood with incredible detail. I can still see His face twisted in anguish. Eyes shut, mouth screaming. His fingers were curled like a bird's claw and His body was eternally writhing in a grotesque, contorted 'S'."

"Why would she have such a thing?" asked Gabby slowly.

"That's what all the other nuns wondered," continued Thomas. "But she explained to me that the image of the dead Christ, although a wondrous sight, lacked the nobility and power of the agonizing Christ. Her crucifix depicted Jesus at the most supremely glorious moment in human history — an eye-blink away from eternity — when he was literally being torn apart.

The God being torn from within the man. In the throes of the ultimate sacrifice. A sacrifice of perfect love."

Gabby had turned away as Thomas finished speaking. He was watching a beetle scamper along the cement step, inching closer to his hand; it had somehow become lost and was searching for escape from the cold. Gabby raised his hand to avoid contact, but then lowered a coarse index finger to rest firmly upon the beetle's hard black shell. He watched the spiny legs twitch under the pressure, as the insect tried to avoid being crushed. "Is that it, then?" he asked as his dark eye turned from the weakening insect back to Thomas.

"Is that it?"

"I don't know."

Thomas began to feel annoyed again. "Are you playing with me? Because if you are, you can fuck right off. I'm doing you a favour sitting here. I don't even know why I've bothered to spend so much time with you. I don't even know you and I'm rambling on like you're my best friend." He dropped his tired head. "Goddamned night . . . ," he whispered to himself.

"Out of the mouths of babes," said Gabby softly as he lifted his finger and watched the little beetle scurry into a crack in the cement.

"What?"

Gabby too suddenly looked very weary. "Nothing."

Getting up to leave, Thomas felt a definite sense of finality to his encounter with Gabby. Such strange talk! He wondered what had ever possessed him to reveal such personal and capricious anecdotes to a stranger.

He felt a hot rush of blood to his legs as he stretched, balancing on the balls of his feet.

The old man looked up at him. The syrupy discharge from his blind eye flowed steadily down his cheek in a straight, silvery line.

Thomas raised a grimy, bloody hand from his pocket to

sheepishly wave goodbye. "I'm sorry for losing it on you . . . didn't mean to yell. See you around."

Wisps of cold breath slithered from beneath Gabby's yellowed teeth as he spoke. "Not likely, son." His tone had a serious bend to it.

Again Thomas felt stupidly caught off guard, needing to explain to himself. "I didn't mean literally. I just meant, you know, goodbye."

"Goodbye, then."

Thomas nodded silently and slowly walked down the stairs to the sidewalk. A gentle snow had begun to fall again, like silt from the sky. His face was so cold that he couldn't tell if the tiny flakes were melting as they brushed his cheek. He stood in front of the stairs, lingering, unsure about leaving now. Something in the gut. An uneasiness that he couldn't explain, mounting like bile. "Are you going to be all right, Gabby?"

"Done all right so far," said the old man curtly. "You'd best be running along now. Time, Thomas, time." And with that he clapped his gnarled hands sharply, twice.

Indeed.

So — oddly out of sorts, like a shunned child — Thomas started down the length of street, towards the corner. He walked heavily, without the brisk anticipation of returning to his warm home that had marked his departure to the library.

His head swam. His return was punctuated by thoughts of the dishevelled street man he had left sitting alone. Such strange, strange talk. Whatever got into me, Thomas wondered. Talking to a street person in the fucking cold.

Just up ahead, a small flock of pigeons lighted and gathered — the wing-beating heard earlier! — to peck at popcorn crumbs in the cracks and crevices of the sidewalk. The mottled birds nervously scattered as Thomas lingered about their feeding spot. He looked up from the sidewalk and recognized this place — the doorway was where he had been asked the time by the woman obscured by shadows. He read the hand-painted glass on the door: Blue Orchi Hotcl; the "d" was completely scratched away and the "e" had been crudely transformed. He glanced up the gritty face of the building; its brown brick was pocked by time and acid rain, lending a certain aged charm. The altered letters, however, made it all look cheap and neglected — much like the reputation of those who dwelled within.

A few doors ahead was the electronics store, its front window still flickering with electric blue light from the single TV. Thomas walked through the pigeons, causing them to flap up to his knees and wait, then drop to busy themselves again with the business of being pigeons. As he lumbered by the store window, the indefatigable Reverend Lucius Del Roberts was still herding the bovine masses on the airwaves — Bible in hand, eyes closed in prayer.

A sharp cold slap of wind carrying snow-dust and street smells made Thomas yearn for his own bed. "Get me the fuck outta here," he sighed to himself. He turned towards his own street, head down against the cold, preparing to cross. He had taken two long steps out into the street when an impulse to look back at the awning-covered steps suddenly washed over his mind. He stopped in the middle of the street and turned, expecting to see Gabby still sitting by himself on the landing.

But Gabby wasn't there.

Thomas's brow furrowed. Where the hell had he got to so fast —?

Then it happened. A mind-numbing sound like the wail of a spurned sea siren pierced his ears. There was something like a minute flash of white light in his brain, then complete darkness.

Like a rifle-shot through the brain, a single neuroelectrical impulse ripped through Thomas's consciousness upon impact with the truck. It filled his mind with an explosion of imagery from a single incident six years earlier — a seemingly isolated moment then, a moment that had trickled into his consciousness earlier at the sight of his barren mantel, but one that now engulfed him like rushing water. For that brief microsecond before he became unconscious, this is what filled Thomas Gorgon's mind:

Elaine.

Toeing a dust-bunny with sandalled feet, she made herself comfortable on one of the many boxes randomly stacked around the large, bare living-room.

Her lush auburn hair was tied back in a thick ponytail. She was clad in an old Grateful Dead T-shirt of faded purple tie-dye, and threadbare cut-off Levis. Weekender beautiful.

"Nice old place," she said, her voice echoing slightly. "Always admired it, passing by."

"Yes, it's lovely, isn't it?" agreed Thomas. He scanned the emptiness around them, filled with mixed feelings of happiness for his newly purchased home and utter dread of unpacking his Life.

She too was scanning the room. Admiring the old fireplace. Thomas noticed a single ringlet of reddish-gold clinging to her cheek in the humidity, prompting him to ask, "Care for a beer?"

"Love one."

He headed for the kitchen and pulled two icy cans from the bottom shelf of the refrigerator. He had had the forethought to put the two six-packs into the fridge before he even lifted the first box off the truck.

"Here you go."

"Thanks." She smiled gloriously.

She pulled her tab with a loud pssshhht and drew a long gulp. She kept her head back and let the coldness trickle down her throat.

Thomas just sat there, enraptured by her wholesome beauty. When she pulled her head back down and opened her eyes, she dimpled coquettishly.

Thomas's eyes snapped back into focus, and the interval of his own *pssshhht* served as an embarrassingly awkward punctuation in time. He felt his face warming.

"Aren't you thirsty?" she asked playfully.

He said nothing, but drank down a number of hard gulps.

"We haven't been formally introduced," she said, leaning forward, her hand outstretched. "Elaine Deerhurst."

"Thomas. Thomas Gorgon." Her hand was soft. He felt a shot of tingling in his testicles. "I'm a teacher. I'll be teaching literature at the community college."

Elaine smiled. "I know."

"You do?"

She took another sip of beer. He could just barely see the golden liquid washing over her tongue. "Yes, I do," she said. "I'll be one of your colleagues. I teach a course in linguistics."

"For what department?"

"Anthropology."

"Been with the college long?"

"About two years. Spent my first year as a teaching assistant."

This was going nowhere fast, thought Thomas. He absolutely hated small talk. He preferred to say nothing at all, rather than engage in a verbal ping-pong match. Especially with a gorgeous woman he barely knew.

She was looking down at the floor, toying once again with that dust-bunny. He thought of initiating a different discussion, in hopes of meatier conversation.

"So . . . you live nearby?" Attaboy, he thought to himself. Sparkling repartee, dickhead.

"Next block. Third house on the north side." Thomas nodded blandly, then quickly raised his beer to occupy his mouth. Elaine followed suit, cocking her head back to expose her smooth white throat. He watched as her throat gently pulsated.

She placed the beer down on the floor between her feet. The sound of the aluminium can was small and hollow, but still resonated within the confines of the empty room. Fearing she was about to up and leave, Thomas spoke quickly.

"Elaine . . . ?"

"Yes?" Her eyes were wide. And green. Green eyes. How

perfect, thought Thomas.

Be cool. Don't fuck it up. The back of his neck felt hot. "Would you like to have dinner with me tonight? Here?"

That smile. "I'd love to, Thomas."

"Great. Um, how does take-out Chinese grab you? I noticed a Chinese restaurant a couple of blocks back, at the four-way stop."

"The Red Dragon."

"Seven o'clock?"

She rose and headed for the front door. "See you then."

Thomas watched as she walked to her car. A canary-yellow VW Beetle. He glanced at his watch. It was just after ten; that gave him almost nine hours.

As his shattered body spun in the air like a grotesque marionette; this too filled his mind before he hit the asphalt:

Her hair was down. Long luscious waves of auburn that moved like fire when she shook her head. "No, really, I've had quite enough. Thanks."

Thomas was clearing away the empty boxes emblazoned with sinewy red dragons while Elaine surveyed the now furnished living-room.

"You must've really put it into overdrive after I left," she said with admiration. "This room looks great!"

As Thomas returned from the still bare kitchen, he couldn't agree more. The living-room did look good. Very warm and inviting. He had even found a florist's shop and purchased some daisies and ferns to place in a vase on the pine coffee-table.

Everything was just about where he wanted it: the two restored wingback chairs on either side of the large bay window; the oriental divan against the adjacent wall, with a pedestal Tiffany lamp to loom over it; and above the fireplace, a wooden clock from a train station.

Elaine returned to the centre of the room and sank her stockinged toes into the wool pile of his Persian rug. "Yup, the room looks wonderful! You've got excellent taste for a bachelor." Again she smiled. Almost dangerously.

"Thanks," said Thomas, returning to the divan. "Collecting antiques is my only real indulgence. Unfortunately, I have no real sense of co-ordinating pieces to keep to a particular era or style. I just sort of buy whatever catches my eye." He surveyed the room. It was true — all his antiques were excellent pieces, some of them quite rare and unusual, but when they were put together it was evident that the room lacked structure and form. The individual pieces couldn't make the room whole. The words "disjointed" and "accidental" came to mind.

"Well, Mr. Gorgon," said Elaine, as she slumped into a wingback chair, "it all looks lovely to me."

And you look lovely to me, thought Thomas. She wore a summer dress of petits-fleurs design and smelled ever so delicately of lily of the valley. Her hair was alive and seemed to dance on her slender shoulders, even when she sat still. He was aroused by the thought of her efforts to look this beautiful tonight.

She rose from her chair slowly. "You know what this room really needs?"

Thomas was savouring her image as she walked over to the fireplace. The ripe curve of her breasts, her long graceful legs. And the waft of perfume as she moved. There was a tightening between his legs that caused him to shift his weight.

"What this room needs," she repeated, "is family pictures."

Thomas's face went blank; he felt as if the wind had been knocked out of him.

"You know, old black-and-white photographs of your ancestors. I bet you have some gorgeous photos in antique frames!"

Thomas sat quiet. Spent.

She rushed over and knelt before him. "Come on! Let's look through your boxes and find them! I'd just love to see them!"

She jumped up and ran into the next room, where most of the unopened boxes had been moved, and began to forage. Her voice sounded distant to his ears.

"I just love old photos! Don't you? The ancient faces staring back at you . . . having them around the house says so much about a person. Who they are, where they've come from . . . don't you think? Thomas . . . ?"

She trotted back into the living-room. "Thomas?"

He just sat there, motionless.

She knelt back down in front of him and placed her hand on his knee. "Are you all right?"

Her touch caused his knee to jump and his pulse to quicken. "I'm fine," he said.

Elaine's smile was beginning to fade. She slowly stood up and walked backwards to the fireplace. The ticking of the train-station clock grew louder. "I . . . I was thinking those photographs would look smashing all along this mantel here." She ran her hand along the length of its bare surface. "They would lend such an atmosphere . . ."

Thomas stared up at her with cold eyes.

". . . to this room," she said, her voice trailing.

"There are no fucking photographs, Elaine."

She opened her mouth to speak but couldn't. She was starting to tremble.

Thomas's face was darkening and his voice was pitched to a yell. "No fucking family! No fucking parents! No fucking siblings! No fucking memories!"

Hot tears welled in Elaine's eyes. Her mouth quivered. She bolted for the door, her face streaming with tears. Thomas rose after her and gently but firmly grabbed her arm at the front door, saying, almost in a whisper, "You see . . ."

But Elaine wrenched her arm free and ran to her yellow car, and sped away without looking back. Leaving Thomas framed in his doorway to complete his apology: ". . . I'm all alone."

This was the last thing Thomas's mind revealed to itself before his bloodied head hit the cold street.

Gabby emerged from a bus-stop shelter and rested his stumps over the curb. He had watched Thomas Gorgon being struck down by the hit-and-run. He rubbed his stubbly chin against his shoulder.

"So this is the unrecognizable . . . the lost," he said, looking at his gnarled hands. "I . . . I just wanted to see. . . ." The dark wind blew through his hair, covering his face. He cocked his shaggy head as if to listen better. "I know, I know. . . ." He sighed wearily. "It won't happen again. Forgive me . . . I'm on my way. . . ."

The old, legless street man grunted as he hoisted himself above the curb, taking one last look at Thomas Gorgon's still body before slowly making his way down the sidewalk.

# Chapter 10

Joseph Langley stood behind Sophia and absorbed the moment. He closed his eyes. In his mind, he isolated the elements that made this moment beautiful: the darkness, the vulnerability, the blood, and the fear . . . especially the fear. He could almost smell it. His head swirled gently, as if blending the components of a fine wine into a heady bouquet. He reached down and felt the length of his erection, testing its readiness. His heart began to quicken.

**Now. Do it now, Azrael.**

Langley raised his arm straight up.

**You've led the lamb.**

With a sharp, circular motion of his wrist the length of the weighted leather belt rose once again and began to beat like a helicopter blade. He ran his thumb over the dewy glans of his penis.

**To slaughter. To merciful slaughter.**

The curved, needle-sharp prong circled high above Sophia's back and shoulders. Langley opened his eyes and said, "Maybe one last indulgence before getting down to business. . . ." He glanced down the cleavage of her buttocks, and with a powerful snapping of his wrist and forearm the deadly belt buckle sliced the air, hooking onto one of the metal bars of the curved footboard, mere inches from Sophia's head.

"Fucking hell," he muttered through clenched teeth, trying to jiggle the sharp prong free. Almost immediately, he was struck by the realization that this helpless woman had not flinched.

Not a bit. He stood for a few seconds trying to comprehend this unnatural reaction, but quickly shook it off, attributing it to her state of shock.

Sophia remained absolutely motionless as the large buckle was worked free and twirled again for another strike. She had plainly heard Langley's comments and the buckle connecting just above her right ear with a loud clank. She was still firmly rooted in the now; however, the imperative of her immediate physical danger had diminished — and the normal impulse to escape had completely evaporated. All this was more than just an act of will or a frame of mind; it was a completely altered state of being. An emergence of nothing new, but of something dormant. Something more real and true than the self she had been living with for the past thirty-six years.

The heavy buckle came down hard. The sharpened prong pierced the skin where her neck blended into her shoulder. She felt it dig in and lodge in her collarbone.

"Ha!" exclaimed Langley, and he jerked back on the belt, breaking Sophia's clavicle with a loud snap, clearly audible even above the blaring choir.

Despite the pain, Sophia uttered no sound. Surprisingly — especially to herself — she was in complete control during this assault.

Her knees did not give out beneath her.

Her mind remained razor-sharp.

And she was not afraid.

The flat, ornate plate of the buckle was snugly pressed to her flesh. Despite the violent tug, there was almost no trace of blood; just a greasy smear of crimson around the edge of the buckle.

Langley maintained a taut rein with one hand. He toyingly pulled on the strap to watch her broken collarbone flick back and forth, like a pinball paddle. This pleased him. With each passing minute, he was becoming more and more deeply immersed in the seductive tow of violent release. He began to pull on the belt, inching his way — hand over hand — closing the gap between his pelvis and her buttocks. He closed his eyes. His lips parted in anticipation.

A mere fraction of an inch from contact, Langley didn't see the large moth land on Sophia's back — the same moth that had caught her attention in the hallway.

The moth poised itself upon her spine and spread its wings, exposing the dark maroon splotches at the tips and the base of its tail. Just then a convulsion surged through Sophia's body. Her spasms sent waves of motion and resistance up the length of taut leather into Langley's hand, startling him just as he was about to violate her.

He straightened his back and stared in horror. Sophia's convulsions were moving the heavy iron bed; her head thrashed, whipping her dark hair about; her spine undulated visibly; and the veins in her hands, arms, legs, and feet were swollen, threatening to burst through the skin.

Langley released the belt and watched it wave and snap with her contortions. The moth rose from her back and hovered near the broken light, barely visible, finally resting on the jagged edge of a shattered bulb.

The choir on the TV had begun another hymn. A baritone soloist broke into an elaborate aria just as Sophia suddenly stopped shaking.

Langley could see that every muscle in her naked body was flexed, stretching the skin. What he witnessed next sent him stumbling to the floor, cowering. He wanted to look away, but found he could not. He also wanted to scream, but something in the room denied him that ability.

The flesh of both her palms suddenly burst open, as did the flesh on the soles of both her feet. She clenched her teeth and shut her eyes. Exhausted, she fell to her knees and rolled onto her hip. Blood flowed from her hands and ran down her arms, dripping from her elbows. She made a conscious effort to steady her frantic breathing, to try to reduce the panic and shock. Fear, real fear, once again crept into her heart. She was confused. The pain in her hands and feet was excruciating, and intense pain shot through her limbs. Deep, slowly drawn breaths filled her lungs; she wished she could remove the duct tape and breathe through her mouth. She wanted more air; she wanted control.

Sophia drew a powerful breath and at the same time lifted herself back to her knees. No sooner had she gained her balance than a sharp pain spread across her side. She gasped for breath. She turned her head towards the pain, expecting to see Langley attacking her again. But he wasn't there. A glance over her other shoulder showed him fumbling to put on his pants. His face registered absolute horror.

The pain in her side was intensifying, and becoming more focused on a pinpoint location between her ribs, just below her breast. She tried to scream and the flesh between her ribs split, leaving a deep gash.

Again she fought for breath. She tugged at her bindings and flung her hair about in anger and fear. Her cheeks bulged like balloons as she tried to force intelligible pleas at Langley, who was gathering up the last of his possessions and heading for the door. She could see him out of the corner of her eye. His shirt-tail was hanging out and his cuffs were unbuttoned. His face was chalky.

"PLEASE . . . HELP ME . . . !" Sophia tried to holler, but it came out as a mumble. This new assailant was even more frightening than Langley. This new attack was coming from everywhere . . . and nowhere. Part of Sophia actually wanted Langley to stay.

Unnoticed in all the confusion, the moth dropped from its perch on the broken bulb; it hung in the air briefly, then spread its wings in a gesture that summoned a blinding pulse of light.

There followed a stillness that was absolute. Without looking, Sophia knew she was alone. Langley was gone. And in that moment of uneasy peace, she yielded to the luxury of weeping.

What had happened in that room, with that flash of light, Sophia did not immediately understand. The incident had been as brief as it was intense: faster than an eye-blink and infinitely more powerful than human love or imagination. In scientific terms, the moment could have been classified as an alteration in the time-space continuum; a sort of sudden progressive hiccup. In the world of the pious, the very same moment was, quite simply, a miracle of intervention.

Sophia rested on her knees. She was completely exhausted and covered in blood, and tears rolled down her face. She remained kneeling for a long period, recuperating from the double onslaught. She felt as though every fibre in her body had been abused. But she was still alive, and for this she was grateful. She remained unclear about the flash of light — hesitant — but the reality was that she had been rescued, and she felt a new sense of hope. She spoke simple words with tenderness: "Merci, Mon Seigneur, pour cette délivrance."

Sophia gradually came to realize that the silk necktie that bound her swollen, bloodied hands to the bedpost had some give to it. She could not tell if it had been loosened by her thrashing, or if the greasiness of the blood was allowing her aching hands to slip out. With some painful tugging she was free. Lying on her back, she tried to remove the thick band of duct tape across her face, but her hands were so badly torn and swollen that her fingers would barely respond. After some delicate picking, she loosened a corner of the tape from her cheek and with one quick twist of her head pulled the tape away. She drew in a long, satisfying breath, enjoying the sensation of air rushing over her tongue and teeth. It felt good. It felt like a small freedom, and she smiled.

She pulled herself up to a sitting position. She looked at her feet, at the pulpy protrusions of flesh that erupted from the tops, and the blood . . . the heavy pool at the base of the bed, dark and shiny.

She examined the rest of her nakedness. Long tracks of blood had coursed down from her head and face, over her breasts and belly. Her hands were ruined. And there was so much blood.

The sight of it scared her again, interrupting her brief celebration of freedom. She needed professional care. The telephone, she thought. I'll dial 911.

She rolled onto her stomach and slithered, propelling herself along the floor with her left elbow and a shuffling motion of her knees. She had serpentined a few feet before she realized that the belt buckle was still embedded in her shoulder. She paused to right herself again, and with her left hand delicately pulled the sharp prong from her flesh; it came out easily, but the jarring of the broken bone made her grimace.

She sat there for a minute staring at the large buckle. Felt the weight in her hand. Stared at the filed-down prong, shaking her head sadly at the type of sick mind that would spend time fabricating such a means of torture. Then she placed the buckle and belt down and proceeded to inch her way towards the phone.

Before she even reached it, though, she lowered her forehead to the floor and sighed in exasperation, "Damn it. . . ." The line had been cut. Even in the muted light, she could see the severed cord. "Shit, now what do I do?" What she really needed was to get cleaned up and dressed. She made her way towards the light of the bathroom.

The tile on the floor felt icy against her skin, and the single lightbulb above the sink was harsh to her eyes. She worked her way onto the toilet seat with a great deal of struggling. This manoeuvring was taking its toll; sitting there, she felt lightheaded. The wet washcloth and soap were still on the floor, as were random drops of sprayed blood; the sink was still partially full of water, now cool; and a faint smear of redness stained the sink where her head had struck it. Sophia closed her eyes and bit her lip, trying to suppress her emotions.

Feeling a little more clear-headed, she hoisted herself up onto the sink with her elbow, floundering with slippery aching feet to catch a glimpse of herself in the mirror. After all that had happened, she needed to see if she was still herself. Something had changed inside her, transformed her, making her inner workings alien.

As she locked her elbow straight, bracing her weight against her stiffened arm, she gazed into the mirror. It was painful but she needed to see, to know. Just as she had feared, her face too had changed.

The change was more than the deep gash across her forehead; more than the broken angle of her nose; more than the dark streaks of blood that flowed down her face. There was a profound change, so profound that it overshadowed the damage Langley had inflicted upon her. It had come, she reasoned, from the second assault, for what she saw in the mirror was a reflection of a reflection. A reflection from within, glowing in her eyes, of the most perfect aspect of her being. It burned like a fire, honing her gaze to an intensity that saw past the ugliness of this world to the very heart of all things beautiful and human.

"Mon Dieu . . . ," she whispered.

When the initial shock wore off, Sophia lowered herself to the floor and crept to the bathtub. She was eventually able to turn the taps on and adjust the temperature. The warm water ran forcefully over her fingers, and her mind filled with the anticipation of a soothing shower. She pulled the shower lever and the water cascaded with an inviting drumming.

Sophia climbed into the tub and lay down, letting the warm water run off her skin and swirl, dark and red, around the silvery ring of the drain. She imagined the infected water rushing down the drain, through the dirty black pipes, to find its rightful place in the sewers, among the rats and snakes and mould. All washed away — all the blood, the fear, the poison; all of Langley's sin, all of Sophia's. Washed away.

She remained under the shower until she felt it turn cooler. Then she eased herself up and adjusted the taps to a hotter setting. The heat brought back some flexibility to her fingers — not much, but some; she gently tossed her long hair under the water, removing the traces of blood. A quick once-over revealed that her skin was clean but her wounds were still bleeding; her hands and feet still dripped blood, and the gash in her side was faintly trickling.

The water was now getting cold, but she had to clean out the deep gashes on her palms. She reversed the shower lever, reduced the water to a bare trickle, and gently cupped her two palms beneath the tiny stream. But despite the pain that raced up her arms, she noticed that there was no weight in her hands . . . the water wasn't accumulating. She looked into the bowl of her hands to see the water pouring through her wounds.

"Oh, shit," she said, trembling. These weren't gashes at all. They were holes driven right through her palms.

Sophia sat in the tub, curled up tight with her knees under her chin. Her teeth were chattering uncontrollably. Deep within her, the impulse to pray tried to surface; but there was a question, or at least something like a question, that remained unformulated in her mind, making her hesitate.

At the sound of a car horn blaring, she bolted upright. There was a long screech of tires, followed by the sound of impact.

Without a thought for her wounds, Sophia rose from the tub and rushed to the window. Down below she saw the form of a man lying in the middle of the street. Dry whirls of snow spun over his still body. In the distance she could plainly see a pair of red tail-lights diminishing.

She brought her face close to the cold pane, trying to make out the victim. Her breath was fogging the glass, so she wiped it clear with her forearm. Her eyes grew wide.

She knew this man! At least, she recognized him by his coat. This was the hatless man of whom she had asked the time! The man with the books in his hand! He wasn't moving, and she wondered if he was dead.

She opened her window and stuck her head out, and the wind caught her heavy hair, whipping the wet, thick strands across her face. She drew the curtain across her body as the cold air rushed in. Several windows were lit and filled with motionless onlookers. A couple of windows over, Sophia noticed a woman talking on the telephone, staring down below; her hands were moving nervously in front of her face. Sophia hoped she was calling for help. Shortly after, the woman hung up the phone, then slowly drew her curtains, though her shape remained still behind the curtain.

Sophia pulled her head back in and closed the window.

As she watched the ambulance pull away, she felt relieved to notice that the paramedics had not covered the man's face, and that they took great care in loading the gurney. He's still alive, she thought. This brought a smile to her face.

It was only after she backed away from the window that Sophia looked at the bloody stains across the floor, and remembered how she had jumped from the tub and run to the window, how she had thrown the window open with her ruined hands. She knit her brow and stared at her bleeding hands and feet. How —? And why —?

Something was strange. Something was very strange.

# CHAPTER 11

The call was received at 4:21 a.m.

"911. Police, fire department, or ambulance?"

"Um. . . ." The woman calling was drawing a blank. Panic. Routinely the operator restarted her monotonous dirge. "911. Police, fire depart . . ."

"Yes! Police!" The caller's voice was frenzied. "And an ambulance! Someone's been run over!"

"What is the address of the accident site?"

"Just south of the corner of Witchurch and 13th Street."

"I am dispatching an ambulance and the police now. Please hold the line." There was a series of clicking sounds; then the operator returned. "What condition is the victim in?"

"I don't know. He isn't moving. I'm phoning from a hotel room above where he's lying. The Blue Orchid."

"Did you actually witness the accident?"

"Well, not the actual hit-and-run —"

The operator immediately cut in. "The vehicle in question is no longer at the site?"

"No. I heard a blaring horn that lasted a few seconds, a hollow thud, some hard braking, and then the sound of a car accelerating. By the time I got to the window, about all I could see were some tail-lights speeding off."

"Could you make out a licence-plate number?"

"No," apologized the woman. "It was too dark and distant."

"What about the make of the vehicle?"

"I think it might have been a truck. A dark truck. The delivery kind."

"All right," concluded the operator. "Is anyone tending to the victim?"

"The street's empty. He's just lying there."

The caller could see light snow settling like sediment on the still body down below. The operator's prattle continued in her ear, much of it lost as the caller was absorbed in rueful observance of the still man. Him lying down there, so utterly alone — broken, possibly even dead — was the saddest thing she had ever seen. She just caught the tail-end of the operator's instructions: ". . . keep the victim warm, but don't try to move him. There may be neck or spinal damage."

The caller responded softly, distantly, "Um, all right. . . ."

"The police and the paramedics should be arriving any moment," said the operator in a conclusive manner, and there was dead air on the line.

"Thank you," said the caller, and she hung up.

No sooner had she done so than she heard the first plaintive wails of the approaching ambulance and cruisers. As their pulsating blue and red lights filled the darkened street, making everything throb with colour, the caller — high above the scene — pulled the curtains closed, opting not to bear witness.

The third rib had broken and jutted upward, tearing the lower part of the lung sac and piercing a small hole in the heart. There was considerable bleeding internally and breathing was becoming sporadic and weaker with each drawn breath.

Thomas Gorgon's pulse was registering a faint, infrequent bleep on the monitor. Suspended above his inert frame, expert hands and life-feeding tubes struggled to maintain life as the ambulance sped towards the hospital.

A sudden cough and gasp from Thomas filled his oxygen mask with a splattering of bright, frothy lung-blood. A paramedic who was administering an IV quickly removed the clear plastic mask as Thomas coughed again, sending a slapping spray of blood into his face. "Jesus . . . !" The paramedic wiped the warm, stinging blood from his eyes and blinked a couple of times to clear his hazy vision; he then blotted the large red bubbles from Thomas's lips with a tissue.

Quickly wiping the interior of the mask, the paramedic reapplied it to Thomas's lower face and watched him feebly suck air. This guy's coastin' in DOA, he thought sombrely.

"Thomas . . . ?"

Thomas was startled by the sound of his own name. The voice he heard — not through his ears, but from deep within himself — was a rich and resonant one. The sound seemed to ripple outwards from his wounded core, surfacing towards his skin to seep out through his pores. His soul hummed.

Although he couldn't recognize the voice, he felt compelled to search for its source.

"Yes?" he answered. There was no response. Only darkness. And then a man came forth from this perfect darkness. He seemed to appear out of nowhere, silently, like a curl of fog. He stood motionless in the surrounding dark, draped in a hooded habit.

Thomas approached the man. He felt no fear, only a burning desire to speak and to know; but he kept his silence despite the incredible urge to pose question after question.

The man removed the hood. He appeared to be in his mid to late thirties. Handsome, with dark olive skin, a high brow, and a strong nose, and intense eyes of aqua, the colour of virgin sea-water. His hands and feet were hidden beneath the folds of his loose garb. He stood and looked silently at Thomas for a long time before he spoke, but, when he did, the strange and wonderfully resonant voice that Thomas had first heard was gone. Now his tone was immediate and warm. "Do you know me?"

Thomas felt his throat tighten. "Are you God?"

The man smiled. "No," he explained slowly, "I am Simon Peter, the Canaanite."

"Simon who?"

The man cast down his eyes momentarily, then raised them when he found a satisfactory answer. "You may know me better as the man upon whom a church was built."

"Why are you here?" asked Thomas.

"I was sent."

"By God, right?"

"Yes," said Simon Peter.

Thomas knit his brow in equal measures of confusion and contemplation.

"I've upset you, haven't I?" continued Simon Peter.

Thomas shook his head. "Not at all. This kind of shit happens to me all the time."

Now it was Simon Peter's brow that knit.

"Simon Peter . . . ," Thomas echoed to himself. "Simon . . . Peter . . . Peter. . . . Are you saying you're SAINT Peter? The Pearly Gates Saint Peter?"

"Yes," responded the saint.

Thomas looked about in the infinite darkness. "I don't see any Pearly Gates."

"No."

Thomas couldn't breathe; his knees buckled. "Oh, f — . . . oh . . . oh, shit." He swallowed. "I . . . I'm in hell?"

"No, Thomas."

"Wait a minute . . . Saint Peter, am I d . . . ?" He couldn't bring himself to say the word.

"No, not yet."

Not yet? "Well, then isn't this all kind of premature?"

"Normally it would be," replied the saint. "But these circumstances are drastically different."

Thomas ran his still bloodied hands through his hair and took in a deep, painful breath. This was not sinking in. "Well, if I'm not — you know — dead, where am I and what are you doing here?"

Saint Peter's smile melted away. "Thomas," he began,

"we've got a lot to talk about."

Just as Thomas had begun to feel more accustomed to the presence of this magnificent-looking man, he was distracted by something he heard all around him. A sound unlike anything he had ever heard before, yet strangely familiar.

He slowly cocked his head back and swallowed the surrounding darkness with his eyes, as he strained to identify the sound that swirled around them. The more he concentrated on deciphering it, the more intense and wonderfully complex it appeared. Finally he could no longer refrain from asking. "What is that incredible sound?"

The saint smiled. "It is called The Song of Man."

Thomas smiled too. "Is it music?"

"Not exactly as you know music."

Thomas wagged his finger in the darkness, like a pulp-fiction detective piecing together a mystery. "I know this sound, it —"

"Sound*sss*," interrupted Peter, emphasizing the plural.

Thomas was growing more in awe, the more this beautiful Song of Man filled his soul with absolute joy. "Sounds," he repeated. "I can't make out any one sound, let alone a multitude of them. Just what is this song?"

Saint Peter paused before he spoke. "The sounds you hear are actually the most perfect thing you have yet experienced." For a moment he spread wide his arms, allowing the folds of his habit to fall open like great wings. "This Song of Man is the harmonious orchestration of all that is audibly knowable to your species. We reveal it to you mortals whenever we come in contact with you. The familiarity of earthly sounds is supposed to calm you."

"Like a lullaby?" asked Thomas.

Peter rolled his eyes as he pondered this. "Yes," he agreed, "something like a lullaby."

The saint continued to watch this mortal consumed in child-like wonder. "Thomas," he said softly.

But Thomas didn't hear his gentle appeal; he was entirely consumed by the immense vortex of sound. "What are the threads in this song, Peter? Help me hear them, please."

Peter bowed his head slightly, swallowed hard, and took a deep breath, while Thomas raised his arms, stretching out his sticky, bloodied fingers as if trying to capture a bundle of sounds. As Peter spoke, he sadly looked into the mortal's ecstatic face. "The sounds contained within the Song of Man are almost too numerous to count. And they vary according to the individual's experience on the planet. Each song is personal. Each man, woman, and child, throughout life — from the very first day — is accumulating the elements of a song, to be catalogued by the Master."

"The Master," interrupted Thomas quickly. "You mean God."

"Yes," replied the saint. "By listening with an accepting ear, a person can hear many wonderful things in his song. Things that brought joy to life."

Thomas stood distracted, his head turning from left to right as he tried to hook a piece of his song with his dull ear.

Saint Peter lowered his deep aqua eyes. He stood quietly, waiting for Thomas.

Thomas pulled himself away from the swirling euphony to ask, "Tell me, what exactly makes up these songs — what does God choose to incorporate?"

"The Master does not choose the sounds, Thomas," replied the saint. "That is determined by the measure of joy any given sound effects upon the individual's soul. As I told you, it is a very personal thing."

"But I can't extract anything from my song," said Thomas, his anxiety mounting.

Peter felt his concern, and quickly responded. "Anything can be part of a mortal's song," he repeated. "Things like birdsong, a child's laughter, the sound of rain, wind, a mother's heartbeat. . . ."

"Mother's heartb—!" Thomas exclaimed

It was done. As soon as it was uttered, it was done. The saint stood in anguish as Thomas's eyes lit up.

Thomas took a fervent step towards the immortal. "Show me! Show me, please! Where is my mother's heartbeat? Help me find it! Please, please, let me hear it!"

Peter's heart ached as he realized it could no longer be avoided. Thomas had to know the truth of his origin, of his self. But in revealing this truth, Peter knew, he was contributing to catastrophe.

"Listen to me," he pleaded painfully. "I was sent to speak with you; to give full account."

Thomas's happiness drained away; his eyes became dark. "What are you saying?" He could hear his voice starting to break. "You're scaring me."

"Please, Thomas —" begged Peter.

Fear the likes of which Thomas had never experienced before was rising in his throat, choking him. Squeezing his words into feeble syllables: "You . . . you said . . . I" — his chest was tightening — "I wasn't going to hell!"

"I said you weren't in hell. Here. Now," replied the saint.

"So you've been sent by God to sentence me!" Thomas's instinct for self-preservation fuelled his rage. "YOU FUCKING BASTARD!" he screamed.

Saint Peter set his jaw, briefly; then he dutifully continued. "Thomas, you will never find the sound of a mother's heartbeat in your song — ever. Because she never existed."

Thomas's eyes darted to and fro as he tried to comprehend Peter's words. No mother's heartbeat? What was that supposed to mean? Some kind of twisted fucking riddle? God's idea of a sick little joke? "Jesus Christ, Peter! What are you saying? Quit jerking me around!"

The saint cast his eyes down, trying to control his emotions. His desire to protect the Master from the outcome of this meeting was clashing with his sense of duty and commitment.

And what of his feelings for Thomas Gorgon? A man completely unaware that his existence had been a threat to the Almighty and the Kingdom. Pity, love, and rage swirled in the saint's heart.

But Saint Peter knew that hesitancy and avoidance could not diminish the inevitable harm this encounter would bring to God. Distressed as he was, he looked up into Thomas's eyes and said firmly, "What I am about to tell you is the truth. The truth of how you came to be, and your eternal fate."

Thomas opened his mouth to speak, but was abruptly silenced by the raising of the saint's hand. "All is about to be revealed," said Peter. His voice rang out strong and clear, and his eyes blazed with a fiery intensity that silenced Thomas. "I have come on behalf of the Master, our King, the great Father of All, to give full elucidation of the emptiness in your soul. I have come to heal you, not to hurt you. So listen with your mind and your heart, Thomas, and you will know who you truly are, and why we are here together at this most important time."

# Chapter 12

Roberts made it in plenty of time to be cued on stage. He was greeted with a dabbing of his shiny brow with a Kleenex. "Really worked up a sweat for such a short jog," said the assistant, smiling. With the deftness of a pit-hand at a stock-car race, she once again touched up his face and hair, inserted his earphone, and attached a cordless mike between his shirt buttons, then gave him a quick once-over for anything untucked or loose. "All set."

The reverend stood waiting for his cue, dead still. Suddenly he tensed. Tersely he asked, "Have today's birds been picked up?"

The assistant's face pursed. "Reverend?"

"The birds. Has maintenance checked the grounds? Nobody has got back to me on this today!" His voice rose in pitch. "I don't want the congregation seeing the cathedral grounds strewn with dead birds! Is this asking too much?"

The assistant shook her head mutely. Don't get into it, she thought.

"Jesus," he muttered. "Get on it after I'm cued!"

A nod. "Yes, reverend." She held her breath, waiting for him to persist. When she realized that he wasn't going to, she exhaled and shook off the needles prickling her neck and hairline.

Birds. He saw them everywhere. Starlings. Sparrows. Grackles. Common street birds. Lying everywhere.

Initially, when Roberts had mentioned the dead birds, the maintenance crew had searched the grounds for the little carcasses and the possible cause; when no birds were found, it was laughed off as a practical joke at their expense. But the order to clean up the dead birds had become a daily ritual, and soon it became apparent that this was no joke. One morning, Roberts even fired an entire day-shift of maintenance people when they politely questioned the authenticity of the request. From that day on, the issue of Roberts' birds had been handled cautiously: a professional nod, and immediate notification that the invisible feathered bodies had been disposed of.

Yet the dead birds had been only the beginning.

Although it seemed so long ago, the change in Reverend Roberts could be traced back to less than a month earlier. In the passage of a few weeks, everyone employed by the SOS ministry had witnessed the rapid transformations: the Reverend Lucius Del Roberts from evangelical superstar to raving hallucinator; the Cathedral of Light from jewel of the ministry to neurotic circus.

The reverend's eyes were closed and he stood motionless; his nostrils flared and a blue vein coursed down from his coiffed hair and fattened around his temple.

The assistant was afraid he was about to explode, so she stepped back. On hearing the director's voice through her headset, she started, quickly composed herself, and relayed the message to the reverend: "You're on."

Roberts remained frozen. Eyes still closed.

"Reverend," she repeated, gently touching his arm. "We're ready for the phone-ins."

At the touch of her hand, Roberts' arm shot up, palm open, silencing her. The assistant caught her breath as she stared at the rigid hand that blocked her words from his ear.

His eyes opened. He pulled the Bible up to his chest, poised to head onto the stage. But before he could take a step, a professional impulse overcame the assistant's fright — she noticed the bandaged finger of his raised hand, sticky-looking and dark. Roberts stepped out into the light.

"Hey . . . hold it, Reverend!" she hissed through her teeth. "What happened to your finger?"

His back was to her as he made his way to the pulpit, but she clearly heard his response above the sounds of the audience and the orchestra. She stood alone in a slant of shadow, mulling it over. "Writer's cramp . . . ?"

Halfway between the stage exit and the pulpit, Roberts heard the tiny click in his earpiece. "Switchboard is on fire, Reverend! On fire! Got some beauts! Don't know what it is this morning. . . . "

The phone-in portion of the SOS broadcast was its most popular feature. What had started out as a simple exercise in interactive television — with a caller offering a confession on air, and the studio audience led by Roberts, an antiphon — had almost instantly become a sensationalist highlight. A decision had quickly been made to "sympathetically showcase the frailty of the human condition" by focusing on some of the more colourful calls. This decision was the result of an on-air confession from a distraught woman who recounted abandoning her newborn baby beneath a highway overpass. The confession sent a shock wave through the studio audience and the viewership. Roberts, however, calmly persuaded the woman to pinpoint the location of the overpass on the air. The child was recovered by the police, Roberts became a hero, and the SOS ministry received good press and ratings share. From that broadcast on, the switchboard had been instructed to screen calls for airing — why not edit to more effectively display God's grace and human benevolence?

"This is just wild! It's like the whole city is on hold, waiting to spill their guts to you! Any time, Reverend."

Roberts approached the pulpit and gently laid the Bible upon it. His head was down. When he looked up, he saw the dark horse and the small girl still standing amid the congregation. But something about the phantom-girl seemed different, making him look more closely. It was her expression; she was afraid. Gone was her calm demeanour. Roberts could tell she was trembling beneath her white dress. The black horse stood motionless, head high. Watching.

The reverend stared back at the two figures in the centre aisle, as the congregation became uneasy waiting for him to speak.

*Click*: "Anytime, Reverend. . . ."

Fuck off, thought Roberts.

He took in a deep breath and exhaled it even more slowly. Then he came out from behind the pulpit of white and gold to hang his toes over the edge of the stage. With hands on hips, feet set apart, he stared down the horse and child. (And fuck right off the pair of you, too.)

The congregation was all eyes. Hungry. Roberts scanned them. When he finally spoke, it was with a trumpet-voice that filled the cathedral and rose to nestle high in the glass dome overhead.

"JESUS!" he boomed. "Jesus wants something from me! I was made to know . . . at an early age . . . I WAS MADE TO KNOW! And it is no secret, good people! My life's work is testament to this ordainment! Jesus wants action from me, He demands it from me!"

Heads in the congregation nodded, many with eyes closed; other people shook clasped palms and brought them to their lips; some genuflected. The great black horse twisted its neck in disapproval, baring its teeth. The young girl only stood with her head bowed, face concealed in her hands.

Roberts avoided making eye contact with the spectres, a gesture now of defiance rather than of fear. He was on the move, working the entirety of the stage lip, face glowing. He was breathing through his mouth, chest swelling, temples pounding.

After stalking the edge of his false heaven, he looped back to stop at centre stage, framing himself between the two massive columns. He raised a shaking fist to the horse and child, blaring, "I AM —" His face flushed with blood, his trembling fist made his whole arm shake. "I AM . . . TOUCHED . . . BY GOD! I AM THE CHOSEN! I AM —" Just then, he blinked. His mouth opened; a tiny silver string of spittle dangled. He slowly straightened his predatory slouch and swallowed hard. His tongue felt thick and useless. He forced his eyes to look about him. Everyone he saw — faces in the congregation, the director, camera men, musicians in the pit — everyone was focused on him. The air had been stilled by his short, explosive rant. He couldn't breathe.

With a quivering jaw, he uttered feebly, "I am here . . . for all of you . . . for all of you who feel . . . shunned . . . cast out by your sin." Sheepishly, he opened his arms wide in a gesture of embrace. "Come to me. . . ."

Silence.

Then a voice called out, "Amen, Rev'r'nd." It was Wendyl. Praise the Lord for the soft-minded.

Roberts stood there with arms out and head bowed for a few seconds. Long seconds that hobbled by as if palsied. Then—

*Click*: "Doreen M."

Roberts gasped, filling his inflamed lungs. He tossed a glance at the black horse half rearing in fury, pounding its hoofs. The small girl remained motionless, still hiding her face.

The reverend exulted in his mind: You can push all you want. I am a rock. Like Sisyphus' stone. Push me and I'll roll back, crushing the pair of you. These people are mine! I won't let them go!

He raised his head and smiled: "Doreen M. . . . We at the Cathedral of Light are here for you. Share your pain with us this morning. God will hear."

Instructed by the switchboard to be succinct, Doreen M. shared her agony, in the hope that her private hell would vanish like a vampire in sunlight. "I found a needle in the lining in my son's school jacket," she said softly, ashamed.

The congregation was moved; there were murmurings of

empathy. Roberts, consciously mocking the phantom-child, shielded his eyes in feigned grief. "Go on, Doreen . . . we hear you," he said.

"I . . . I'm terrified, Rev —" The woman's voice broke and the sound of her sobs filled the cathedral. "What is my boy doing, Reverend? He won't talk to us. What did my husband and I do wrong?"

*Click*: Let's move it along, Reverend. Cut her off.

"What about AIDS? What if my boy . . ."

"The Lord knows your pain, Doreen," said Roberts, interrupting. "We at the Cathedral of Light send out our prayers for your son and your family." His dismissal was echoed by the congregation:

"O LORD, BLESS AND SHIELD YOUR SERVANT."

One after another, anguished souls known only by their phone-voices and aliases sought drive-thru forgiveness, love, and a sense of the communal; sought a mainline connection to God, a plug-in to the Almighty.

*Click*: "Arnold S."

"I'm a retired widower. I volunteer part-time as a crossing guard."

"Arnold, we hear you."

"I've been luring boys into the woods . . ."

"O LORD, BLESS AND SHIELD YOUR SERVANT."

*Click*: "Dennis N."

"This morning . . . around four I hit this guy with my truck . . . he just stepped out in front of me. . . ."

"Dennis, we hear you."

"I didn't stop to help him . . . left him lying there . . . I . . . just kept going. . . ."

"O LORD, BLESS AND SHIELD YOUR SERVANT."

*Click*: "Amanda B."

126

"I forged the signature of another loan officer at the bank where I work . . . put her into a world of sh(*bleep*) by authorizing a risky loan."

"Amanda, we hear you."

"But I really wanted that promotion. She was in the way. I was raised to know better. I know I've done wrong. But . . . I . . . it was so convenient."

"O LORD, BLESS AND SHIELD YOUR SERVANT."

The switchboard had screened thirty-five calls for Reverend Roberts before the last caller's voice came in over the speakers. It was a Mr. "Harold J."; his voice was still shaken as he related, "Found a dead woman this morning, Reverend. Think she was murdered. Beat up real bad."

"Harold, we hear you."

"She was just lying there, all busted up. Covered in blood."

*Click*: "Running late, Reverend. Wrap it up."

Subtly Roberts twirled his index finger by his pantleg, indicating that he wished to go on with this caller. "Where did you find this woman, Harold?" he asked, anxiously.

"Where I work. In the church. St. Peter's. I do cleaning in the early mornings. St. Peter's is my last stop."

"Do you know who did this?"

"No. But she hadn't been dead too long. Police say she was a local hooker."

"Who could have murdered a prostitute in a church, Harold?"

"Don't think she was."

Roberts cleared his throat. "Don't think she was what?"

"Murdered in the church, Reverend. All kinds of blood trails and marks in the snow outside, up the aisle, all over, like she'd been there a while, moving about before she died. Can't figure out how she got in, though. Place is always locked tight."

Roberts was becoming bored with "Harold J." He had hoped to air a murder confession; instead, the Cathedral of Light was hearing a janitor outline the sort of cheap mystery that fills the pages of a dime-store novel. Although the congregation was captivated by this tale of a murdered prostitute, the reverend wished he had followed the director's orders to wrap it up. In the hope of making a quick segue out, he said, "So, Harold, why do you think a battered prostitute chose a church to die in?" The elaborate speaker system above the stage was silent for a moment. "Harold?"

The congregation heard Harold exhale. "Dunno," he eventually said. "I remember as a schoolboy learning this poem. Very small poem, with small words. It was beautiful. Don't remember the poet's name. A lady poet, I think. Anyway, she wrote: 'Hope is the thing with feathers' —"

Clenching his teeth, Roberts asked, "What are you getting at, Harold?"

"Maybe this woman went looking for that special part of herself to see if it could fly again. . . ."

"Like a bird?" asked Roberts, with poorly concealed derision. "You're something of a romantic, aren't you, Harold?"

Another silence stilled the speakers. Then, "Maybe that's all it takes . . . for starters."

"I can assure you that the business of human salvation has very little to do with romance and fantasy. Jesus did not die to open the gates of heaven for sinners to dream themselves beautiful again. . . ."

"That's not what —"

"Harold, listen to me: we are fallen. Flawed. We cannot change what we are."

"What do we do, then?" asked Harold.

*Nothing. We are all lost. Fucked.* Roberts had a detached expression as he looked up to the glass-domed ceiling. The dark morning sky was beginning to pale with the dawn. "We pray," he said softly.

"O LORD, BLESS AND SHIELD YOUR SERVANT."

The orchestra music filled the cathedral as the stage lights dimmed and Reverend Roberts walked back to the pulpit.

*God is a sham.*

*Love is a sham.*

*Hope is a dead thing.*

*There is a nothingness and there is only this.*

*Amen.*

The black horse and the small child had never left the centre aisle throughout the phone-ins. By the time "Harold J." was cut off, the behaviour of the two spectres had altered; in fact, there had been a complete conversion, as each apparition seemed to have taken on the other's demeanour: the little girl was now deeply disturbed and weeping, while the horse had become eerily calm. Roberts had been aware of all this, but no longer cared.

While the orchestra played, the reverend took notice of a silk marker protruding from the middle of his Bible. He hadn't inserted the marker. Or had he? He couldn't remember. He paused. The frayed tongue of dark silk begged to be released from its captivity; it drew him in like a schoolyard dare. Without even questioning his feelings, Roberts grabbed the marker and opened the great book — at the prophecies of Isaiah.

Isaiah? Roberts knew something was stirring. It was years since he'd read these ancient prophecies — full of parables and warnings of deliverance from oppression, and cautions that sin is the hurdle to final salvation; these Old Testament prophecies read uselessly, like a safety sticker on a machine designed to maim. Utterly futile.

Without raising his head, he could see the horse's head in the darkness — black on black; it stood motionless, ears pitched forward. He looked back down; the small, soft light on the pulpit revealed chapters forty through forty-four. Roberts gazed to the right and down the column to stop on the nineteenth verse of the forty-second chapter:

Who is blind, but my servant?
Or deaf, as my messenger that I sent?

A burning cold surge of blood ran through Roberts' body. His eyes skipped down:

and they are hid in prison houses:
they are for a prey, and none delivereth;
for a spoil, and none saith, Restore.

The sensations of fire and ice intensified, tormenting Roberts' nerves. He loosened his tie, felt his face redden. He looked out into the centre aisle and saw the girl in white down on her knees, crying pitifully. The horse stood over the child, broad-chested and legs apart, and raised its muzzle sharply — a controlled gesture that Roberts interpreted as a command to keep reading. He did so, fearfully. As his eyes scanned for his place in the verse, he felt the same anxiety as when he'd first been faced by the monkey. The black horse, it seemed, was no longer just a reactive presence; it was now communicating with him. The reverend's eyes hooked onto these words:

Therefore he hath poured upon him the
fury of his anger, and the strength of
battle: and it hath set him on fire round about,
yet he knew not; and it burned him, yet
he laid it not to heart.

Roberts stared at the page without seeing; his eyes could not blink. A drop of cold sweat rolled down his ribs.

Without his realizing it, uncertainty and fear had gradually sent hairline cracks through his suit of soul-armour. Pride and denial had continued to distract and propel him, making him overlook the vulnerability of his state. A tear of rage fell from his eye onto the prophecies of Isaiah.

The music from the orchestra pit was concluding and the massive lights overhead were changing intensity throughout the cathedral. Within Roberts too there was a change of intensity.

Deep within the reverend's soul was issued a final call to arms, mere moments before the entire congregation erupted into a panicked stampede at what they witnessed next.

It all happened quickly, like a chain of falling dominoes, culminating in a screaming exodus from the Cathedral of Light.

The first of these events went unseen by the congregation. Only Reverend Roberts saw and heard the small child in white speak. As he wiped away his tears and looked up from the open Bible, he saw the child, still on her knees, wailing beneath the great horse. She raised her arms and screamed, "WHAT HAVE I DONE?"

At the hearing of this, Roberts' heart stopped momentarily; his knees gave way. It was his mother's voice.

Trembling violently, he whispered, "Mom . . . ?" He collapsed and began to pull himself towards the edge of the stage. As he approached closer, the lost man yielded to the lost child: "Mommy . . . ? Mommy . . . ? Is that you?"

The congregation was startled; like a fog, anxiety drifted over everything. The director was trying desperately to speak with the reverend. The orchestra was anticipating a cue. Camera men were unsure whether they should follow Roberts. Technical personnel nervously waited for word of how to proceed.

Roberts gripped the edge of the stage and stared into the teary face of the little girl. "Mommy . . . ?"

Just then, the black horse reared high and stood with its sharp hoofs poised above the child.

Roberts' face went ashen and he screamed.

Arms waving, the director immediately ordered the broadcast stopped, pulling the plug on all cable affiliates. The SOS ministry was silenced beyond the walls of the Cathedral of Light. Severed.

Roberts witnessed the black horse come down upon the child's head and shoulders as all the lights in the cathedral suddenly went out. There was complete darkness. Some of the congregation screamed sharply, and there were sounds of movement and wails. Nothing could be seen.

All the while, in Roberts' head, he could hear the sound of the child's agony and the repeated stomping of heavy hoofs. Through the layers of scar tissue on his psyche, a tiny urge — something distorted, something like love — surfaced, filling him with a desire to protect. He cried out against the sound of the horse's fury: "I'LL KILL YOU!" The darkness pressed him to threaten the other apparitions as well, wherever they were: "I'LL KILL ALL OF YOU!"

He lunged from the stage into the darkness.

There was a loud whirring sound, and the lights pulsed twice as the generator kicked in. When the interior of the cathedral was fully illuminated, the frightened congregation saw the reverend holding the bloodied body of a small child.

Roberts was on his knees, crying, cradling the battered little girl; her white dress was blood-soaked and torn. A deadly silent fermata stilled the cathedral before the first screams heralded the charge for the rear exits. Men and women clawed at one another and stepped on the fallen in their frantic dash. Even the cathedral staff who were witnessing this terrifying scene, either live or on the monitors, fled. It took just a few wild minutes to empty the Cathedral of Light.

Reverend Roberts rocked the broken body in his arms; felt the sticky warmth of the child's blood through his shirt, making his shirtfront greasy. He felt nauseated. He felt faint. He wanted to drop the body, to remove himself from it, but he couldn't. Instead he raised the child up to place her matted head against his shoulder. He hugged the body gently, feeling the bones move. The reverend could not remember the last time he had held a child in his arms, and this tiny intimacy moved him. Some part of him yearned, stretched, and scrambled to see beyond the hideous; like a parched man lapping at the edge of an oasis, he wanted to swallow deeply the waters of this, the most genuine of human moments ever to occur beneath the dome of the cathedral. But the waters were a mirage, and the reverend's tongue was never soothed; and that small humanness — so frail — dried to a handful of dust.

Then the child stirred; her bloodied head twitched, brushing the reverend's cheek. Roberts tensed. When he heard her soft release of breath, he lowered her to the carpeted aisle, and looked down into her broken face.

The little girl's eyes fluttered, then opened; like bottomless pits, her dilated pupils further darkened with ravaged innocence. She coughed once, a cough heavy and wet with blood; it poured over her chin and down her throat. Her lips parted and the sound was again the voice of Eleanor Roberts. Weakly she said, "What . . . have I . . . done . . . ?"

The voice of his mother stabbed at Roberts' chest, arresting him. Warring emotions and memories raged in his heart and mind; he could only stare at this dying child, his mother.

The girl coughed again, her face registering pain. "I'm . . . sorry . . . ," she whispered.

Roberts shook his head vaguely, feeling both angered and drained.

I was just a little boy.

"Forgive me . . ."

I won't.

". . . please . . . Lucius . . . forgive me. . . ."

I can't.

"I . . . need you to . . ."

You killed that in me.

The small girl twitched. "I thought . . ."

Nothing. You thought *nothing*.

". . . it was . . . a sign . . ."

*Taming the animal-wild.*

". . . a sign from . . . God . . . oh, Lucius. . . ."

*Fuck God and fuck you.*

The child's darkened eyes rolled back and her broken body jerked; again she spewed blood. Gasping, she forced a plea through her arched neck: "Lucius! . . . please . . . say . . . speak to me! Forgive . . . !"

Roberts was overcome by a madness fuelled by the sound of his mother's voice. The lost man re-emerged — a black sun eclipsing the lost boy. Arms gesturing to the great interior of the cathedral, he said, "I don't have it in me to forgive! So I can't dish it out! But all this! This I have within me! This I have to offer!" Now tears flowed like fire, burning his cheeks.

The little girl rocked her head weakly.

The reverend leaned forward, his face close to the child's, and through a sneer he hissed, "Thank you, Mother."

He sat back on his heels, with a mien of forced relaxation and detachment. As if ignoring the dying child's presence, he wiped uselessly at the stain of blood on his shirt. After a time, he exhaled long and slow, then said, "So . . . what's with the company you're keeping?"

The child's frail chest heaved once in response. Waiting for a more enlightening answer, Roberts rubbed his red hands, then raised his fingernails for close inspection; sniffed the bloody cuticles. He looked down at the girl. She was barely breathing.

"It almost worked," he added. "Almost had me on the run." He grinned. "Just what did you think this could accomplish, hmm? What the fuck was all this about?"

The grin cracked into a laugh. "Not happy with your little boy? Not what you expected?" He shook his head, and his eyes became vicious. "Your boot camp groomed one bitchin' foot soldier for the Lord, didn't it, Mother?"

The little girl did not respond.

Roberts' throat tightened with self-pity and his voice became squeezed, pathetic, and private: "Done all right for myself . . . considering the damage you inflicted."

Nothing.

He doubled over onto the floor, shaking. With his face pushed into the carpet, he erupted: "YOU TOOK . . . !" His eyelids fluttered and his face ignited with a rush of blood. "YOU TOOK AND YOU PUSHED! YOU PUSHED AND PUSHED AND PUSHED! YOU PUSHED ME AWAY FROM ME! MAKING ME INVISIBLE INSIDE!" His tears and snot flowed heavily; his mouth was stretched large, wet and angry. "WHO AM I? WHO THE FUCK AM I, MOTHER?"

He reached out and grabbed the warm, wet front of the child's dress, pulling the limp body closer, and pressed his face deeply into the blood-soaked folds. Coughing and choking past his sobs, he whispered, "I am this, Mother . . . this is all I am . . . all that's left. . . . And I wasn't going to let anyone push me out . . . no man, no God . . . nothing. . . ." He swallowed and sniffed. "Regardless of how I re-created myself . . . regardless how ugly I am . . . you can't push me out, Mother . . . neither can your fucking petting zoo. . . ."

The child's mouth moved, but the reverend couldn't make out her words; he only felt a tiny hum through his cheek, felt her effort to speak. He pulled away and stared at her lips.

Finally, her lips parted and words floated out, soft as a wingbeat. Roberts drew his ear practically against her mouth to hear her say, ". . . didn't . . . come" — she exhaled weakly — "to . . . push. . . ."

Roberts closed his eyes. "What are you saying?" he whispered. "What do you mean?"

"They came . . . to . . ."

"To what?"

"to . . . anchor . . . you. . . ."

Roberts' head snapped up, his eyes large. He saw that the girl's eyes were open too. "Anchor . . . ?" he repeated. "Anchor me . . . ?"

"To moor . . . your . . . soul. . . ."

The reverend shook his head in disbelief. "And you too, Mother?"

The child turned her head feebly to empty her mouth of blood; she wheezed painfully. "I . . . came . . ."

Roberts trembled as if naked in a blizzard.

"I . . . came . . . ," repeated the child, ". . . in . . . hope. . . ."

Roberts sat mute, watching her chest rise once more, then settle in death.

A sound came from directly above. A crackling, splintering sound.

The great dome of glass that gave the cathedral its name was being fissured by a silver crack that raced across its immensity.

Roberts looked up. Slowly he stood, and tilted his head slightly, examining the cleft in the glass. Suddenly it sprouted a million tiny cracks that coursed outward across the dome to its edge.

He inhaled and held his breath, as if it were to be his last. There was a moment of stillness inside the cathedral. As he stared up at the broken lens to the heavens, he noticed a patch of darkening outside — like a storm cloud passing. This darkness intensified and expanded, as if something outside the dome was approaching rapidly.

As the falling darkness came upon it, the dome shattered into countless pieces.

Roberts raised his arms to shield himself as he was covered by a torrent of glass, cold air, and the falling darkness of dead birds. Thousands of dead birds.

# CHAPTER 13

"That re-entry's a bitch, isn't it, son?"

Joseph Langley lay stunned on a high mattress of green garbage bags. He shook his head and raised himself on his elbows. His breath was frozen and billowed out in front of him, which confused him. He blinked hard and shook his head again.

"Lucky you landed where you did," added the voice. This time Langley heard it clearly. He was startled. He backstroked over the garbage bags and fell off the other side of the mound. Cautiously he looked over the garbage heap to spot the speaker, while his still-clouded mind tried to figure out why it was so dark and so cold. Just a second ago he'd been in a warm and moderately well-lit room. . . .

Room. The Blue Orchid.

Langley quickly looked up to see dark sky. He felt a chill wind blowing through his hair and untucked clothing. The impossible and the incongruent suddenly clicked into reality — as if he had skipped frames in a poorly edited film. His heart felt about to explode from his chest. He wanted to scream. "Jesus Christ!" he gasped.

"Close. But no cigar," replied the voice, starting to laugh. It was a coarse laugh.

Langley raised his head from between his hunched shoulders, but all he could see was a wall of old brick, the angular lines of a fire-escape, and shadows.

The laughter continued.

Langley closed his eyes and tried to will his frantic breathing under control. He swallowed. Opening his eyes, he scanned his immediate surroundings and confirmed that he was in an alley. Smells filled his nose: rotting fruit rinds, furnace oil, and urine.

He looked at his watch. It read 5:39 a.m. His mind tried to backtrack to the last moment he could remember knowing the time . . . it had been at the Blue Orchid. On the staircase! Trixie had asked. His memory locked in: it had been 4:07. An hour and a half ago.

His mind flipped through the events at the hotel, then stopped abruptly. The very last thing he could remember was the sight of Trixie tied up, convulsing, trying to scream something at him through the duct tape. Then . . . then what? He couldn't recall how he had got away. Couldn't recall his departure, or running down the stairs.

But I must have, he thought. How else did I get here? Could shock or fear have wiped out the memory of my escape? But why would it? No — if anything, I would have blocked out the sight of the bitch's bleeding and seizure . . . wouldn't I?

It was all a blank. He had absolutely no recollection of how he had arrived at this alley.

His arm was still extended and bent in front of his face. "In a hurry?" asked the voice in the darkness.

"Who's there?" countered Langley. "Come on out." There was a sound of stirring. A dragging sound. A slow approach.

Langley placed a hand below his stomach, but didn't find what he had hoped for. Instead, his thumb wiggled in an empty belt loop, and his heart heaved. The buckle was gone! Where the fuck was it? He couldn't remember if he'd taken it with him. Was it still at the Blue Orchid? Was it somewhere in the alley? He ran his hand over the cold asphalt, feeling for the belt or the buckle. His fingers discovered pebbles, aluminium pull-tabs, cigarette butts, bits of paper, but no buckle.

How could I have been so fucking careless, he thought. My prints are all over it! I've got to get it back! If that cunt's still alive, she'll . . .

138

The sound of laboured breathing interrupted his train of thought. It was close — right behind him. The vapour of frosted breath swirled around his head and misted his eyes. He leapt to his feet and spun his head around.

"Boo!"

Langley's nose was practically touching the face of a grinning old man with wild eyes and a mane of grizzled hair. He screamed and sprang away, bracing his back against the brick wall behind him. The old man laughed and shook his head.

Langley stood there gasping for breath. He pointed a finger at the old man. "YOU . . . STUPID . . . OLD . . . FUCK . . . !"

The old man just smiled pleasantly. "Go easy, son." He had his arms folded in front of him as he rested against his side of the garbage pile. "Hey, you all right?" he asked warmly.

The sincerity of tone calmed Langley like a tonic. This was just some harmless old wino. "Yeah," he replied. "But you really scared the piss out of me, old-timer."

The wind whipped the old man's long white hair. He just stared at Langley. "I mean," he said slowly, "are you *all right*?" He made this simple question sound almost dangerous to answer.

Langley became nervous thinking about the old man's enquiry. He shook his head. "What . . . what do you mean?"

The old man smiled again. The weak light revealed a broken, ugly mouth. "Just look at yourself," he said.

Langley hesitated to do so, but then he slowly cast his eyes down. Finally he understood what the old man was referring to: the blood. It was all over him. He raised his hands to his face and realized that they were dark and greasy with gore; his untucked shirt and pants were splattered with fine red specks. His eyes grew wide as he went to feel his face.

"Don't bother, son," said the old man. "It's all over your face too. You'll just make it worse."

Langley stood leaning against the wall. His mouth hung open, slack with terror: not only could he not remember how he had arrived at this alley, but he had no idea who might have seen him in this state. He imagined himself walking dazed through the city streets, covered in a whore's blood. Such sloppiness, he said to himself. Such sloppiness!

The old man watched Langley's face. Even in the poor light, he could tell that Langley's expression had changed; had hardened.

*You can't go back after her. What to do?*

"Where are you off to now?" asked the old man.

*Run.* "What?" asked Langley.

"Maybe you should get to a hospital. Maybe the police can help."

*Fuck, look at you. You can't.* "No! I'm fine. Everything's fine!"

"By the way, your coat is over there," said the old man, gesturing with his head. "Just up the alley a few feet."

"Thanks."

Langley walked to the spot where his coat lay; his black hat was nearby. He shook the snow and grit from the fine wool coat and put it on. The weight felt good across his wide shoulders, and the coat concealed most of the blood on his shirt and pants. But he still needed to clean his face and hands. He picked up his hat and ran his thumb along the stiff brim, as if testing the sharpness of a blade.

Langley's quiet manner hid his gut-impulse to create a whirlwind of violence. He wanted to destroy! Kill anything that got in his way! He needed release! Needed it because, once the rage is vented, the aftermath is calm, is peace. Tabula rasa. Newness and potential spring from destruction. Violence purges, it cleanses. Think of the phoenix. Think of Jesus Christ. After violence, anything is possible.

But the donning of his coat and hat stifled the impulse. Violence requires a sense of itself — and that can only exist in a mind set in a clear course of action. And right now, Langley's mind was fragmenting into distant camps.

*You're trapped.*

With his coat done up, he had a sense of impending departure. It was unnerving; as if he were being forced out of the alley.

"I'm not going anywhere," he said, in a flat tone. The utterance came out like a private thought voiced accidentally.

"So you're staying?"

Langley stood puzzled for a moment. "Yeah. I guess I am."

"How wonderful." The old man clumsily pulled himself over the garbage heap to join him. Standing on the knuckles of his fists, he came up to Langley's mid-thigh. Langley looked down at him in shock.

"The name's Gabby."

"I'm Joseph Langley."

"Charmed, son." Gabby's smile broke open, filling the alley once again with coarse laughter. "Charmed."

Langley could not remember ever having seen a more repulsive human specimen in his life. He watched as Gabby walked on his fists — his torso dangling like the clapper of a bell — towards a large cardboard box with a square hole cut in front. Gabby entered the box and lowered himself onto his stumps.

Langley took in the image of the street-dweller in his cardboard hovel, and it conjured up thoughts of wise old men in mountainside caves. However, he doubted that Gabby possessed anything even remotely resembling wisdom. In all likelihood, the old cripple was insane. Schizophrenic. Just another fucked-up street freak.

"Come on over, son," offered Gabby. "Grab yourself a seat."

Langley twisted his neck and rolled his thick shoulders, unknotting the tension. He grabbed the neck of a plump garbage bag, carried it over to the box, set it down, and punched an indentation in the top for a seat. Gingerly he lowered his weight upon it, to see if it would support him. It seemed that it would, so he relaxed his leg muscles to sit. But as soon as his buttocks met the resistance of the bag's contents, he shot straight up.

"Problem?" asked Gabby.

Langley had been sharply reminded of the wounds he had inflicted upon himself when he sat on the broken glass at the Blue Orchid. "No problem. But I think I'll stand."

"Suit yourself."

The wind gusted through the alley, pushing bits of scrap over a dirty sheet of puddle ice. The debris flitted across the surface like tiny birds trying to penetrate the ice to wash themselves. Langley watched this with detached interest.

Gabby sat in his box, his dark eye rotating. Scanning. His leathery face showed no expression until Langley finally turned his head. Gabby greeted the eye-contact with a quick grin.

This odd street-person had an unquestionable drawing-power over Joseph Langley. He stared into the old man's weathered face — stared into those wild eyes and watched the dark globe shoot back and forth in its socket, while the milky eyeball remained still, moist and shiny with discharge. Langley stared but couldn't penetrate the source of the allure. It was something much deeper than the desire to linger over Gabby's physical curiosities; it was something generated by the old man's presence, something that hovered in the air between them. Whatever hold Gabby had over Langley, it charged the area like a magnetic field. It was very real and alive.

Gabby interrupted Langley's musing, asking, "Something wrong, Joseph? You've got far-away eyes."

"No. I'm —"

"Mind if I call you 'Joseph'?"

Langley turned his collar up against a gust of wind that was running its tongue along his neck. "I guess not." Normally, rushed familiarity with a recent acquaintance bothered him. He had grown to hate intimacy. It angered him. However, this disgusting stranger somehow overrode his usual impulse. It was as though the impulse wasn't allowed to surface — if indeed it still existed within him at all.

"Mind if we talk?" asked Gabby. "Don't get much conversing out here in the streets."

Langley pulled the brim of his hat closer to his nose and dug his hands into his coat pockets. "That'd be all right," he muttered.

"You sure, Joseph?"

"Yeah. I'm in no real hurry."

"I guess not," said Gabby, revealing yellowed teeth.

"What's that supposed to mean?" replied Langley quickly. "And quit smiling like that."

Gabby tucked his long white hair behind his ears and continued to smile. "Just teasing you about your appearance. Whatever did you get yourself into? A car crash or something?"

"Just never fucking mind where I've been, old man, all right?"

Gabby raised his gnarled hands in a gesture of surrender. "Sorry, Joseph. Just asking." His cracked lips pulled back again into a slow, sly grin. "You don't moonlight bleeding livestock in an abattoir, do you?"

Langley took a menacing step forward, his face flushed with anger.

Gabby sat perfectly still. "Thought you wanted to talk," he said, in a strong, firm voice. The tone resonated deeply, like a growl rolling in a lion's chest. It caused Langley's bold approach to recede; he raised a heel and set it back a step.

"You're the one who wanted to talk," he replied.

"I do. I have been."

"You talk shit."

Gabby said nothing at first to this, but his dark eye with the curious oblong pupil stopped rotating. "Didn't wish to offend or mock you, Joseph. It was just talk. Tell me, what kind of talk do you want?"

"I don't know. Just cut the crap."

"You prefer some fancy twenty-questions party talk?"

"Anything but your bullshit," replied Langley.

Gabby lowered his gaze momentarily and nodded in agreement. "You're right, Joseph. Absolutely right. Who am I to mess around with such a bonding human tie? And we having just met . . . what was I thinking?" He glanced up to catch Langley's reaction.

Langley stood like a monolith. Something was registering within him. Tumblers in his mind were falling and clicking into place.

Gabby watched him silently. "What was I thinking?" he repeated softly, still watching Langley's taut, funeral-drum face.

"What . . . are you talking about . . . ?" asked Langley.

"Joseph — ?"

"What you said. About ties. Bonding ties. . . ."

"I was just agreeing with you, Joseph."

"Agreeing how?"

The corner of Gabby's mouth pulled up. "Agreeing with you that the crap should be cut. So much is 'out there', working against us, while we're down here; dividing us, severing us. Human talk should be something that pulls us together. After all, talking is what separates us from all other animals, isn't it? We ought to put it to good use."

Langley nodded. His mind was becoming saturated with thoughts and feelings triggered by Gabby's remarks. The same thoughts and feelings he had exorcized at the Blue Orchid just a few hours earlier were resurfacing, bubbling to the top. As the bubbles burst, his mind became coated again with psychosis, with a new layer of old fears: the shock of exposure; the collapse of the communal; the loss of the tribal; isolationism; divorce from the self and from God; heaven and hell, the womb and the mind.

"In the end," said Gabby, "all we've got is each other." He could see the breadth of Langley's shoulders heave with mounting agitation. A silence grew between the two men. "Joseph," said Gabby softly, "I'm sorry."

The gentle croak from the legless man evaporated the tension and drew Langley back in. His great shoulders seemed to curl in like the edge of a withering leaf.

Gabby adjusted his weight on his stumps and rubbed the white stubble on his chin before he spoke again: "Son?"

Langley was still backed against the wall for support, but his frame relaxed. He looked weary.

"Should I shut up now, Joseph?" asked Gabby. Although Langley was darkened by the wall's shadows, Gabby could plainly see him shake his head. "You sure?"

Langley did not respond.

"Joseph?"

A quiet charge of frozen breath emerged from the dark figure against the wall, bearing a whisper: "Yes . . . all we've got is each other. . . ." The words drifted across the alley. "Speak to me, Gabby. Lead me out. . . ."

"Out? Out of where?"

"This fallout zone."


Gabby had gradually coaxed Langley out of the shadows and into a flow of conversation.

". . . so you're not from around here?"

"Out of town," replied Langley. "Out west."

"Is this your first time through?"

"No. I return periodically."

"Business?"

Langley visibly twitched. "Personal. Sort of a reunion thing."

"Family, huh?"

Langley's expression hardened again. "Yeah, sort of. Actually I've been trying to reunite with him for years, but he's a difficult person to hook up with."

Gabby looked confused. "How difficult can it be to visit family?" he asked. "I mean, this person does live here, doesn't he? You know where he is, don't you?"

"Yes! I know where he is!" said Langley harshly. "I told you: he's a difficult man to reach." He turned a shoulder to the old man in the box. "And sometimes," he added, in a low, almost confessional tone, "things get in the way . . ."

Gabby stared at Langley's back, watching the hem of his coat sway. Waiting for him to continue.

Things do get in the way, thought Langley, staring at the frozen ground. Like the last time I was in town. I had the focus. I was prepared to meet him. But then she appeared. Why did I turn my head in her direction? Why did I look? I tried to resist her, I did. I tried. But I couldn't. She was too obvious. Sitting there in that coffee shop, smoking. With that hair — a bright orange crewcut. Shitty dye job. I had to approach her. We left together but we never made it to the hotel. Bony little bitch lured me behind a restaurant. Went down on her knees. Had my pants down in seconds. Kissing me through my boxers. Licking at the silk. Then she noticed the buckle. Asked what that plastic tip on the tine was for. She found out. I lost control. Lost the focus. So I tossed her in the dumpster and I had to leave town. That — that was the last time.

". . . but this time," said Langley, turning around to face Gabby, "this time I won't be leaving until I see him. Come hell or high water."

## Chapter 14

After drying off and dressing, Sophia made her way to the bed and pulled the top sheet off. Sharp bits of glass flew to the floor. The bloodstains from Langley's buttocks added a noticeable weight to the end of the sheet when Sophia shook it clean.

She sat down and began to make tiny cuts, with a safety razor she had procured from the medicine cabinet, along the edge of the sheet: about a dozen half-inch starter cuts. Then she tore long strips of clean white linen for bandages.

Sophia had begun to wrap her left foot when she stopped and sighed. "This isn't going to do. . . ." She needed something heavier to protect the wounds. She thought for a moment, and remembered something she had forgotten about — in the vanity beneath the bathroom sink. She carefully limped back to the bathroom and opened the vanity doors. There it was, beside a canister of cleanser, a sponge, and a can of Raid: an almost full package of sanitary napkins.

As she lumbered back to the bed, she remembered how they had been left in her bathroom. Quite some time ago, another call girl had frequented the same all-night coffee shop that Sophia stopped in after turning tricks — a petite woman with brightly dyed hair cropped in a mannish crewcut. Her name was Cassandra Wilkes, but she was known on the streets as "Jessie".

Sophia and Cassandra had become friends, often trading stories and laughter over wine and bad take-out. On one such evening, Cassandra — who suffered painful and irregular periods — had unexpected cramping. Sophia purchased sanitary napkins and a bottle of Midol at a twenty-four-hour pharmacy. After popping a couple of relaxants, Cassandra had decided to head home, leaving behind the bulky package of napkins.

Sophia never did see Cassandra again. About a week later, the news of her death made the papers. The narrow column of words described her death as just another trick gone bad. She was found in a dumpster behind a restaurant, with multiple stab wounds to the throat — deep punctures.

Sophia stared sadly at the sanitary napkins in her hands. Left under her sink, they had remained unused and unneeded, for Sophia had been rendered sterile after a foolish adolescent tryst. She had not menstruated in seventeen years.

She placed the napkins on both sides of her hand and foot wounds, wrapping them with the torn strips of linen; she secured the loose ends with a safety pin. Then she tied a long piece of linen into a hoop, fashioning a sling to support her arm beneath her broken collarbone. The utter clumsiness of the procedure almost reduced her to tears.

The dressing of the wounds was a painful and slow process, once again taxing her energy reserves. She felt so tired. But a quick glance at the condition of the apartment, and the memory of all the violence, prompted her to hobble to her jacket and shoes. She awkwardly slipped the short, patchwork, rabbit-skin jacket over her injured shoulder, but cursed to herself when she looked at her shoes. The pointy red heels would never fit over her bound feet. She chewed on the inside of her cheek as she thought for a moment, and perked up as she remembered an old pair of canvas hightops in the closet by the door. She managed to put them on, but even with the laces cut they proved to be a painfully snug fit.

As she opened the door to take her leave, she noticed small stains of blood already seeping through the dressings on her hands. She needed to get home quickly and properly attend to her other wounds; there was no way she could walk into a hospital in this state. How could she explain the holes in her palms and feet when she couldn't even reason them out for herself? Touched by God? The doctors would never believe her story. She definitely had to get home. The less anybody knew of her condition, the better.

I'll just have to lie low for a couple of weeks, she thought. That's what I'll do. Those holes will heal and I can get on with my life with no questions asked.

She locked the door and headed for the stairs, dreading what she knew was going to be a painful descent down seven flights of stairs. Resting the elbow of her good arm on the railing for support, she took her first cautious step. The pain made her grimace. She peered down the squared spiral of the stairway to the patch of floor that was the foyer below.

"Shit," she said wearily. "This is going to take some time."

By the time Sophia reached the foyer, a considerable amount of blood was visible beneath the floppy tongues of her sneakers. Her feet were throbbing with a deep, dull ache. She sat herself down gently on the last step, to catch her breath.

Tenderly she poked at the blood-soaked wrappings on her feet. The stress of walking down the steps had aggravated the wounds, causing the bleeding to become profuse once again. As for her hands, the bleeding seemed controlled; on the back and palm of each wrapped hand was a red stain the size of a silver dollar.

Sophia stared out the glass doors of the Blue Orchid, watching the snow latch onto the wind as if to ascend back to the clouds. She too wished she could be whisked away on a wind — to another place, another time; away from all the hurt. But her adult mind reminded her that wishing doesn't work; it doesn't mend; it doesn't heal.

Lifting herself up off the step, Sophia could feel her body beginning to stiffen from the abuse. She straightened her back and headed for the doors, and filled her lungs deeply with the icy air.

She hobbled directly to the place where the body of the man with the books had lain. There remained evidence of the hit-and-run: snow-blown footprints, tire treads, and something ghastly that made her once again worry for the welfare of the fallen man. She lowered herself, kneeling above a stain on the asphalt. The cold had thickened the stain, and tiny snow crystals were starting to cling to its surface, eagerly accumulating, trying to erase yet another ugly human imprint on the earth's surface.

Halfway up the block, Sophia stopped in front of the electronics store, cupped her bandaged hands around her eyes, and peered in the window. Behind the service counter she saw a large digital clock that read 5:17 a.m.

She closed her eyes. It would be another hour and a half before the sun rose, she thought. At her rate of progress, she would just make it home as dawn broke.

She crossed her good arm gingerly beneath her sling, trying to tuck her hand under her armpit. The flimsy rabbit fur of her jacket was providing little warmth, and her feet and hands were becoming unbearably cold.

As Sophia pulled away from the window, she noticed what was flickering on the TV screen. She recognized the broadcast as the SOS Network from the unmistakable image of its founder. The Reverend Lucius Del Roberts was standing alone on an immense white stage, sandwiched between two huge columns of white fluted marble; incredible, vibrant floral bouquets accented the vastness. The camera man pulled in for a closer shot, honing in on Roberts' dripping face.

Sophia stared at the reverend's lips forming words of salvation for his studio audience. His mouth was slow and deliberate.

The camera angle then changed and panned back to reveal that Roberts held a Bible in his hands. The good book was wide open on his palm, and was held at a dramatic distance from his face. His eyebrows drew tensely together as he read something to himself. He raised his eyes to the audience and began to speak forcefully, and a line of yellow words glided across the bottom of the screen:

> St. Luke 17:20–21 "And when he was demanded of the Pharisees, when the kingdom of God should come, he answered them and said, The kingdom of God cometh not with observation:
> "Neither shall they say, Lo here! or, lo there! for, behold, the kingdom of God is within you."

The reverend closed the Bible and bowed his head. When he raised it again, Sophia saw tears streaming down his face.

Sophia grimaced as she shuffled along the sidewalk. With geriatric propulsion she distanced herself from the store window and headed towards the corner. The soles of her sneakers echoed with each step she took. But the sound could not drown out the violating words from Luke's gospel, boring into her brain:

*God is within you*
*God is within you*
*God is within you*

No matter how hard she tried, she could not stop the encroachment, the violation. Her brain had absorbed these last words like a sponge; there was no wringing her memory clean. She thought of Langley and what he had said about the magnetic mind becoming a hell, an indiscriminate receptor.

*God is within you*
*God is —*

Could that be? If it wasn't true, why could she not clear her mind? Where was her control? She shook her head. Langley was insane, sick. And so were his words — infected. Firmly she reassured herself that his ravings contained no truth, no reason.

I'm tired, she told herself. It all means nothing. My brain is just tired and playing with the last thing it saw. Just because I can't shake these words doesn't mean I've lost control.

Still, this one notion remained, coiled in the back of her mind: she wondered if Langley's delusion had begun like this. A self-assuring pep talk.

Before she reached the corner, Sophia paused again to lean against a building. She wanted desperately to sit down and rest, but feared that if she eased her weight off her feet — even for a moment — the pain would be intensified tenfold when she set off again.

She stared at her feet. The wrappings were now completely saturated with blood; they were beet-red and pulpy. "Oh, Mon Seigneur . . . ," she whispered; thoughts of not making it home started to fill her mind. Then a small sound from almost directly across the street distracted her from her thoughts. She gazed up to pinpoint its origin.

There. Again. Coming from a second-storey window, open just a crack — a baby's cry. The rectangular patch of light cast a soft ruby glow from the red sheers. The infant's cries rolled out into the street.

Sophia stood there looking at the window, and the form of a woman with a child in her arms appeared behind the curtains. The motherly form cradled the baby by the open window. The red sheers billowed inward with cold air.

Probably trying to lower a fever in the little one, thought Sophia. She remembered her own mother taking her onto the porch for a short spell on cold nights, to relieve a burning brow, to help settle her back to sleep.

The baby's cries faded gradually and the image in the window became hazy as mother and child drew deeper into the room. The short distraction evaporated, and Sophia was left alone with a sharp, hurtful feeling for her own barren incapacity — a feeling that seemed to merge too comfortably with the obtrusive bit of Luke's verse emblazoned in her mind.

Anger suddenly flushed inside her. She felt once again violated. Where's my control, she thought. These feelings I'm having . . . my mind . . . my mind is no longer my own. Maybe I'm going mad. Clearing my mind, my heart, should be easy enough. Especially of such stupidity. Just words. . . .

More than anything, she wanted to scream, to stop the carousel of impressions her alien mind forced upon her:

*GOD IS WITHIN YOU*
*GOD IS WITHIN YOU*
*GOD IS WITHIN YOU*

Initially those words . . . swirling and swirling and swirling . . . but now . . . now accompanied by the sound of a baby's cry, and a most particular anguish, which only a woman can have: the knowledge that your gift of creating life has been destroyed.

How she wanted to scream! Needed to scream. The most primal of human exorcisms. But a glance at her hands and feet, the pain in her side, her collarbone, the memory of her reflection in the bathroom mirror, kept her jaw clamped. No one must see me, she reminded herself. Questions must never be asked. So she endured. She did not even exercise her will to give up — doing so would only have amplified the intrusion.

She hoisted herself away from the face of the building and gave a sharp cry as she once again set her torn feet in motion. She reached the corner and turned, heading north. A quick backwards glance showed that her slow progress was now marked by the occasional smear of blood from her saturated sneakers.

Ahead she could see the old wrought-iron fence of the church lot. She looked up to see the cross set against the morning sky, black on black. The cold wind rushed past her ears carrying the sound of only the deepest of silences.

*GOD IS WITHIN YOU*

"I'm going mad," she said, as she came to the iron gates of St. Peter in Chains.

By the time Sophia stopped at the gates of the old stone church, the pain from her wounds had become excruciating; especially from the wounds on her feet. The cold and the blood loss were beginning to make her feel light-headed, so with her good arm she steadied herself against the black bars to keep from toppling over. She closed her eyes to rest.

The wind was picking up, starting to gust; it tossed her hair across her battered face. Then, suddenly, it carried a noise from behind her. She turned.

One of the heavy church doors was moving on its hinges. In her worn state she didn't bother to question why; she quickly fumbled with the crude lift-latch and walked through the open door.

She approached the old stones; she allowed her eyes to course along the mortar, penetrate the texture and colour of the fieldstone. She drew even closer and stopped, her nose mere inches from the wall. An axiom from her youth sprang to mind: of how perfect a thing a fieldstone wall is, a perfect earthly thing.

She raised her bandaged hand to the wall, so that her bloodied fingers could absorb the stones. Stones like the ones that supported Papa's barn, the very stones she had contemplated as a young girl establishing a contrariety to Papa's views on man and nature and farming.

"No, Sophia," he would say, leaning on his fork, "we don't farm out of love for the land."

"Why not, Papa?"

He would always toe the dust with his boot when he spoke of such things. "Because you cannot, in the end, love what does not love you in return. . . ."

Confusion. And the usual response: "Why not, Papa?"

One time in particular, Ezra knelt down, bringing his sun-browned face to his young daughter's, and what he proceeded to say inspired a tender mind to see beyond seeing. "Do you see our house, Sophia?"

A nod.

"Mama's garden, my tractor, the barn?" he continued. "And

even our clothes?"

"Yes, Papa."

"All the stuff people use to live and work are made to control nature. Understand?"

The young Sophia registered only blankness.

He smiled. Another attempt: "When we move calves around, what does Papa use?"

"A halter."

"Why?"

"So they don't run away."

"Everything people do is to keep nature from running away. So we can control it. You see, nature doesn't love people very much. It doesn't care what happens to us."

"Is that for really, Papa?"

He stood up and gazed at his dusty boots. "Yes, sweetheart, it is. . . ."

"Is the farm bad?"

Looking down, Ezra sensed that the depth of enquiry was too much for his little girl. He smiled. "No. The farm is good. But it is only good because Papa controls it. And control is not love, sweetheart. That's all. Okay, now run along and let Papa finish his work."

Weeks later, insight struck when a fierce thunderstorm forced a herd of cows into the shelter of the barn. Sophia sat and watched the herd find safety within the high borders of her father's rebuilt fieldstone walls. Intimation sparked in her young mind, and over time was transformed into belief, and then finally into knowledge: knowledge that there was love between people and nature, but that the love had to be developed, by establishing a middle ground with compromise. Same as the love between a man and a woman, or between a person and God.

Many years later, the image — whenever it recurred — of those frightened cows safely nestled within the barn gave pause to Sophia, and led her to challenge her father's beliefs. She came to realize that his observations had never blossomed beyond mere belief because his mind had been for ever clouded by the harshness of the work, and the sweat that filled his waking hours.

Made blind by the process. Never coming to know; to know that, through the toil, the process of his life's work stood as true testament in the cultured earth, wood, and stone of their farm. The very foundation of love itself: compromise. A perfect earthly thing.

No. Control was not love.

Sophia withdrew her wrapped hand from the church wall. "I hurt, Papa . . . ," she whispered sadly. She entered the stillness of the church. "I hurt."

# CHAPTER 15

Surrounded by infinite blackness — blackness without stars or any perceptible boundary — Thomas felt like a lost child, forgotten. Frightened and alone.

Saint Peter stood motionless with his eyes closed, his breathing slow and meditative.

Afraid as he was of what Peter was about to relate, Thomas began to feel an odd sense of anticipation that seemed perversely self-destructive and at the same time liberating. This had a curiously sedative effect as he prepared himself to deal with the inevitability of reckoning with the Eternal. Shaking his head, he thought: Catechism and Dante never prepared me for this shit.

And then, as if Saint Peter knew his readiness and relative ease of mind, he began: "Thomas, a man's life is not an easy thing to sum up; his influence and importance can be either far-reaching or, in some instances, insignificant."

Thomas was stunned, but instantly his defence mechanisms were raised. "Insignificant!" he exclaimed. "That can't be right! I can't believe it." He was overcome by shivers that made him shake visibly. "No man is insignificant!"

For the first time since they had come face to face, Saint Peter began to pace. Thomas stayed put. He felt as though his veins had filled with black lead — heavy and numbing. Peter continued to walk about contemplatively in front of him, occasionally diverting his gaze from the black heavens above to the sway of material at his feet.

Thomas couldn't stand the silence now — if this is going to happen, then get on with it. The anger and fear rising inside him burst out as a sob, causing the saint to stop in his tracks.

Peter turned to face him again. "As you fear — or, more accurately, as you know, deep in your heart — you fall into the latter category."

Thomas felt his heart heave painfully. He fell to one knee and toppled over, eyes closed. Saint Peter stood above him, unsure of what to do — leaving him unattended seemed no less inappropriate than offering comfort. The strangeness of this paradox bothered the saint. He waited in the darkness for Thomas to awaken, so they could resume.

After a while, Peter squatted beside the fallen man and stared into his pale face. He put his hand gently on Thomas's head and watched him breathe slowly and shallowly. The saint stood up again, but Thomas's appearance — so small and frail at his feet — stirred feelings that further interfered with Peter's objective. Despite his reluctance to offer any gentleness, he lowered himself once more and placed the mortal's head in his lap.

Within his heart he felt a bitter urge to curse all of this: the darkness, his own frailty, his fears, and God's design. A design that allowed a man like Thomas even to exist.

Into the blackness above and beyond, he raised a plea: "Master, Thomas is a lost aspect. There will be more, many more. If You will this dangerous condition upon Yourself . . . what will happen to You after the gathering?"

Only a deep silence ringing with melancholic resonance answered the saint's question — a question undermining a fundamental pillar of faith. Peter had spoken in doubt.

His bloodied head cradled in a cervical collar, Thomas was expertly rushed from the ambulance through the sliding glass door of the Emergency bay. The bearing on one of the gurney wheels rattled like metallic bones over the beige linoleum floor.

A crossfire of medical jargon split the canopy of synthetic air above him. He was hoisted "on three" onto a cool white table; his stained and tattered clothes were cut away from his broken torso; a tray of cold surgical instruments was wheeled beside him; he was hooked to a bank of monitors.

"CLEAR!"

A pair of arms reached across his chest and slapped two electrodisks above his torn heart. Hot volts slammed into his body, making his spine arch like a fish thrashing out of water. The green line on the heart monitor registered a series of strong sharp peaks, then tapered off again.

"CLEAR!"

Again Thomas contorted as the current seared through his system.

"What's going to become of me?" asked Thomas wearily. He awoke exhausted from the effects of the shock brought on by Peter's words. His head still rested in the saint's lap, and he gazed up into the immortal's warm face and brilliant eyes. The saint seemed to him to be the most beautiful man he had ever seen. "Am I going to suffer for ever, Saint Peter?" He lifted his head from the saint's lap, rolled up on an elbow, and pushed himself back a few feet.

Peter too was feeling the strain of this encounter; he wished that it were over, that he had never been chosen to speak to this mortal — who was no mortal at all. Such a wretched, wretched business. The saint closed his eyes and drew his legs in, deer-like, beneath him. He sat motionless in silent communion, seemingly oblivious of the question posed to him.

Thomas leaned forward and looked into his closed face. Gone. Once again alone. He sat back and noticed that his breathing had become thicker and more laboured, the air pouring into his lungs like heavy syrup. This filled him with a rising sense of panic, and he brought a hand to his tightening chest and closed his eyes.

What is all this, he wondered. Nightmare? Vision? Something beginning? Maybe ending?

Reason had nothing to cling onto. Certitude was a withered

balloon. And now dread was beginning to creep, like a water-stain across a ceiling, into the expanding void that Thomas Gorgon's soul was becoming. With each passing moment of silence, he felt hollower inside. In a further effort to find consolation, he immersed himself in the Song of Man that flowed within and beyond his soul. The music of his life filled his being, making him homesick. He was starting to pick individual sounds out of the dark space around him. Sounds of his youth; his loves; sounds of his whole life, celestial and terrestrial, all so wonderfully orchestrated. But Peter was correct; there was no sound of a mother's heartbeat in this song. What could that mean? Although Thomas had grown up never knowing who his mother was or what she looked like, she had to have existed.

I'm living proof, he reasoned.

"No, Thomas," replied the saint. "You are not proof of anything."

Thomas was startled by Peter's retort to his private thoughts. "You're awake!"

"I was never asleep."

"Tell me what you meant about my being insignificant," Thomas begged.

Peter slowly slid his folded legs out and pulled his knees up to his chin, smoothing his habit neatly towards his feet before he spoke with contrived firmness: "All men are not equal." He wrapped his arms around his knees; there was a painful pause. "Even in the eyes of the Lord, Thomas."

"But, but we were always told the opposite. Human equality before God is fundamental."

"That is not entirely true," explained Peter cautiously. "It has become a half-truth, at best."

"So God doesn't love us?" probed Thomas.

"Yes, the Master does. Very much."

"But not equally."

Both Thomas and Saint Peter could feel the convergence gathering momentum, like a locomotive. Who would utter the first sound? The first recognizable syllable leading to the pronouncement of Thomas's fate? They sat facing one another, two small figures: one silenced by mortal fear of eternal damnation; the other by anguished compassion.

Thomas felt his larynx tighten painfully with each attempt to part his lips in speech, but this silence was killing him; he had to ask it. The question. Four small words. With every nerve frayed by fear, he willed himself to do the most difficult task he had ever done; in a voice that was barely more than a ghost-whisper, he asked, "Does God love me . . . ?"

Saint Peter's mouth hardened, but in his eyes was a depth of sorrow beyond the flow of tears. "Thomas," he began, "God does not even know you."

Never in the history of mankind had there been a cry to heaven more wrought with pain than the one that erupted from Thomas Gorgon's soul. It was the most horrendous and piteous sound Saint Peter had ever heard. The wails seemed to carry with them the entire burden of the human condition: everything from the weight of Adam's deception to the splitting of the atom.

Such pain must take its course. Saint Peter felt helpless; he could do little more than bow his head in grief, close his eyes against such torment until it subsided. If it ever did.

The screaming reached a final crescendo and abruptly ceased. Saint Peter sat frozen — eyes squeezed shut, chin buried in his chest, hands sealing his ears — afraid to behold the man. Now he was silent — but in what state? Slowly Peter opened his eyes. "Dear God — no — Thomas!"

Curled in a tight fetal ball, Thomas lay shivering, wide-eyed. He had screamed so forcefully that tiny blood vessels in his throat had burst, leaving a faint stain of crimson in the corners of his gaping mouth.

Peter wanted to comfort him, but could not bring himself to reach out and touch him. He felt wholly responsible for this man's suffering; he had managed his charge poorly. Commissioned to enact the Master's will upon this mortal, he had grown infirm with doubt and quandary. Questions had arisen in his mind, when faith alone should have governed the deed, obscuring the end. Questions he had never before posed to himself regarding the Master's judgement.

Saint Peter stood up and looked down at Thomas still quivering in shock; his heart was pounding as he spoke, in a voice tinged with bitterness, to God. "Is THIS your will, Master?" he asked, gesturing to the bereft man at the hem of his garment. "Such torment on one small man? Who — by the very fabric of your design, which allows free will to govern human actions — was created and lived outside the realm of your love? Is this just? He is still a human! And should be reckoned as one! A by-product of scientific vanity should not be judged mortally sinful!"

Peter's rhetoric rose through the darkness, with what effectiveness he could not say. His heart ached for the shattered mortal lying crumpled at his feet; and for the God he himself so loved, but could not obey this time. "Forgive me, Master; My Father; My Lord; I do love You with all that I am, but I cannot follow You with a pure and true heart. Standing here, I feel divided, without a centre or focus; and my mind — like the collective mind of my kindred species, YOUR truest church — is divided, distorted, unrecognizable to itself or to You. O Master, this cannot be right, this decision. I . . . I know my place . . . I do, but to me this judgement rings with injustice. Forgive me . . . please . . . but I cannot find the comfort of rightness in this mortal's fate." Saint Peter swallowed with difficulty; his hands were clenched in tension. "But I will obey. I will concede to Your bidding. I will yield. My faith falters, but my love for You is firm. I will adhere to my duty, Master."

The darkness suddenly felt colder to Peter. He felt the urge to pray for strength and direction, but felt unworthy and dirty, so he kept a silent mind.

There was a stirring at his feet that caused him to jump. He looked down into the despairing eyes that gaped up at him.

"Don't leave me, Peter . . . ," Thomas pleaded faintly, reaching up with a trembling hand. Peter swore he could hear a hollowness, like an echo, in his words when he said, "I won't leave you, Thomas. I won't."

# CHAPTER 16

Joseph Langley shifted his weight from one leg to the other. The wounds in his rump were beginning to throb, and he wondered if there was any glass still embedded in his flesh. He wanted to check it out, but this was hardly the time or place. It would have to wait.

A snow had begun to fall, from the strip of black sky left by the two buildings. Gabby had been watching the snow gather gentle momentum since the first lone flake had caught his eye; now it fell like sprinkled talc. But Langley's movements distracted him and he smiled. "Your feet getting cold?" he asked. "You look like you're trying to remember the steps to a jig."

Langley stopped moving. He looked away, embarrassed. In an attempt to hide the truth of his discomfort, he said, "Yes. My feet are a little cold."

Gabby stretched his neck out to look at Langley's footwear. "Pretty fancy boots. I like that stitching and coloured leather. Guess they're not too warm, though, are they?"

"No, not really."

"Is that real silver on them pointy tips?"

"Yeah. It's real."

Gabby shook his grizzled head in admiration. "Awful nice," he said.

An uncomfortable silence settled between them. Langley grew increasingly irritable as the silence was prolonged. He paced the narrow span of the alley, kicking a crumpled Coke can, his jaw muscles tightening beneath his cheeks. Finally, Gabby spoke: "So, who is this person you're here to see?"

Langley kicked the Coke can hard; it bounced off the wall and landed at his feet. Slowly, he raised a boot heel and crushed the can beneath his weight. "My brother," he replied.

Gabby's dark eye rested on the image of the flattened can, then rolled up to look at Langley's face before he asked, "What about the rest of your family? Any of them live here as well?"

"No. There's only my brother."

"You haven't seen him in a while, I take it."

"Been years."

"What happened? You two have a fight?"

Langley shook his head sadly, eyes closed. The resurfacing memories were subduing him. "No," he answered. "My parents split up and I went to live with my dad."

"And your brother stayed with your mother?"

"Yes." Langley's mouth hung open, mute with sorrow. He finally added: "But he was just a baby. . . ."

The words fell from his lips like a crippled bird, and the raw nakedness of his pain moved Gabby deeply. Gabby sighed, then said in a faint voice, "Yes. I'm so sorry."

Joseph Langley fired a hard look at the legless man in the box. "What did you say?" he asked.

Gabby's dark eye registered alarm. "What?"

"What you said. What did you mean by 'Yes, you're sorry,' like that?"

Gabby swallowed uneasily and looked away. "Nothing," he said. "Nothing at all." He closed his eyes and hid his head. He could feel Langley's gaze on him, could hear the insistence in the grit under his boots as he stepped closer.

"Why did you say you're sorry that way?" asked Langley again, standing at the opening of the cardboard box. Gabby kept his head down and didn't reply. "Answer me, damn it!"

Slowly Gabby turned his face up to meet Langley's; and when he did, it was with an expression so full of human warmth, gentleness, and empathy that even Gabby's horrid face was beautiful. His eyes radiated a compassion that seemed boundless, despite their grotesque appearance. "'Tell me about your father," he said quietly.

Joseph Langley looked down at the legless freak. His anger evaporated and a single desire saturated his will — he wanted to dive deep into the old man's face to find and know the source of such profound beauty.

"My father . . . ?" he asked vaguely, still mesmerized by Gabby's new radiance. "Which one?"

"You had two fathers?"

"No," answered Langley. "Well, one man, two fathers."

Gabby paused, then said, "Tell me about the father you know best, I guess."

Langley's eyes flickered with memory. "My father," he began. "The father I was fortunate enough to know was a handsome man. A large, gentle man who loved me very much. He was a ranch hand. He worked for a man named Cummer Lee who owned the Weeping Cedars Ranch. It was a big operation . . . over two thousand acres. Green and cattle everywhere. My father used to help manage the herds — you know, culling sick and injured animals, helping heifers calf out, branding . . ."

As Langley spoke, wading deeper into the pool of reminiscence, his face softened and became youthful. Gabby smiled at the change. "Like a cowboy in the movies," he suggested.

Langley's smile widened with pride. "Kind of . . . yeah." Gabby stared into his eyes, shiny and distant with joy.

Langley shot a look at Gabby. "My dad had this horse!" he exclaimed. "Stood over sixteen hands!"

"That's big?" asked Gabby.

"Yeah. It's a good-sized animal. My dad called him 'Blackstrap'. He called him that because he was black as molasses. My dad loved that horse."

Gabby nodded, enjoying the ease of the conversation.

"Such a beautiful animal," Langley said fondly. "I can still see my dad riding him. Such a graceful mover . . . like floating. . . ." He looked at Gabby in great earnest. "You know," he said, "I truly believe that horse actually loved my dad back. Do you think that's possible?"

Gabby shrugged. "I don't know much about animal ways, son. I have a tough enough time understanding people."

"Well, I think it's possible. And I know my dad thought so too. He used to say how he and Blackstrap were as one. My dad green-broke him, trained him, and worked every day with that animal. He told me once that the horse had become him, and he the horse, joined as one, like a single soul. He even told me once that when he died a part of his soul would fuse with Blackstrap's spirit . . . or energy, or whatever it is that drives animals."

"I guess some people get very attached to animals, to their companionship. Thinking of them as near human," said Gabby.

Langley shook his head vigorously. "No. What you're talking about is . . . um" — he tapped his forehead with a knuckle — "anthro . . . something *or* . . . pomorphism! Anthropomorphism! Yeah! No, my father didn't think of Blackstrap that way, as a human extension of himself. He just believed all things were linked."

"Linked?"

"By any invisible thread — like some great strand of DNA — that everything's a part of. He believed that every single thing in the universe is part of a greater sum. The pulse and poetry of life with all its diversity is designed to urge the mind into discovery. To search . . . to know . . . it was his religion."

"His religion?" puzzled Gabby.

"He worshipped the connectedness of things, the kinship. It was how he defined himself — by discovering the links to all 'otherness'. Doing so transformed him."

"You mean it changed him as a person," offered Gabby.

"More than that," replied Langley. "You see, this quest of discovery actually transformed him. Physically."

"No shit?"

"Yes, and drastically, too. It was because of the absorption."

"Absorption?"

"That's how he described it: absorption. This absorption changed the colour of his skin to a deep dark copper that never faded — even in the winter. His hair turned like fire, auburn and gold. But it was his eyes. . . ."

Gabby's head tilted slightly as he saw Langley engrossed in the images surfacing in his mind. "What about his eyes?" he asked.

Langley's stare was fixed and his fingers moved gently, undulating like a current of water. "They became brighter . . . honey-hazel . . . I believed that his eyes had soaked up the sun's rays . . . he used to stare into that ball of fire . . . into the eye of God. . . ." Langley said the last words softly, too softly for Gabby to catch.

"What was that, son?"

Langley blinked. "Hmm?"

Gabby just shook his head.

Langley drew in a deep breath of frozen air. "That was the absorption. The change in his appearance was the physical absorption of the landscape — the sun and the air, the rain and the wind, the grasses of the plains, the dust and the dung — these all became actual parts of his blood . . . consumed as sacrament, filling his lungs and strengthening his heart."

"Sounds like quite a man."

"Oh, he was — he became a beautiful man."

"But this was the father you knew; what about the other father?"

"Him?" Langley's face grew strained at the mention of his father's alter ego.

"What was he like?"

"He was an investment banker, and an excellent provider. He was very business-wise, managing money well . . . always prepared for any eventuality. . . ." Langley's voice trailed off slightly. Gabby sat quietly, attentive. "But," continued Langley, in a stronger voice, "I pieced this together years later. I was quite young when I left to live with him so I really hadn't been aware of what he did for a living. All I knew was that he left in the morning wearing a suit and tie and carrying a briefcase, and came home for supper looking the same but with a folded newspaper under his arm. On weekends we would throw a baseball in the back yard, or go fishing, maybe do some yard work . . . but my memories of him at home with my mother and brother are little more than that — recurrent images and vague patterns.

"My home life was safe — boring, I guess, but the good kind of boring. Stable. Typically suburban."

"But not the lifestyle he wanted, right?" proposed Gabby. "That the reason for the breakup?"

Langley grimaced as he shifted his weight to ease the throb in his buttocks. "Maybe partly," he answered. "I guess, like most people, he found his real self denied by obligation and commitment. It's a fact of life — married life — and he accepted it. He concealed his true nature beneath a Brooks Brothers suit Monday through Friday, and a polo shirt and a pair of chinos on weekends."

"You're losing me, Joseph."

Langley smiled sadly. "Even as a small boy, I was aware of how other people were struck by my father's presence. Underneath the suburban polish was a lion. An athlete. A rogue. It was in his walk, his eyes, the shape of his hands. As a child I couldn't see all this . . . he was just my dad. But it's funny . . . I do remember other people reacting to him. It wasn't until I grew up that I saw these things in him myself, and understood my memories."

"But you think he left your mother because he needed to bust loose?"

"No, not really. As I said, he accepted his family obligations. He was very pragmatic that way. Cautious. It was largely how he showed his love for us, I think: camouflaging his dreams to ensure a steady paycheque."

"You make the ordinary sound somewhat heroic."

"Not heroic. Tragic. I think it's true of most people," said

Langley. "We go through life in a state of a compromise."

Gabby sat silently, nodding.

Langley tipped his dark hat back and gazed up at the narrow black heaven above them. "It's tragic because the surface life often takes over, erasing the dreams and the raw energy that feeds the true life within each of us. So it can never emerge. But in my father's case, it wasn't tragic," he added firmly.

"Why's that?"

"Because my father didn't let his choice of compromise kill his spirit. He managed a difficult balancing of his two lives; he kept them apart."

Gabby smiled as he began to understand Langley's notions. "And that," he said, "is what people saw glow from his surface."

"Yes," agreed Langley. "He became charged by the tension. Beneath his conventional surface of manners, education, and responsibility was a supernova."

"I see," said Gabby. "But" — he lowered his eyes and cracked a grin — "if I may play devil's advocate here. . . ."

Langley wasn't sure he liked the way Gabby had cast his eyes away, but he conceded to the request: "Sure."

"Well, it seems to me that your father could be seen as a cop-out. You talk about him 'happily' camouflaging and balancing; talk about him being in control, above the bullshit of modern life — but it all sounds like a lot of lip-service. Like your father was a charismatic man who lived a life of . . . oh shit, how does that go? . . . 'quiet desperation' . . . yeah, that's it. All that talk he fed you is window-dressing, son. All that talk is one frightened man seeing his pathetic state, and trying to compensate for his . . . ordinariness."

There was no sound from Langley, no response. He stood as if pole-axed. His mouth was a thin line; when it parted, his words were slow and menacing. "Fuck you, old man," he said in a whisper. "You don't talk about my father that way."

Gabby smiled gently. "Devil's advocate. That's all, Joseph.

Calm down, son."

Tears of rage rolled down Langley's cheeks. He was shaking. "Don't you ever . . . !"

"Listen, Joseph, I'm sorry if I struck a nerve. I didn't mean your father was lying to you."

Langley closed his eyes tight and clenched and unclenched his fists, as if firing bolts of lightning from his fingertips. Through his teeth he said, "My father never compromised. Never deviated."

Gabby stared up at him as if plotting his next words — or a course of escape. Softly he replied, "Of course he didn't." His dark eyes rolled once, slowly, then he added, "He never compromised."

"YOU'RE GODDAMNED RIGHT! TO DO SO IS DEATH! AND MY FATHER WAS ALIVE!" Langley put his hands on either side of his head and appeared to be squeezing. "He never compromised, old man!" His eyes opened wild and fierce, but his voice strained for composure. "Compromise is not about a lifestyle. It's about what you let that lifestyle do to your inner self. *That's* the fucking compromise! *That's* the death!" He dropped his hands and paced briskly from one wall to the other. Gabby sat quietly and watched the silver boot-tips flash back and forth.

Abruptly, Langley stopped pacing. In a trembling voice, he whispered, "Compromise is deviation . . . and deviation leads to distortion. . . ."

Gabby looked into his tortured face and said in a nurturing tone, "All right, son. But where do you lay the blame? Where's the cause of it all?"

Langley shook his head in despair as his mind drew its conclusions. Tears began to form in his eyes as he answered. "Modernity is humankind's forbidden fruit; and our weakness of will to resist it is our Eve. Our whore."

He fell to his knees and cried.

Gabby raised himself onto his gnarled hands and emerged

from his cardboard sanctuary. He approached Langley, setting himself down beside him. Gently he reached out and placed a hand on his shoulder.

At the touch, Langley collapsed and wailed like an abandoned child. The legless old man removed the black hat and tenderly wrapped his arms around Langley's head, temporarily shielding him from the jaws of his demons.

"But all this wasn't why he left your mother?" asked Gabby, when Langley's sobs had subsided.

"No," replied Langley. He spoke softly now. His eyes were red and swollen.

"What was it, then?"

"He could no longer live with her. She" — he paused, trying to find the right words — "she made it hard for him to want to stay. She changed."

Gabby leaned forward slightly, intrigued.

"She even changed her name and my brother's after we left. She changed back to her maiden name: Eleanor Roberts."

Langley's hands moved in front of his face. Expressively, poetically. His palms and fingers were re-creating in space the billowing waves of white in his mind. "I can't remember if the change in her was gradual or sudden," he said. "But I do remember the day it dawned on me — that something was odd. The laundry. . . ."

Gabby raised an eyebrow. "Laundry?"

"Yeah," said Langley pensively. "You know, it must have been a gradual change because, as I recall, noticing the laundry was like suddenly seeing something that had always been there."

"What are you talking about?"

"The laundry. My mother's laundry. It was all white. Everything of hers was pure white cotton: bedsheets, underwear, blouses, skirts, sweaters, socks. Every stitch of clothing. Whiter than the whitest snow."

"That is kind of odd," conceded Gabby. "But hardly grounds

for abandoning a wife and child."

"Oh, her obsession with cotton wasn't the reason he left," explained Langley. "She had to wear cotton because of an affliction she kept hidden. An affliction that grew and spread all over her body. It tortured her."

"What was it?"

"An acute case of eczema. Apparently she had always had mild patches of it here and there. Nothing serious."

"But it got worse?" asked Gabby.

"Yes. Much worse. It spread almost overnight, covering most of her body in raw, weeping flesh."

Gabby rubbed his furrowed brow. "But why the secrecy?"

Langley shook his head. "I guess we'll never know. The truth of it went to the grave with her. Much of what I know I learned later on, as a young man . . . but initially I learned of my mother's peculiarities from my father."

"He kept in contact with her?"

"By one-way correspondence. He used to send her brief notes about my progress in school, my health. He also sent her money . . . not that she needed any. He'd left her financially secure."

"So what did he tell you?"

"Not very much, actually. When I reached twelve or thirteen he began to tell me the details, as far as he understood them," said Langley. "My mother had once been a warm and affectionate wife. But at some point she suddenly turned it all off. He told me she became reclusive and introverted. Wouldn't speak with him, sleep with him; their sex life came to an abrupt halt. She completely severed him from her life. I later realized that this was when the disease spread and she took to wearing white cotton. I guess it felt most comfortable against her raw skin."

"Tell me, Joseph," begged Gabby, "how could your mother keep this a total secret?"

"Well, aside from her isolating herself from my father, there was the way the disease spread."

"Oh?"

"It was a curious thing," said Langley distantly. "The infection began at the base of her neck, covered the entirety of her torso, and ended just above her wrists and knees."

"That really is strange," said Gabby. "How she must have suffered," he added sympathetically.

"I saw photos of her flesh. It must have been excruciating. But you can see how easy it would have been to conceal the affliction. I can remember her wearing her collar and cuffs done up all the time. She was very fussy about it. Later I understood that she was checking to make sure her disease was concealed."

"I can understand the pain and embarrassment she endured, but I still don't get why she hid it from your father.

Langley looked at Gabby with an unsettled expression. "Everything I knew at that time was so piecemeal." He turned away and became — within the borders of his imagination — a small boy again, remembering flashes of moments: like the cool, smooth surface of his bedroom wall against the curl of his ear, as he listened to his father:

> Please, Eleanor. . . . I'm trying to understand . . .
> these silences of yours . . . makes it hard. . . . I have
> needs, Eleanor. . . . What is happening . . . I need to
> feel you . . . to be close . . .

And there was his mother's anger, when she was cornered and forced to speak to her husband:

> Damn it, Clayt! Don't. . . . Don't!. . . . You wouldn't
> understand . . . just something I have to figure out
> . . . I need time. . . . I need to go through this . . .
> alone . . .

There would be yelling, mostly from his father. And tears, mostly from his mother. The bedroom wall would hum frighteningly against young Joseph's ear — but it was the silences in between that made his small heart race.

After one of these silences, as the floor vibrated with Clayton's departure downstairs, Joseph Langley first heard the words "animal-wild" through the wall. His mother was alone, crying and speaking to herself, asking questions.

> Why . . . why am I to suffer? . . . The pain is sometimes more than I can bear. . . . Why did you do this to me? What have I done? . . .

She cried louder. Moving around the room. Frantic.

> He doesn't want to understand. . . . He isn't patient, he just wants sex . . . doesn't know You've touched me . . . won't let me sort it out. . . . I need solitude, but he's just wild . . . wild with his need . . . animal-wild . . . his needs are distracting me from You . . .

Langley rubbed his eyes and exhaled deeply. He looked at Gabby, who was staring at him, waiting for him to continue. He looked down at the cold ground. "It was all so piecemeal," he repeated. "In the end, the physical torment drove her mad. Her mind tried to deal with the reality of perpetual pain by finding a cause for it. A reason to justify such anguish. And she came up with one."

"Which was?"

"That God had chosen her."

"Chosen her? For what?"

"As some sort of instrument to spread His will on earth. She came to interpret her affliction as a sign, a puzzle to be figured out."

"How can you know all this?" asked Gabby. "You weren't around any longer."

"When I was older, I took to returning to my hometown from time to time."

"You'd check up on your mother?"

"Just to see her," replied Langley. "From a distance. There was a void I could never fill, but at least being close eased the pain a little."

"You loved her very much, didn't you, Joseph?"

"She was my mother."

Gabby nodded. "So what happened?"

"She became very ill. My brother was away at school most of the time, so she had professional in-home care. One day a van pulled into the driveway; it was an oxygen-supply company delivering fresh tanks. A nurse greeted the van driver at the door. I felt compelled to approach, hoping to hear something. I crossed the street and stopped by the fence that bordered our property. I heard fragments, but I couldn't catch it all. But I remember my heart pounding. I hadn't been that close to my home in years." Langley swallowed. "The man was beginning to unload the van. He was getting out a number of tanks. I asked him if he needed a hand."

"He accepted your offer?"

"He did," said Langley, through trembling lips. "I . . . I followed him in. Stepped back into my boyhood. There was new carpeting up the stairs and the walls were painted a different colour . . . but much of the furniture and lamps and pictures was familiar." His eyes filled with tears. "I was home. . . ."

Gabby placed his rough, spindly hand on Langley's. "And your mother, Joseph?"

"I saw her. . . ." He wept openly, gasping occasionally. "She . . . she was in the kitchen . . . by the bay window . . . in a wheelchair, her back to me . . . wearing a white housecoat. . . ." He choked at the memory. "Her wrists and hands were so thin. . . ."

"I'm sorry, Joseph."

Langley looked into Gabby's eyes. "An angel from heaven could not have been more beautiful to my eyes."

Gabby smiled.

"I . . . I just stood there in the kitchen. Staring at her back. I

176

wanted to hold her so badly. . . ."

"What happened?"

Langley wiped his tear-stained face. "I don't know how long I stood there — probably not very long — but the delivery man called out to me after he'd finished setting up. I turned from my mother without ever looking into her face, and began to walk out. And as I did I noticed a book on the table. Brown covers, with gold-edged pages and a brass latch . . ."

"A diary?"

Langley nodded. "No one was watching. So I slipped it under my jacket and walked out."

"And the diary filled in many of the gaps."

"Yes, it spanned years. It detailed her suffering, her separation; it traced her fall into madness and her life alone with my brother."

"And was that the last time you saw her?" asked Gabby.

"Alive, yes. After she passed away, I identified myself at the morgue. I saw her corpse and read the coroner's report. Said my goodbyes . . . my apologies. . . ."

"Did you ever show your father the diary?"

Langley shook his head solemnly. "He was killed about a year before I took the diary. He died without ever knowing what had driven my mother away from him."

Gabby's dark eye began to wander again. "You say he was killed?"

Langley's mouth became hard. "He was murdered. By a woman named Yvonne Wilcox. He used to keep her company."

"They were friends?"

"Lovers — they became lovers. At first their relationship was . . . I guess you'd say 'business'. But over time it developed into more than that."

"She was a ranch hand too?"

"No. She worked in town. My dad would go and visit her . . . employ her . . . her services. Did so for years." He shook his head and sighed heavily.

"No shame in that, son," said Gabby. "A man has his needs. He wasn't hurting anyone."

Langley stared at his boots. "It's not that. . . ."

"It's the fact they fell in love?"

"Not even that, really," said Langley.

"What is it, then?"

"I fell in love with her too." Langley raised a hand to stop the old man from speaking. "Not," he assured him, "in any competitive way. But my dad loved her very much, and eventually she came to live with us."

"Like a family."

"Not 'like' — we were a family. Yvonne's presence filled an emptiness in me. I loved her for that. I thought I always would."

"Why did she kill your father?"

"It was an act of desperation. She needed money. A lot. There were these men. They'd phone at all hours. They threatened her family, threatened their lives. My dad swore to protect her and her family, as best he could, but she went crazy with fear. . . ."

"But why did she have to kill him?"

"My father lived simply. He had no money. Everything he'd earned in his previous life, he'd left for my mother and my baby brother. All he had was a couple of hundred bucks in his savings account, and . . ."

"And what?"

". . . an insurance policy for $250,000." He dropped his face into his hands.

Gabby's eye stopped rotating. "She killed your father for the insurance money?" he asked. "Didn't the money go to you?"

Langley shook his head. Through his fingers he explained, "He had changed it, made her the beneficiary. I guess he thought she'd always take care of me."

"Dear Lord . . . how did she get away with it?"

Langley raised his head, his face showing the years of pent-up grief. "She didn't kill him herself. She had it done. Contracted it out."

178

"How can you be sure?"

"My dad was shot point-blank in the back of the head with a .32 calibre handgun. We didn't own one, and there wasn't a handgun of that calibre anywhere on the ranch. Mr. Lee had a legally registered .44 in his office, but that was the only handgun around. And Yvonne was conveniently out of town. She'd gone visiting somewhere. . . ."

Gabby shook his head. "Now hold on, son — it sounds to me like your father was murdered, all right, but I'm not convinced this Yvonne had anything to do with it."

Langley laughed scornfully. "Then how do you explain her disappearance after the insurance cheque arrived?" he challenged. "When the cheque arrived, she vanished. The bitch packed her stuff, left town, and was never heard from again! I complained to the police, but they had no grounds to look for her. There was no evidence against her, and she was the rightful beneficiary, and I was no longer a child requiring a guardian."

"How terrible," said Gabby. "What did you do?"

"I continued to work on the ranch, earned my keep. I managed to save some money and put myself through college, business administration and then part-time university studies."

"So you've done all right for yourself."

"Done all right for myself? Like I had any fucking choice?" snapped Langley. "THAT FUCKING WHORE ABANDONED ME!" He began to pace back and forth across the alley, slapping the brick walls with open palms. With each crossing his shoulders grew more hunched, and his face became redder and more distorted. He stopped abruptly in the middle of the alley to face Gabby. "WHY DID SHE LEAVE ME? WHY? WHY? I THOUGHT SHE LOVED ME! LIKE A MOTHER WOULD! SHE LOVED MY FATHER. . . ." His mouth hung open and quivering, and he could hardly draw breath. "WHY DIDN'T SHE LOVE ME TOO?"

Gabby was rendered speechless. Langley was trembling, and despite his large physique and savage eyes he looked pitifully frail and vulnerable. The legless man raised his arms in a gesture of comfort.

Langley's knees buckled and he laid his head on Gabby's shoulder, exhausted. "I only wish I could have killed it. . . ."

Gabby took Langley by both shoulders and eased him back. "It?" he asked. "You mean Yvonne?"

Langley wiped his nose and shook his head. "No. That thing within her — the Eve-canker on her soul," he said flatly. "The whore within the whore. Maybe . . . just maybe I could have saved us all."

# CHAPTER 17

The interior of St. Peter in Chains was muted by darkness, but the moon cast enough light to reveal the subtleties of its grandeur.

Sophia shuffled painfully up the polished wood of the centre aisle. The warm stillness of the air coated her face and felt good to her. She came to the nearest of the rear pews and eased herself into it. The darkness, the serenity, and the warmth enhanced her relief. She sighed, creating a slight echo. All she could think at that moment was: Here is a little peace. . . .

Her muscles jolted in a spasm that made her legs spring forward. She sat upright and looked about in a momentary panic, and shook her head. "Can't fall asleep," she mumbled wearily. She rubbed her face against the fur of her sleeve. "Can't get too comfortable. . . ."

She yawned. All she would have to do was lie back, and she would fade away — she knew that. The warmth was seeping into her pores, melting her bones. She stretched her eyes open and took an exaggerated breath. "Gotta stay awake." She shifted on her seat, sending a wave of pain through her body. Stiffening up, just as she had feared. Carefully she slid her tailbone back into the bowl-like curve of the pew, and straightened her shoulders, panting from the effort.

She undid the buttons of her jacket and gently fanned herself. Her feet and hands were burning as they warmed, throbbing, feeling thick.

Again she closed her eyes. Tilting her head back, she

stretched the muscles in her neck. After two revolutions on each side, she opened her eyes. Even in the poor light, she could make out the fresco on the arched ceiling: a vast, pale blue sky backing clouds tinted salmon-pink and cream. Kind of unreal . . . forced in its perfection, she observed. The curved ceiling added a further dimension of the infinite. Around the fresco was an ornate border of thickly entwined gold grapevines with winged cherubs at each corner, blowing long trumpets.

Sophia straightened her head and looked at the walls. Above the caravan of pews were more paintings, also framed in gold. Squinting, she concluded that they were the stations of the cross; although she couldn't be sure, they appeared to be oils on canvas. Above the paintings was stained glass — long, curved windows that came to a peak, depicting saints and martyrs. There were statues everywhere. And spiral staircases of carved wood. Ornamentations of gold and silver. Icons. As in many old Catholic churches, the opulent decor was more conducive to slack-jawed gawking than to prayer. Sophia felt as though she were sitting in a warehouse for a museum of fine art. As beautiful as the individual pieces were, together they formed a grotesque tribute to human excess.

In her mind she summoned up a reordering of the church interior. St. Peter in Chains would be erased. Gutted. Broken free of its yoke of convention. A blizzard of fragmentary images and emotions tore through her imagination, swooping and merging. Colliding, confronting, evolving into an intuition, a shadow-whisper, that spoke to Sophia's soul:

Allow infinity to be expressed in the swirl of a garden snail's shell. Immortality in the promise of a kernel of corn. Hope in the mingling of rain with dust. And let the word of God be known in no tongue, which is every tongue. Eventually coming to see and know God more intimately in the world, allowing His kingdom to lie like a lover upon the earth. Decorate the house of the Lord with the truth of what is plainly revealed and what can be plainly perceived. A perfect earthly thing. A perfect divine thing.

A compromise. . . .

Sophia blinked, breaking her frozen stare. She sat back in the pew and stared at her wrapped hands. The imaginative burst of energy had left her exhausted. She closed her eyes.

Silence. Peace.

She opened her eyes. It was gone! Her imaginative redecorating of the church seemed to have cleared her head of St. Luke's verse. It was gone. . . . She breathed a sigh of relief.

Although she felt somewhat better without the parasitic piece of verse, a bevy of dark emotional sucklings still swam around her heart; she could almost feel their old, frayed mouths trying to clamp onto her again. Eager to feast on the blood, the wound. To nourish themselves on her pain. The most painful blow she could imagine, and made even more painful by the knowledge that hers was self-inflicted — her infertility, her barrenness. She remembered her sin vividly. Nothing is recalled with such clarity as one's fall from grace. Her mind rolled back to the terrible moment. Seventeen years ago.

Swirling pipe organs. Popcorn in the air. Red-yellow-red-yellow on the windshield, reflections of the carousel.

The car radio glowing green. Neil Young crooning shrilly; something about Mother Nature on the run.

Wet breath. A clumsy chin against my temple. A promise: "You'll pull out, won't you?" "Yeahyeahyeahsure. . . ."

Scared. Feel scared. In too long, much too long. "Come on, get off me. Stop! You said —" Palm in my face, pushing hard. Bending my nose, my mouth. Twisting my jaw.

Finished. My dress around my throat; panties around my ankles. Hear him pissing out behind the bushes. Whistling. Returning, peering in. "Hey, hey shake a leg. C'mon, the night's young . . . hello . . . ? What'syerfuckingproblem?"

Then later: shame, fear, and the testing. Blood. Urine.

"So you're saying I'm not?"

"No, you're not. Tell me, when did this happen?"

"The last Friday of the spring fair."

"The fair? That was three months ago."

"Yeah . . . well, okay . . . but you said I'm all right. You said so."

"That explains the severity."

"Of what?"

"You have gonorrhoea. You can sit up now."

Stirring. The wide ribbon of white paper on the examination table crinkled.

"Quite advanced. You're very sick, Sophia."

"I. . . ."

"We'll begin treatments imme —"

"I don't feel sick. Are you sure?"

"The infection is deep-seated. Often there are no obvious symptoms."

Tears down my face. Papers pulled from a desk, a file started.

"I'm going to need his name, Sophia. He'll need looking at too —"

Crying. "I . . . I don't. . . . Just a . . . a boy. . . ."

The treatments lasted almost three weeks. Heavy doses of antibiotics and frequent checkups. But the damage proved to be significant. The disease had worked its way into Sophia's fallopian tubes, resulting in massive scarring. The doctor told her she was highly unlikely to conceive. She was shattered by the idea of being a dead end, an arid island. Severed. Her most precious ability erased. She no longer felt plugged into the network of life; she no longer belonged to that vast sorority of regeneration that kept the planet breathing. "I'm empty. . . . Useless."

The greatest power in the universe, flippantly destroyed in the back seat of a car. The vulgar absurdity of it all only magnified her mortal sin.

Sophia kept her fall to herself. She spent her days brooding over the stupidity of her actions, hating herself, until it all became too much. The pain acted as a spur, forcing her to heed her cues to leave. Papa had become a ghost who didn't have the courtesy to remain hidden; Mama and Joelle had been lying in the cold earth for years; the farm had all but died, spilling out its innards of weeds, peeling paint, rust, and scrawny cats. There was nothing left that resembled home.

In the dark of a spring morning she crept out of the house with two hundred dollars she had taken from the tobacco tin in her father's top dresser drawer. The last memory she had of her escape was the gassy wheeze of his breathing following her down the hall. That same memory was also the last she had of her father alive — detached, invisible, vaporous — which was something of a tender mercy.

The days that then passed — her new life, her life alone, her "adult" life — were a pathetic continuation of ugliness, fear, and desperation. Days spent cold and alone; nights in hotels; eating in soup kitchens; wearing thin clothing; always dirty.

In three months the little money Sophia had was almost gone. She turned her first trick — a blow-job for ten dollars — in the locker-room of a hostel. It was so easy; too easy. The solution became a habit, and the habit became a lifestyle. As Sophia slipped deeper into the ways of the street, becoming proficient at selling her body, her suppressed hatred turned into spite. And that spite bred another habit: she sought to appease the God she had been taught to love and fear, by ritual self-torture. Prostitution was no longer just a means of survival on the streets; for Sophia it was a means of atonement. The degradation, filth, danger, and loneliness were a small measure of suffering compared to the anguish she believed she had caused God.

Early morning light was beginning to add sharpness and contour to the interior of St. Peter's in Chains. Sophia shuffled out of the back pew and walked up the centre aisle towards the altar. Her feet made sloppy noises, like a wet mop. The bed linens that wrapped her hands hung in scraps.

This is all just more of the same, she thought. More pain,

more suffering, more punishment. There hasn't been much good in my life. Papa was probably righter than I gave him credit for: nature — this life — maybe even God Himself doesn't love us very much. But why should He? There's nothing lovable about me. I'm a whore . . . I'm dirty . . . I. . . . She looked at her hands. Who was she kidding? Why should she hide them? Who in his right mind would suspect a whore of being touched by God?

She stopped in front of the altar. To her right were rows of candles with twisted little black wicks. She made her way to them and pulled out a long wooden match and struck it. The flame cast a gentle light. She held it up to her face and felt the tiny warmth against her wet cheeks. Then she dipped the flame towards a candle and watched it grow slightly as the wick ignited. She smiled to herself: a small living light for the soul of a departed. "Bonne fête, Joelle," she whispered.

She was about to blow out the match when she decided to add a few more resurrections. With each new flickering light she uttered a name and a sentiment: "Mama, I love you . . . ," — "Cassandra, I miss you . . . ," — Langley, this is for the part of you that is hurting you. . . ." Here she paused, then said, "This is for the man who was hit by the car. . . . I hope he's all right and doesn't need this prayer."

Her hand moved to the next candle and the flame hovered above the wick, quivering, until indecision yielded to the weight of compassion and her wrist bent to ignite the candle: "Papa. . . ." She swallowed and concluded with a blessing: "I hope God keeps you all well . . . amen."

She blew out the match and watched the six little flames become longer and stronger. She was amazed at the amount of light these candles cast. Slowly she backed away and eased herself down into the front pew, and looked at the bloody bandages on her hands. The image of blood mixed with firelight seemed appropriate: a symbol of mortality illuminated by a hint of everlastingness. Another compromise.

But no sooner had she acknowledged the simple beauty of

the image than she imagined the ring of light shunning her vile blood and leaving her in darkness. And why not? Nothing beautiful sticks to me, she thought. Nothing beautiful should. I've abused my life. I've abused God. I'm so ugly that God Himself interrupts my dreams. No part of beauty will ever belong to me, even in my own head . . . even in my dreams. I'm just a whore.

As she sat there, the rising sun was slowly conquering the darkness. Now she was able to decipher the elaborate structure that towered above the altar. Looming in front of her was a triumphant Christ, fashioned in gold, at least seven feet tall; clenched in one hand, like a shepherd's staff, was a large crucifix, while His other hand was poised in a theatrical gesture. Behind this Christ were moulded clouds and dramatic shafts of light, also in gold. The giant Christ stood heroically on a large sphere of polished gold that was supported by five ornate extensions that came down like a spider's legs, to rest on the shoulders of winged angels, their hands clasped in prayer.

Sophia shook her head. Such an overwrought tribute to Christ's triumph of spirit over flesh and sin; it was all wrong. She raised her arm towards the golden Christ and wagged her hand: "No, you're not even close. . . ." Her whispers sounded loud to her ears. "Whoever made you had no idea. You look like a sideshow; you're almost uglier than I am. . . ." She leaned forward, squaring off against her mute adversary. "His victory was for the small and weak and frightened . . . because God allowed Himself to be all those things when they nailed Him up. . . ." She could hear her voice rolling against the painted clouds on the ceiling. "He descended to such depths . . . to show by example . . . the heights we need to rise to . . . to meet Him halfway. . . .

She cast her eyes back up to the Christ. "His dying was a quiet thing. His triumph was without fanfare . . . that's what matters. . . . We HAD to take notice of such greatness in such a small package. . . ."

Then she was struck by a pang of self-consciousness that

silenced her dialogue with the statue. Feeling foolish, she painfully lay down in the pew, drawing her knees in. As she lay there, the golden Christ towered above her, even more grotesquely un-Christlike.

She began to rock, and draped a heavy arm across her eyes. "Led astray . . . I have been led astray . . ." She pulled away her shielding arm to finally see the golden Christ for what it truly was: a forgery, patented and peddled by the church. Her voice was tight with anguish as she confessed, "God was never within me. . . ." Her eyes burned with the sight of her careless soul cartooned in false gold. "You," she murmured sadly to the giant Christ; "*you* were always within me."

Now Sophia could feel death settling on her skin. "I don't want to die here," she told herself. "This place kills the soul. I couldn't stand two deaths tonight . . . especially that deeper one." She worked herself upright and began to shuffle back to the great doors, wondering, And just how do you think you're going to save that deeper self? Loudly she addressed the domain of her misguided soul: "THERE'S NOTHING LEFT! NOTHING TO SALVAGE! THE WELL IS BONE-DRY!" She began to laugh, and tears ran down her face. Between sobs and painful laughs she urged herself on: ". . . someplace to curl up . . . hidden . . . so no one can find my poor body. . . ." Her hysteria gradually faded as she proceeded down the aisle: "All this time . . . all this time . . . the wrong kind of god. . . ."

A sudden weakness melted her legs, and she fell to her knees halfway down the centre aisle. She lowered her head to the floor. "I'm going to die here," she said weakly. "I really am. . . ." She couldn't summon the strength to rise, so she let herself collapse onto her side. "My God, I feel so alone. . . ."

The change in the golden Christ was subtle at first — so subtle that it went unnoticed by Sophia. It wasn't until she rolled over onto her back that she saw the metamorphosis. The once rigid folds of the statue's tunic were beginning to move, to gather and bunch up. She stared mutely, not believing her eyes. Then she realized that the movement was mainly in one area of the statue: the groin.

The golden folds of the tunic continued to gather up, and then they parted, forming a cleft that slowly opened and closed, as if breathing. Sophia brought her hand to her mouth in horror as the transformation took on clarity, for from within the folds of the Christ's tunic a fully developed likeness of a woman's vulva emerged.

The sound of Sophia's screams hit her ears at the same time as a shaft of light shot from the statue's genitals, stabbing her eyes, hurling her into blackness.

Breaking the surface and emerging back into the realm of consciousness, Sophia felt pressure on her shoulder — the weight of a hand; the sound moving like water rings in her head was the beckoning of her own name.

"Sophia?"

In a panic, she tried to roll away from the face that peered down upon her. But her condition would not allow flight. She closed her eyes again.

"Sophia, don't be afraid." The voice was one of incredible gentleness. "I am here to help you."

A scent filled Sophia's nostrils, like a perfume, only not so synthetic. It was more intimate, more organic; it was a pleasant smell that made her want to draw more in; a smell that brought to mind things exotic and Eastern.

"You are not alone," said the voice. "Please, open your eyes and look at me."

Sophia acknowledged the voice as female. She opened her eyes. Kneeling beside her was a woman. "Let me help you up." The woman slowly assisted her to a sitting position, placing her shoulders against the side of a pew, and sat back, smiling.

Sophia was grateful for the tenderness, but remained apprehensive; the woman's appearance was unnerving. Although she sounded "modern", she seemed out of time and place. Sophia stared at her, admiring her quiet beauty — the smooth mocha skin; the shimmering black hair pulled back and arranged in intricate braids; the wide cheekbones that supported soft brown eyes; the fine, slender neck that suggested a delicately boned frame beneath her simple gown of deep purple.

Sophia felt an overwhelming urge to reach out and connect with another human being, one last time. The easy gentleness of this beautiful woman's presence wiped away all desire for isolation, banishment, and death. "Who are you?" she asked. "Are you a nun?"

The woman smiled. "No, Sophia, I am not. I've come here for you."

"How do you know my name? Who are you?"

The woman averted her gaze and appeared to search for a suitable answer. Then she spoke:

"I am the first and the last. I am the honoured one and the scorned one. I am the whore and the holy one. I am the mother of my father and the sister of my husband, and he is my child. I am the barren one, yet many are my sons.

"I am knowledge and ignorance. I am shame and boldness. I am strength and I am fear. I am war and I am peace. I am the silence that is incomprehensible and the idea whose remembrance is frequent. I am the voice whose sound is manifold and the word whose appearance is multiple.

"Give heed to me. I am the one who is disgraced and the great one. . . ." She paused, then said with a weighty sadness, "I am the utterance of my name."

Sophia sat in shock. This strange, lovely woman must be stark raving mad, she thought.

The woman herself realized the effect her personal introduction had had, and tried to make amends. She looked Sophia in the eye and said, with a soft, steady voice, "I am God. And my name is Mary."

Sophia struggled to get up. She had no interest in spending

her last moments with some nutcase. "I just stopped here to rest. I think I'll be moving on. Nothing personal." But as she tried to pull her legs in to rise, she fell back in agony.

"You are dying, Sophia. You cannot leave."

Sophia was gasping for breath; this woman was right, there was no way she could muster enough strength to go any farther. Too much blood loss. Shock. Just go with it, she thought. You're on your way out. Go easy . . . just avoid the God-thing with this woman. "Thank you," she said. "For your kindness."

"You're welcome, Sophia," said Mary, smiling.

She hasn't even offered to get help, thought Sophia. She just smiles. This made Sophia nervous. At the risk of prompting the woman to even stranger behaviour, she asked, "What do you want?"

A look of concern changed Mary's face. "I have come here to be with you, Sophia. So that you will know you are not alone. That you have never been alone."

"Where did you come from?"

"Through the statue."

In her state of shock and confusion, Sophia had forgotten the incident with the statue. She looked up. The transmuted likeness of the golden Christ was still there. She turned to Mary and asked, "You saw that too?"

"I caused it."

Sophia began to tremble. "No. . . ."

Mary leaned forward to wipe away the tears overflowing Sophia's eyes; as her hand reached out, Sophia gasped. On the long, slender palm was a horrible, knotted mass of scar tissue.

Mary curled her hand shut, concealing the ancient wound, and spoke with nurturing firmness: "The last time I walked on this planet, my friendship was rejected. Now I have returned, as promised, to reclaim the remaining goodness that lingers."

Sophia had stopped shivering. The raw memory of the altered Christ, and the scar on Mary's hand, lent powerful credibility to this dark woman's claim of being the Almighty. At the

191

same time, something was happening to Sophia's consciousness. She had a sense of clarity and vision that overcame her fear. She felt the need to engage with this encounter, for her soul spoke to her of reaching out and reclaiming. But even with this expansion of her awareness, even in her feeble state, there were questions she had to ask.

"But if you are Mary, why are your hands . . . ?"

"I am the mother and the son," replied Mary. "I am extensions of the Master's true self."

"The Master?" asked Sophia. "You mean God, right?"

"Yes. The elemental source of All."

"But you said you were God."

"I am."

Sophia leaned back and closed her eyes for a moment, then pressed Mary for clarification: "*You* . . . ," she said, "are God . . . ?"

"Yes, Sophia," Mary said patiently.

"Then . . . who was Jesus?"

"He too is God."

Sophia sat quietly for a few minutes with her mouth open. "But we were taught that you were . . ."

"Human?" asked Mary.

Sophia nodded.

"Well, to a degree I was . . . I was every bit as human as my son. The Master willed that both Jesus and I walked this planet as perfect human incarnations . . ."

"Of Himself . . . right?"

"Not *Him*self," said Mary, shaking her head. "The Master is not male or female, but possesses all essence of masculine and feminine. All creation has sprung from the Master's dyadic self. All of life is but a manifestation of the Master."

"But I . . ."

"It is the truth, Sophia."

Sophia began to feel something lift within her; there was an honest directness to Mary's words. Yet it was difficult to give up everything she had been taught about God and eternal life.

192

"What about the churches? The bibles? Priests and nuns? How much does all that have to do with God? They can't all be wrong, can they? Some of it must be true."

Mary bowed her head. "No," she said flatly. "There is very little truth left in the whole of Christendom."

Sophia felt her heart heave. "It's all a lie?"

"It happened so long ago," said Mary sadly. "So very long ago. The deception . . . the deliberate alteration of the Word." Her voice fell to a whisper. "So many were lost. . . ."

"What do you mean?"

"There was a great divorce in Christianity," said Mary. "It was during a time of social change and reordering. Of course, the damage was done over an expanse of time . . . but the very beginning of the deception can be isolated to a single man and a single piece of parchment."

"Who was the man?" asked Sophia.

"He was Clement I, the Bishop of Rome. In the ninety-fourth year after the execution of Jesus, Clement wrote a letter to the church in Corinth, after an uprising stripped the bishops there of power. A group of Gnostic priests —"

"Gnostic? What's that?"

"The Gnostics were early Christians; they were labelled heretics by the orthodox church. They believed in dualisms and even pluralisms when it came to understanding God, unlike the monotheistic view of the Roman church. But even more threatening was their tendency to describe God in sexual terms."

"Sexual? What do you mean?" asked Sophia.

"Many Gnostic Christians saw God as a creative force fuelled by the power of both sexes. They believed in the equality of God's dual sexual nature, and extended it to equality between men and women in their communities . . . which was not what Rome had in mind."

"You mean this Clement wanted to keep women out of the church?"

"Not just the church, Sophia. Although he perceived the

193

overthrow in Corinth as an attack against the 'spiritual hierarchy', he took advantage of the incident to start a campaign for the subjugation of women generally. At that time the Roman church was one of the most powerful institutions of government. And like any other human administration, it was inevitably destined for corruption. Clement used his office to dictate a twisted theology, and that theology was the subject of the letter to Corinth . . . which was a most crucial deviation in human history."

"Why?" asked Sophia. "What did it say?"

"Basically he charted the course for the repression of women ever since then. He said that the God of Israel alone rules on high; that He is the master we must obey, the final judge who lays down the law, punishing the heretical and rewarding the pious." Mary leaned forward and asked Sophia, "But how do you think the Master's law was to be administered?"

"Well, through the church, I guess," answered Sophia.

"Precisely. You see, Clement claimed that God had willed the authority of his reign to the bishops, priests, and deacons of the orthodox church. Whoever refused to bow to the church leaders was guilty of insubordination against God Himself."

"And of course all the administrators were men."

"Of course. And from that point on, for the first time in the Christian community, there was a division between the clergy and the laity. And this division grew to separate the Gnostics from the fold."

"And no one fought against all this?"

"Sophia, literally an army of men and women tried to contest it. But the Roman church made sure there was no repeat of the Corinth episode. The policy was enforced with fearful rhetoric, and even secretive torture and murder. It all became very ugly. But the worst was yet to come."

"What was that?"

"The final blow against Christianity and truth," declared Mary. "About a generation after Clement, another bishop in Syria, Ignatius of Antioch, defended Clement's principles and enforced an even more rigid version of the church hierarchy. Ignatius developed the principle 'One God, one bishop'; he professed that humanity could *only* access God through the church, and *only* through the men who administered the church. Ignatius went so far as to warn people to revere the bishop as if he were God Himself."

Sophia nodded silently. "So the church isn't the way to rejoin God," she said wearily.

Mary met her eyes steadily. "The church is a path that leads in the opposite direction."

# CHAPTER 18

Through the barrier of shock that walled in Lucius Del Roberts' brain, a tiny familiar sound penetrated.

*jingjingjing*

It took a few seconds of floundering for the reverend to realize that he was laid out on his back. As he scrambled to his feet, thick shards of glass and dead birds fell from his chest, arms, and legs. He staggered on quivering legs, vision blurred; his heart was racing. He grabbed hold of a pew for support.

Despite the coldness blowing into the cathedral, he was sweating profusely. The wintry wind wrapped tightly around his damp body, burning his flesh with ice-fire. He fell back to his knees, shaking violently.

*jingjingjing*

Roberts turned his head and blinked, then squinted for focus. The goat had returned and stood a few yards beyond, up the centre aisle. Beside the goat was the black horse.

The reverend couldn't move; he just knelt with his arms around his torso, shivering, teeth clacking. All he could do was stare back, puffing short bursts of frozen breath.

The goat and horse stood silently, motionless, watching him from behind a rising curtain of their own breath. From the gaping hole above, brown withered leaves, old seed pods like tiny sarcophaguses, and powdery whirls of dusty snow gathered around Roberts' shivering form, as the cold stiffened his wet clothing. His muscles ached from tensing against the cold. He wanted to shrivel up inside the freezing shell of his clothes. But a movement behind and above him startled him into turning around. What he saw made him scream.

"Ave, frater."

The monkey sat on the edge of the stage, one leg dangling. A crown of thorns — a heavy, twisted halo of vine with needle-sharp quills — was perched on its head with an arrogantly comic vaudevillian tilt; strapped to its chest was a hurdy-gurdy. Painted all over the organ were hellish images of humans and animals engaged in acts of dismemberment and copulation.

Roberts stared at the monkey with an open, shivering mouth; he cried loudly, and raised both arms in a plea for mercy.

The monkey's eyes became shinier and darker; it barked, and Roberts screamed again.

He closed his eyes and wept. "Please . . . ," he begged.

The monkey gripped the edge of the stage, then slipped its rump over to lower its dangling leg until the leathery foot silently touched the carpet. It lumbered forward, stepping over the dead birds and glass. In its other hand was a length of electrical wire that stretched back up on the stage. Roberts noticed that the wire was taut — something was being dragged. As the monkey neared, it gave a few tugs on the wire and the large, silvery fish with the torn spine dropped heavily from the stage. The wire was crudely looped through the fish's mouth and out its gill; it continued beyond.

The monkey stopped in front of Roberts and squatted, then scratched its testes against the carpet, grunting. It stared at him and grunted once more, with an intonation that made him examine its face. The brute's flat black nose twitched a couple of times, and it peered through the reverend's pleading arms, homing in on the little girl's body. It snorted, rose, and took a step around him, its eyes locked on the small, bloodied corpse.

"NO, DON'T!" Roberts found himself yelling.

The monkey bared its fangs and snapped at his face. Roberts fell back to the base of the stage and the beast squared off, facing him where he cowered, as if daring him to interfere again.

Roberts hid his face in his hands and wailed.

The monkey approached the dead child and brushed off a pair of dead starlings from her chest, and a severed fox-sparrow's wing that fanned her cheekbone.

The beast tilted its ugly head, seemingly examining the broken body from head to toe. It sniffed at the blood in her hair and on her face, and recoiled, adjusting its crown and snorting the scent from its nostrils. Next, with a long, black finger, it gingerly poked at the child's eye; getting no reaction, it sniffed at her cold lips.

As if finally satisfied, it pulled on the wire, drawing the fish up past the child. It drew in a couple of yards of trailing wire, then raised the child into a floppy sitting position, lifting her by the hair, and proceeded to wrap the wire numerous times around her neck, under her arms, and across her chest, like a spider trussing a fly. After securing the wire to the child's body, the monkey gathered a dozen or more dead birds from the floor and pews and tied them to the trailing wire, spacing the feathered bodies a foot or so apart.

The reverend sat still, his mind unable to absorb any more. His vacant eyes scanned a length of space while his mouth moved continuously, leaking wisps of breath.

When the last bird was firmly fastened to the wire, the goat and the black horse walked down the aisle towards the monkey, who picked up the front end of the wire and waited as they approached. The horse stopped and turned with easy majesty, readying itself to be mounted.

With its free hand, the monkey grabbed hold of the horse's tail. It climbed up the great legs and massive rump to sit at the croup, then busied itself fastening the wire to the horse's tail just below the dock; that done, it walked along the wide back and straddled the withers.

The goat positioned itself in front and looked over its shoulder at the monkey, who responded by bobbing its sloped head. The monkey then grabbed the crank of the hurdy-gurdy and began to turn it, filling the Cathedral of Light with a distorted symphony of shrieking notes and mournful musical phrases that jarred the ear.

The noise stirred Reverend Roberts out of his stupor. He stared at the pageant arranged in the aisle, and the bizarre sound somehow lured him to speak; he asked, in a low, cautious voice, "What is that sound?"

The monkey continued to play the hand-organ, but it turned and replied, "Canor hominis."

Roberts cast his eyes down. "Canor hom. . . ." He looked up at the monkey with a perplexed expression, asking, "The Song of Man? What the hell is that supposed to mean?"

The handle of the hurdy-gurdy continued to go round and round, cranking out the noise that the reverend found so compelling in its ugliness. Nothing about it was soothing or beautiful, but there was no avoiding it: this vile song *belonged*. While his mind fired impulses to block the song, his barren soul opened itself as if receiving a lover.

"Ave in perpetuum, frater," the primate called out from atop the black horse. "Ave atque vale." And with that the monkey bowed to Roberts, tipping its crown of thorns, bidding him adieu.

The goat trotted out first, ringing its bell as it went. The black horse shook its mane and followed, as the monkey continued to crank the hurdy-gurdy strapped to its chest. Behind the rump of the horse followed the fish; then the child, dragged along like a rag doll; and the dead birds, one by one, in tow.

But the Song of Man continued to penetrate Roberts, not through his ears, but through his chest — it felt like a burrowing worm. It sickened him. It was alive inside him, probing at the cleft his soul had prepared. After boring through him to his core, it finished hollowing out his soul — sucking at the black residue — leaving a cavity that ached more intensely with each beat of his heart.

As the last of the entangled grotesques disappeared from view, the tremendous emptiness of the cathedral swooped and fell upon his psyche, tripping his mind into free-fall — a plummet that brought final awareness.

There was no confusion.

Only absolute clarity.

Reverend Lucius Del Roberts now knew what had befallen him; now knew what all these visions, these apparitions, were about; and the knowledge weighed upon him with a fear beyond human endurance.

These past weeks of strangeness and anxiety had been a process, an unfolding, as the soul revealed its contents. Purging itself. Emptying itself. The diablerie that had paraded out the back exit of the cathedral was the very contents of his soul, made visible. The monkey had told him as much when it first confronted him in the dressing-room — "Ego sum ego" — thus is the Devil ever God's ape.

All the other spectres had also been aspects of him, all "I", and the terror they had generated grew not from their strangeness but from their affinity. This final awareness imploded the reverend's consciousness, securing him absolute isolation.

He sat cloaked in the finality of self.

I am I.

I am.

Remains.

A figure stood in the doorway of the cathedral's back exit. The morning light that seeped in revealed it to be that of a man. He looked over the state of the cathedral, taking in the ruin.

A strong gust of cold wind blew in from the broken dome and tousled his hair. He pulled the wide collar of his coat closed over his plaid shirt, doing up the top button, and pushed his crooked glasses up the bridge of his nose. Then he walked down the centre aisle towards the stage, avoiding the dark stain in the carpet, and knelt before the shivering shell of the reverend.

Roberts' clothes were now frozen, as was the hair on his head. Two thick cords of mucus hung from his nostrils. His lips continued to shape words.

The man pushed up his glasses again and brought his face close to Roberts'. "Rev'r'nd?" he asked. "It's me, Wendyl. Wendyl Gudhart. Can y'hear me?"

Roberts remained still.

"What's goin' on, Rev'r'nd? Things're strange. The TV say it's 'pandymonium' an' 'a state of emergency'. People's jus' droppin', all over. For no reason. Some people's goin' round screamin' an' others is jus' standin' and' starin' all blank like ... like yer doin'. What's 'pandymonium', Rev'r'nd? Is't like bein' scairt? I think lotsa people is scairt this mornin', 'cause they's jus' droppin' dead. The life sucked right outta them. Sumpthin' inside's evaporatin', or sumpthin'."

Wendyl pushed up his glasses and scratched an ear. He tried to catch some movement in the reverend's eyes. "You scairt too, Rev'r'nd? I ain't. Maybe's I should be, but I ain't. People's goin' crazy, screamin' an' hollerin', but I ain't scairt." He tapped his forehead and snorted. "Pro'bly 'cause I'm too daft." He smiled at his own self-deprecation. "That's what m'mom says 'bout me. Not in no bad way, jus' plain out. Weren't born too quick in the head. So m'mom says, so use yer heart fer thinkin', Wendyl, 'cause your head's not too quick. That's what m'mom says."

Roberts' face was greying. Tiny ice crystals formed in his hair and eyelashes, and on his cheeks. Traces of breath curled from his cold mouth and messy nose to nest in his frozen, blood-ied spikes of hair.

Wendyl's smile faded and he felt the cold penetrating his folded legs. He rubbed his thighs. "Y'cold, Rev'r'nd? Y'ain't got much on. Here y'go." He removed his heavy coat and gingerly draped its weight across Roberts' hunched shoulders. Again he leaned his face in front of the reverend's dull eyes. "No, it's okay. Gotta shirt an' sweater on, so it's okay."

His brow knit and his eyes shifted nervously with thought. "Rev'r'nd? 'Bout what happened with that girl" — he cast a fearful glance at the bloody patch of aisle in front of them — "y'didn't ... didya? People's screamin' an' runnin' away ... no one could find out nothin' fer sure. So I come back. After the lights went off I was pushed out by the crowd, but I come back. T'know."

Wendyl stared into Roberts' frozen face; watched his moving lips, waiting for audible words to spill out. He sat patiently. But the prolonged silence finally convinced him that he was in the wrong: "Shouldn't'a asked . . . ! Y'don' need t'answer, Rev'r'nd . . . 'specially t'the likes a' me. Sorry, Rev'r'nd. But I did come back to ya."

Wendyl nodded to himself and pushed up his glasses. He looked around the empty cathedral and up at the broken dome. The jagged edges looked like the jaws of a shark trying to bite the sky — the thought made him laugh. But when he caught Roberts' fixed glare and stern mouth, he stopped laughing, lest his humour be misinterpreted. He swallowed and put his face close to Roberts' again. "It's gonna be okay, Rev'r'nd. It'll all get fixed. It'll be right agin, don' worry. Cathedral'll be fixed like new an' the congr'gation'll come back. Jus' like I done."

The cold was beginning to make Wendyl shiver. "Gotta go, Rev'r'nd. But y'can keep my coat till I come back, okay?" He stood up and looked down at Roberts staring up the centre aisle. "It's gonna be awright, really. Soon y'can get on with the good fight. The Lord'll provide, 'cause yer givin' so much t'us all. Like the Bible says: y'shall reap what y'sow. Ain't that right, Rev'r'nd? The Lord'll help ya fix it. The Lord'll help ya 'cause yer givin' so much t'everybody. So much hope."

Wendyl shoved his hands deep into his pockets and began to walk up the aisle, huffing clouds of frozen breath.

"Birds. . . ."

Wendyl turned around. "Say somethin', Rev'r'nd?"

Robert's voice was distant and small: "Hope . . . thing with . . . feathers. . . ."

Wendyl came back and crouched in front of Roberts' unblinking eyes. "What're y'sayin', Rev'r'nd?"

"Birds. . . ."

"Birds?' Wendyl looked around the cathedral. "Lotsa nothin'
and broken glass in here, Rev'r'nd, but ain't no birds. No birds.
No birds in here at all."

One tear gathered enough fullness to brim and fall from
Lucius Del Roberts' eye.

Wendyl looked puzzled. Shocked. "Jeez, what's wrong,
Rev'rend?" he asked. "Doncha cry. Everything'll be fixed an'
made right. Doncha fret." He quickly wiped away the tear from
Roberts' face and rubbed it hard into the pile of the carpet —
obliterating all trace of weakness. Then, with resolve, he proceeded to undo the collar button of his plaid shirt, removing
something from around his neck. "Yer in a hurtin' way, ain'tcha,
Rev'rend? So I got somethin' fer ya." The simple man put his
opened palm almost directly under the reverend's heavily running nose. On it lay a silver chain and medallion. "M'mom gave
it t'me long time ago. She used to say it were my patron saint.
Wearin' it's s'pposed t'guard me or somethin'. Seein's yer sorta
scairt like all the others . . . I want ya t'have it, okay? I don' think
my mom'd mind."

Wendyl pushed up his glasses, then carefully placed the
chain around Roberts' frozen head and laid the medallion on
the reverend's chest. "There," he said.

He took a moment to admire the result, smiling, then looked
at the reverend's cold lips still mouthing their silent phrases and
nodded. "Yer welcome, Rev'r'nd."

Wendyl raised his chin, rebuttoned his shirt collar, and stood
up. "Really gotta go, Rev'r'nd. Be seein' ya, okay?" He paused.
"God bless."

He pushed up his glasses again and slowly walked up the
centre aisle towards the back exit. The sound of glass crunching
underfoot echoed loudly throughout the cathedral.

Roberts jolted with a spasm. He lowered his head and tried to
focus on the silver medallion on his chest. He moved his arm up
and took the medallion between stiff white fingers and raised it

to his face, and slowly turned it around. The silver disc was embossed with the likeness of Saint Jude.

Saint Jude. Patron saint of lost causes. His cold hand curled around the medallion. "No . . . birds . . . at all. . . ."

## Chapter 19

Langley looked at his watch; it read 7:06. The morning sky was still black and cold, but a grave impatience was dawning within him, illuminating his purpose. "I've got to be going now," he said as he rose to his feet.

Gabby nodded solemnly. "Very well, Joseph."

"Goodbye, Gabby."

"Bye, Joseph."

Langley didn't move. He stood still, his gaze distant.

"Off to see your brother?" asked Gabby.

Langley blinked without making eye contact. "My brother . . . ," he said slowly. "Yes . . . it's time. . . ."

"Here then, just a moment," said Gabby. He turned to gather up something from the ground, and raised his cupped hands to Langley. Inside was freshly fallen snow that had powdered the ice of a puddle. "To wash that blood off your face."

Joseph Langley looked at the offering cradled in the twisted hands. He said nothing.

"Quick now, Joseph, it's melting."

Slowly, Langley cupped his hands below Gabby's.

"Now rub it all over your face. . . . That's it."

Langley mopped his face with his coat sleeve, then silently walked away. When he arrived at the mouth of the alley he stopped and turned. From the street, the interior of the alley seemed that much darker — just a tunnel. He called back, "Gabby?"

"Yes, Joseph?" replied the blackness.

"Do you really want to know what happened? How I got

covered in blood?"

There was no response.

"You still there, Gabby?"

"Yes, I'm still here."

"Well? Do you?"

"If you wish."

Langley cracked a grin at the dark alley. "What would you say if I told you I almost killed God tonight?"

There was no response.

Langley's grin evaporated. He lowered his head and walked away.

A bitter wind passed before the opening of the alley. "I would say, you are indeed killing Him," replied the blackness finally. "Very slowly and very painfully."

Back in the alley, behind the cardboard box, Gabby dug out a briefcase from between a stack of wooden fruit crates and some garbage cans. He dragged it up to the opening of the alley, into better light, released the latches, and placed it on his stumps to check out the contents. Lengths of nylon rope, handcuffs, a metal file, kitchen and carpet knives, a small jar of Vaseline, and a roll of duct tape were in the bottom half of the case; in the filing pockets of the lid were newspaper clippings about dead women, mostly prostitutes, with dates and times written in pen across the top. Some of the clippings had words jotted along the borders — "Eden Restored", "Purified", "Suffer the Lambs", and, most disturbingly, "Touched by an Angel".

In the top pocket of the lid was Eleanor Roberts' diary. Gabby pulled it out and thumbed through the pages, tilting them towards the street to read better. The elegant penmanship revealed horrific details of mental and physical anguish, prayers and poems to God, heart-breaking laments for her missing older son, and documentation of a young boy's torture as penance — page after page of human suffering.

Gabby closed the diary and put it back in the briefcase,

snapped it shut, and bowed his head, whispering, "Such frailty. . . . Such pain. . . ."

A soft glow moved within the alley; occasionally a tiny light, like a spark, flashed in the darkness and flew upwards.

Gabby sat in the middle of the alley with his arms outstretched, palms up. Around his head was a swirling mass of flickering that spun faster and faster, causing his long hair to rise and flow. He closed his eyes. "Master?" he called out. "It is I." Tears began to seep through his closed eyelids. "Their courses are chosen. The brothers are meeting. O Master . . . there are so many scared . . . made blind by fear . . . their souls now camouflaged from You . . . to be eternally forgotten. . . ." He opened his eyes wide with foreboding and sadness. "Master, the gathering . . . all the lost aspects . . . I fear You reap an empty harvest. Why did You will this to be? All may be lost. . . . Will there be enough aspects?"

There was only silence. And darkness.

The swirling mass of lights that surrounded Gabby's head dispersed and floated skyward. He lowered his head into his shaking hands and continued to cry. In a small voice, he spoke in dread: "I know nothing. . . . I fear, Master . . . I fear. . . . Less and less is recognizable. I can barely recognize myself, Master . . . this semblance, this semblance I fear may become more than just a cloak . . . it feels more like a coffin. . . ." He wiped his wet eyes. "What am I? Who am I, Master? Nothing seems certain. . . . "

And the Master responded: "You are Gabriel, the Annunciator. Gabriel the Merciful. Gabriel the Vengeful. Gabriel, the Revelator. You are he who heralds death, he who occupies the seat to My left. You are My beloved angel."

"Oh Master," replied the archangel, "how will all this end?"

"Carry on, Gabriel. The Gathering continues."

Gabriel wiped his eyes again. "Yes, Master."

The fear and anxiety vented by the archangel caused the

sheath of his human semblance to become uncomfortable, warm and sweaty. He itched at his moist neck and loosened the collar of his ragged coat for relief. In doing so, his fingers caught something that made a sound — a tiny sound muffled by the layers of grimy clothing. With his thumb, he pulled out a strap that circled his neck. He cast his dark goat-eye down to see the small bell dangling from it, and gave it a tiny shake.

*jingjingjing*

He closed his hands around the small bell, and tears gathered in his eyes as he accepted the Master's command: Thy Will Be Done.

The dawn settled grey and still over the empty Cathedral of Light. Joseph Langley stood on the frozen lawn and stared at the great building of sculptured stone and concrete. He was in the middle of an elaborate topiary garden. The ornamentals were trimmed into human forms with arms raised in silent hosannas, but the cold weather had reduced these tree-people to skeletons of metal and bare branches. Through the torso of one tree-person, Langley could make out the broken glass dome. The longer he stared at it, the more it looked like a large mouth screaming to the heavens.

**Azrael . . . ?**

So few have reclaimed the divine, thought Langley. Rediscovered the God within us. It's not your fault, little brother, you can't — Mother's Eve-canker killed it in you. But you are one of the fortunate. You have me.

**AZRAEL !**

Langley covered his ears and spoke aloud in a forceful tone: "I won't let you suffer any more. Won't let you be overlooked. . . ."

**AZRA** — ! Langley squeezed his head. *Stop it!*

**Azrael . . . ?** He clenched his teeth. *Fuck you!* He began to shake, unable to control himself.

**Azrael ?**

"Okay, I'll listen," said Langley. He collapsed, grabbing hold of a tree-person's leg, crying silently into the dead, sculptured branches.

**I sense hesitance.**  "I know," replied Langley. "I'm scared."

**It's no different.**  "It is! He's my brother."

**Perhaps you are right.**  Langley nodded.

**His salvation is paramount.**  "He was just a baby. . . ."
**The others were meaningless**
**in comparison.**

**Don't fail him.**  "I'M SO SCARED!"

**You are scared because you**  Langley was choking on
**won't admit to it — who**  his sobs. "I. . . ."
**you are, what you are.**

**Azrael, listen to me. Once you admit the truth, the righteousness of your quest will become apparent again. It will wipe away your fears. It will save your brother. Admit to it — who you are, what you are.**

"I know, I know," said Langley, pulling himself up. "Only I can do this. Only I can save him." He wiped away his tears as he made his way out of the topiary garden and headed for the Cathedral of Light.

An exit door on the east side of the cathedral was slightly ajar, wedged open by a hymn-book dropped during the panicked departure of the congregation. Langley pulled the door open and entered quietly, easing the door back to close on the slightly crushed hymn-book.

He stepped into a long, brightly lit corridor with grade linoleum flooring, cinderblock walls painted grey, and fluorescent lighting — a utility corridor. A cold wind was blowing from within the cathedral. Langley could feel his heart beating in his chest, and his face was hot and prickly with anxiety. Somewhere inside this building was Lucius Del Langley. His throat tightened as he thought of his baby brother, and memory-flashed popped in his brain like flashbulbs.

*I'm coming, Lucius. It'll be all right.*

At a canter, Langley blindly approached the end of the corridor. He didn't feel the pain this caused his injured buttocks. He took no notice of the scattered stuff that littered the floor: clipboards, headsets, papers, a woman's shoe, keys — evidence of frenzy. He saw none of it.

The wind was now stronger and colder, slapping his face. He slowed his pace to a walk. In front of him was a drawn curtain of heavy black material. Slowly he peered around it to see a vast white stage and fluted columns. Like a deer venturing out of a thicket, he stepped onto the stage. He walked past the pulpit and gazed out at the rows of seats, the TV cameras, the shattered glass.

Langley looked up at the broken dome and felt the hard, cold air swirling around the brim of his hat. He closed his eyes. *Where are you, Lucius? It's all over. The pain. The fear.*

He was about to turn and look elsewhere when something caught his eye. In the centre aisle — a dark patch in the carpet. He took a couple of steps forward to get a better look. It seemed like blood. Was it Lucius's? Had something happened to his brother before he could make things right? Was he injured? Dead? Langley's mind whirled with scenarios explaining the vacancy of the cathedral, the damage, the blood. Impulsively he called out, "Lucius . . . ?" His brother's name sailed on the echo, but there was no reply. In a high, trembling voice, he whispered, "It's Joey."

It was then that Langley saw it. Through the burning of his tears, rising thin, almost invisible, over the edge of the stage — a wisp of frozen breath. He waited, his stomach tightening. There, again. Ever so faint.

Langley quietly made his way to a set of six white steps and walked down. In the face of the stage wall was a large fire extinguisher; he opened the glass door and silently removed it, and ran his hand along the thick metal base. He walked along the curved stage, raising the extinguisher with each step, side-stepping the shards of glass. The carpeting made his approach silent. As he neared the centre of the stage front, he stopped and stretched his neck forward to see the source of the breathing. His eye caught a pair of shoes, cuffed trouser hems, and bent knees.

Langley snapped his head back and held his breath. Somebody was sitting there! His arms shook from holding the extinguisher up high; his grip tightened. He waited to see if the person would move, if the person had seen him peer around the stage. But there was no sound. Again he looked around; this time he took in more than the shoes and knees — an elbow and an extended forearm with a clenched fist. Dangling from the fist was a thin jewellery chain. The person remained seated, motionless.

Langley's back and shoulders tightened as he stepped forward, the extinguisher raised above his head. What he saw paralysed him.

The huddled, freezing man didn't move or react to Langley standing above him. His wide eyes didn't blink. Only his blue lips moved slowly.

"Lucius . . . ?" asked Langley, shocked.

There was no acknowledgement.

"Lucius Del Langley," he repeated, louder. "It's me. Your brother."

The hearing of the almost forgotten surname stirred something within the reverend. He looked up. His dilated pupils were

*211*

unseeing at first; then they became black pinholes of recognition. "Joey?" The reverend's eyes grew shiny with tears of joy. "That you, Joey . . .?"

"Yes, it's me — your brother —"

**The last lost lamb.**

" — Azrael."

The fire extinguisher came down on the reverend's head, caving it in, as Joseph Langley's soul resonated with a howl of haunting for what once had been.

## CHAPTER 20

Thomas lay sprawled on his side, limp and exhausted. He could no longer muster the strength to gather himself upright. A chill was coursing through his body, making him shiver.

Saint Peter dreaded the thought of pressing on, of revealing the balance of Thomas's fate; each word brought the Master's conditioned decree closer to fulfilment.

But what could he do? How does one actually deny God? And how did one cast an objective eye upon such a matter? Love seemed to be acting as the impetus for disobedience. Could this be? Love turning against its source? The perversity of these musings frightened Peter, but his love for the Master and the protective instincts aroused by the circumstances could not be denied. Failure to reveal Thomas's fate would be a transgression of God's will, but obedience threatened the Master and the hereafter. This should have never been allowed to happen. Peter felt sickened once again, wanting to blame the Master for all this. He foolishly wanted to conceal the thought, but knew too well that, the instant it was fabricated in his mind, it was out there — looming over his head like some vast, gloomy storm cloud. He yearned for a complete cessation of thought, language, feeling, and love; he yearned for the sanctuary of stasis. But it wouldn't come. God would have none of it; this frailty, this inability to obey. Peter was sure that his Master would punish his irresolute soul.

Whether it was his own guilt or the Master's displeasure — Peter couldn't tell — some powerful urge prompted him to proceed. "Thomas . . . we must continue. . . ."

"STOP! Please, please . . . why don't you just kill me?" pleaded Thomas. "Get it over with!"

"I can't."

"Why do you insist on torturing me?"

"I don't want to torture you," explained Peter. "I don't even want to be here. But you have to know. And I have been" — he wanted to say "forced", but suppressed his rising anger — "appointed . . . to ensure that you understand the circumstances that governed your life and ultimately divorced you from the Master."

"Divorced?" asked Thomas ruefully. "I never rejected God from my life. I'll admit I didn't exactly embrace Him with open arms, but I thought about Him; wondered what He was like. I often questioned His existence, but I sometimes prayed in earnest; I never flat-out abandoned Him. I mean, I always maintained hope that God was around, that there was an order or a reason for the way things are, but I also had my doubts . . . I mean, shit, Peter . . . that's normal, isn't it? Human, right?"

Saint Peter's vibrant eyes became distant and hollow; his voice took on a menacing resonance. "Well, the Master abandoned you, Thomas."

"But why? Was I that bad a person? I wasn't evil, was I?"

"No, Thomas. You weren't a bad person and you certainly weren't evil. You were abandoned because you are not of the Master."

Thomas weakly lifted his head from where he lay. "Not of HIM? How can I be not of Him? Isn't He the creator of all things? I was born and lived on His earth as one of His creations."

"No, Thomas. Your relation to the Master is a remote and distant thing. To the Master, you are like a lost pup approaching an unfamiliar bitch with whelp."

"How do you mean?"

"The Master, your God, recognizes you in type and form," explained Peter sadly. "But you are not from Him, so you are not welcomed for comfort and nourishment."

Thomas was becoming weaker with each retort, waning with each attempt to elevate the status of his soul before God. "But what could I have done? How could I have become closer to God? What does it take to gain His favour?"

Saint Peter shook his head sadly. "There was nothing you could do, Thomas. No prayer could have saved you. No magnanimous act or thought could have protected you from His apathy. Your fall from grace was caused by interference. Human interference."

"Then why am I suffering?" Tears of despair were filling Thomas's eyes; he felt as though he were experiencing a new form of death. "Why aren't the people responsible being punished?"

The immortal knelt down and placed his hand upon Thomas's head. "Understand that their fate is none of your concern; it is the business of heaven. The Master will deem their eternal fate."

"What will He do?"

Saint Peter drew in a painful breath. "I do not know."

"And what about me? How much longer do I have?" asked Thomas despondently.

Saint Peter clasped his hands and shook his head heavily. "I could not even hazard a guess," he replied. "Your remaining time as a man is not controlled by me. I do not drop the black veil."

"So God is milking my existence to the very last beat of my heart? To the final gasp of air? Is this mercy, Peter? Why doesn't He just end it and send me off?"

"The Master won't end your tenure in this life," explained Peter. "He has chosen not to know your fate. By the hands of men were you created, and by their hands you shall be extinguished."

Thomas's eyes rolled back in their sockets from fatigue, the hazel irises flickering like a wind-blown candle flame. "Why is . . . that . . . ? What does . . . that mean . . . ?"

"Thomas," said Peter, in a hushed tone that was almost a whisper, "you must listen to what I'm about to say. This is it — I am handing down your fate. Bare bones, my lost friend. You see, you were created outside the realm of the Master's design . . . put together piece by piece by men's hands . . . an artificial man, an empty shell in the eyes of the Master."

Thomas continued to lie motionless; his eyes were closed now.

Saint Peter bent down on one knee to see if his mortal charge was still earth-bound; single tears squeezed through Thomas's lids to trickle across the bridge of his nose.

Then something must have died within the immortal, for Peter no longer felt compassion for the fading man at his hem; just a sickening objectivity. It was as if all feeling had ceased to exist in his heart; he felt like an unruly beast who was finally broken. He had witnessed enough; he wanted no more of this.

Complete the reckoning.

Obey.

The Master's will was an iceberg. Cold, pure, and immovable, it tore through the hull of Peter's hesitant soul and ensured that Thomas's fate was handed down.

"You were pieced together beneath an artificial eye. Human hands with cold instruments shredded the fabric of life, re-ordered it, and implanted it into surrogate wombs. . . ."

There was a sharp gasp from Thomas's pale lips, and a moan followed by an utterance that Peter had to ask him to repeat. "I said," wheezed Thomas, "Mary's nightmare . . . taken to . . . extremity. . . ."

Saint Peter furrowed his brow. "What does the Virgin Mother have to do with this?" he pressed.

Thomas shook his head and coughed feebly. "Not the Virgin . . . Shelley . . . Mary Shelley's creature . . . the lonesome monster. . . ."

"You're not exactly alone," said Peter. "You were one of six babies created for an experiment that never took place."

Thomas lay like a whipped dog, shaking his head in misery.

"It was an experiment intended to improve the retaining capacity of the human mind; to open barriers; to tap into mysteries," explained the saint. "Vain humans delving into areas they had no business tampering with. What . . . what has become of the human animal, that it wants to improve upon what is already perfect?" He shook his head. "So short-sighted . . . lacking faith . . . unable to accept the fact that imperfection — regardless how great — is part of the design, part of the beauty of the life pattern." He paced around Thomas's still body. "Creating human life outside that pattern . . . idolizing transcended knowledge . . . becoming gods. . . ." The saint stopped pacing, struggling to control his incredulity. "But the nursery in the laboratory caught fire . . . and your crib being closest to the door was your salvation." Peter paused at the vulgarity of this irony, and felt a wave of nausea. "The five other babies perished in the fire — burned alive."

Thomas stirred, speaking as if in a fevered nightmare: "My dreams! The white room . . . the burning babies. . . ."

Revelation as incubus. Truth without peace. Darkest of enlightenments. Like a spring violet cringing from an arctic blast, Thomas shrank from the horror of the saint's disclosure.

"Since that time," continued Peter, "your life has been a sad little puppet act, your strings dangling, limp. Without guidance you walked the earth alone. Detached from everything. And all the while, the Master remained unmoved, wanting no part of such self-idolatry. Innocent as you are of your own existence, the Master — your God — has chosen not to see divinity mirrored in your elemental parts." The saint shook his head at the misery of it all. "Because you were never intended to exist, because your parts were fashioned beyond the Master's alchemy, and because you sprang from the golden calf of technology, the Master cast a blind eye upon you, Thomas Gorgon, and decreed no part of the Kingdom yours."

Thomas's face was becoming dry and cold, pale as clay; his eyes were grey and coated. "I am . . . a man, Peter . . . ," he hissed. "I . . . I am not" — it was a great strain to finish this assertion — "*nothing. . . .*"

Saint Peter waved his hand through the blackness and terminated the Song of Man that had been hovering about them. He stood in absolute silence and darkness, waiting for Thomas Gorgon to die.

"Time?"

"6:17."

The anesthesiologist removed the mask from Thomas Gorgon's face, as bloodied surgical instruments were wheeled away from the operating table.

"What was his name?" asked the surgeon.

"We don't know," replied the head nurse. "He had no ID."

The surgeon nodded sombrely, peeling off his rubber gloves. "Another John Doe," he said, rubbing the burn of fatigue from his eyes. "Coffee. My kingdom for a cup of coffee. . . ."

A white sheet was lengthened from its fold and pulled over Thomas Gorgon's face, covering him like a drift of snow.

There was a period of transition — from flesh to spirit — after Thomas Gorgon exhaled for the last time; a tangible metamorphosis from his pupal human vessel to a fleeting imago.

Saint Peter watched in awe as the corpse purled with activity, like a small child playing beneath a heavy coat; he could hear soft, short bursts of gas issuing from Thomas's dead mouth; he could see the cold, chalky flesh rippling. Thomas's back rose and his spine arched grotesquely to the sound of splintering and tearing, as the top of a translucent bubble emerged.

The bubble pulsated slightly, coloured like watery milk with a bloodswirl; it remained motionless for a few moments, and then, with a final violent thrust that buckled the lifeless shell, pushed through to reveal itself as a head, followed by an anatomy loosely akin to human; it stepped out of Thomas's twisted, empty body like a new Adam into a new Eden.

Saint Peter recoiled, speechless.

The creature was lanky and of short stature, standing no taller than four feet, with a long neck; from narrow, sloping shoulders hung limbs that were gangly and smooth; it possessed no genitals; although its facial features were recognizably anthropoid and intelligent, hairless brute shadowings lent a fierceness to the brow, jaw, and nose.

Peter sat trembling as he watched the creature scrutinize its own nakedness; watched it scan its surroundings with opaque eyes, measuring the blackness with slow animal gestures. Then, suddenly, the creature locked in on the sight of Thomas Gorgon's corpse. It sidled over to the broken body and crouched to examine the tattered hole in the back with a slender, milky finger.

Peter could see the back of the creature's head pulsating rapidly beneath the bloodswirl, where the brain pan should have been. Was it pulsating in fear? Thought? Perhaps anger?

It snorted and turned towards the immortal, approaching with a simian gait. "How long have I been dead, Peter?'

"Thomas . . .?" replied the saint faintly.

"How long, Peter?" asked Thomas again, squatting chimp-like.

"Just a moment, Thomas. Are you in pain?"

"No. I feel all right." He looked at his long fingers and short palms. "What's happened to me?"

"I don't know. You've undergone some sort of regressive conversion . . . to some primordial origin . . . an elemental starting-point."

"Starting-point?" mused Thomas. "Of what? I've come to an end, Peter. God has forsaken me and has turned me into this . . . this thing. . . ."

Saint Peter gathered himself up and straightened his habit. He stepped up to Thomas and reached out his hand. "May I . . . touch you?"

Thomas felt a pang of self-consciousness, and bowed his head in embarrassment at his new form. Peter quickly retracted his hand. "Forgive my crassness, Thomas. I wasn't thinking."

"It's still me, Peter. Just reborn, I guess. Why has God changed me this way?"

"I really don't know. I wasn't sure what to expect when you died, but I never expected . . . well . . . *this*."

"So this isn't the usual transformation?"

"No," replied the saint, vexed. "I don't know what any of this means."

Thomas slowly scratched his apeish brow in thought. "Is there any way of finding out?"

Saint Peter had begun to pace in a quick and agitated manner, his hands tightly clasped behind his back.

"Thomas," he said, in a grave murmur, "a word in communion with the Master is in order."

Thomas sat absorbed, troubled by the realization that he no longer had a gender. He tenderly touched the spot where his long milky legs met in union, feeling the smooth patch where an appendage had once hung — and something caught his eye, something like a firefly or a popping cinder from a campfire punctuated the bleakness. He looked up to see Saint Peter sitting in a meditative position, with a flurry of tiny lights circling his head, like satellites. With each revolution more and more lights appeared, burning brighter and brighter. The orbiting pinpoints gathered such momentum and density that they almost completely enveloped Peter's head, in a vortex of radiance that swirled at an incredible speed.

Thomas flinched at the sight, covering his smooth head. "Peter . . . ?" He crouched beside Saint Peter and placed a hand on his shoulder. "What just happened?"

"I was in communion with the Master," replied the saint. "He has revealed your fate."

"And — ?"

"You are to be cast into the Parahian Latitude."

"The Parahian Latitude," echoed Thomas. "Is that . . . hell?"

"No, Thomas, it's not hell. It isn't even a place. The Parahian Latitude is not of space or time or dimension; it's less than a void."

Thomas folded his long fingers and placed them on his head, covering the bloodswirl. "Less than a void? How . . . ?"

Peter raised a hand and shook his head. "Don't even try to rationalize it or ask me to explain it, Thomas; it's ineffable. The very ineffability of this latitude actually lends reason to your new form. You see, the Parahian Latitude is in need of being invented. Do you follow?"

"No. I don't understand at all."

Peter sighed. "Unlike being . . . how can I put it? . . . unlike being 'saved' or 'damned', whereby one's eternal fate and all its consequences are handed down from another source, your destiny remains undetermined."

"I'm afraid that doesn't help much."

Peter placed both hands firmly on Thomas's sloping shoulders and looked him straight in the eye, speaking with deliberation. "Everything must be reinvented, Thomas. Everything. Even yourself. You are at the cusp of a primordial alpha. That's why you look the way you do — your eternal necessities are to be furnished by yourself, from yourself, and for yourself. Every one of them. However fulfilling or incomplete these necessities become is entirely dependent upon you."

"Reinvent everything?"

"Yes."

"Even . . . myself?"

"Yes."

A long silence hung between them.

"But . . . how . . . ?" asked Thomas.

"I don't have an answer."

"Well then, how do I get to this Parahian Latitude?"

Peter smiled sadly. "It doesn't exist yet. You have to

establish it."

"When should I start? How do I begin? I'm scared, Peter."

The saint opened his mouth to speak, but couldn't find any words. He turned his back and stepped away in contemplation.

Thomas stood alone, watching Peter walk away pensively; then he looked over at the hunkered mass of his own mortal remains. He sat down and drew a deep breath to help steady his quivering nerves; fearful and unsure of whatever frontier lay ahead, he closed his eyes. The bloodswirl on the top of his head slowly began to stir.

Peter suddenly turned to address him. "Perhaps you —"

But Thomas Gorgon was gone.

Standing alone, Saint Peter felt a sadness seeping back into his heart. The cold mask of objectivity could now be lifted; it was over.

A warm tear trickled down his cheek as he whispered, "Goodbye. . . ."

The first strains of the Master's beckoning caught Peter unaware and startled him; they reverberated through his frame and tugged at his soul, calling him back to the Master's realm. Dread washed over his mind, thick and heavy, like black oil. He could not think to act.

It is over now.

It is over now.

The summons was becoming increasingly insistent and forceful within him, making him quake with indecision and foreboding. But he called upon the reserves within himself, his inner sanctum of strength, and with slow purpose lowered himself on bended knee, in prayer for one misbegotten lamb. He prayed that Thomas Gorgon, wherever he was, possessed the symmetry and scope to conjure up a greener and more tranquil pasture on which to lie.

The immortal pulled the hood of his habit over his head.

*O Master, I am lost.*

*O Master, I am lost.*

The beckoning persisted as Saint Peter's heart hammered in his chest.

## CHAPTER 21

The two women spoke at length of the men, the politics, and the historical events that had turned the Roman church into a spiritual vacuum. Sophia then asked Mary, "If the church is not the way to salvation, surely the Bible offers the truth?"

Mary fought back tears; she couldn't speak.

Sophia felt uncomfortable with her silence. "Don't tell me the Bible is not the word of God. . . ."

"The fragments that were chosen to be canonized, the fragments that became what you now call the Holy Bible, are indeed the Master's Word" — Mary wiped tears from her face with her sleeve — "but they represent only part of the truth."

"I can't believe this," said Sophia softly.

"You see, after the year 200 there is virtually no record of women as prophets, teachers, healers, or evangelists . . . with the canonization of a Bible stripped of female contributions, the subjugation of women was complete. The men who controlled the church controlled every aspect of the Christian community, and they deliberately obliterated women as active spiritual citizens."

"Whatever happened to those writings?" Sophia asked. "The ones that contained the female aspects of God?"

"Many were destroyed by the church — burned. Others faded to become oral mythologies; still others were locked away or buried, to be lost for centuries."

Sophia brooded quietly. "Why was there such a need to suppress anything female?" she asked at last. "Was it done for money, status . . . what?"

224

"The money and the social status were secondary benefits. The real reason was to conceal the most elemental and obvious of truths. But in concealing it, the bishops and their church destroyed relations between the sexes, and the purity of human faith and worship as well."

Sophia sat absorbed, her eyes wide with astonishment. "What truth?"

"The truth that the power to create life exists because every female, of every species, contains the entirety of the Master's genius inside her. The church was determined to distract people from that power, and from thoughts of the Master's sexuality, so it forged a campaign that removed all sexual powers from its presentation of God. The first step was to strip women of their spiritual life; the second was to change the perception of the sexual act itself. Sexual union was reduced to base, animalistic behaviour. People were gradually brought to believe that copulation was something they had in common with other animals, when in fact . . ."

"It was something animals had in common with God," answered Sophia.

"Exactly," said Mary. "And the sight of a woman full with child was never again truly revered as a divine and holy thing. You see, Sophia, each bearing of young — from the tiniest mouse and sparrow to women like you and me — is a duplication, in miniature, of the process the Master endured in creating the universe. The sight of it should always be worshipped."

At the mention of herself and pregnancy, Sophia cringed. Mary proceeded with her explanation, apparently unaware of her withdrawal. "The passage of time only strengthened the bishops' deception. The hidden mystery of creation in the womb became Envy's object of scorn, while the pain and bloodshed of labour become Ignorance's object of ridicule and debasement."

Outside, the howling wind had died and left a solemn silence around St. Peter in Chains. The naked trees were black and cold in the red smear of dawn. All around there was

225

stillness and quiet; no birdsong welcomed the rising light.

Mary and Sophia sat together in a profound silence. The gentle, dark-skinned woman read the anguish and sorrow in Sophia's face, but said nothing; she closed her eyes as if to rest.

Sophia felt cold to her core. She thought of what Mary had just said, and let it settle upon her weakening heart.

"The Master's genius," she repeated to herself. "There was no genius of any kind running through my veins . . . or if there was any, I infected it long, long ago . . . killing it."

Her body had slumped somewhat since being propped up against the pew, and she felt like a deflating parade float, almost ready for storage. She took another look at herself; she was almost completely covered in her own unholy blood. She was amazed by how much of it her body had had in store; like the excess that decorated this church, plenitude was the swap for worthlessness.

She exhaled slowly. "Mary," she said softly, "I think I need to be left alone now."

Mary continued to sit quietly with her eyes closed. She feared for Sophia — feared that she was waning, that her clarity was fading. She wondered how much longer Sophia could hold on.

"Mary . . . ?" repeated Sophia. "Please. . . ."

Sophia's fears are shutting me out, thought Mary. Despair is setting in, cannot come to know. . . . She opened her eyes. "Sophia — ?"

The dying prostitute barely moved.

"Sophia!" Mary said again. "What is it you need? Tell me. I must hear it from you. What is your last wish?"

Sophia's lips barely parted, and her words were fragile: "Alone . . . leave. . . ."

"I told you, Sophia — I am here to help you. I won't leave you now. Tell me, Sophia! Tell me! What do you want from me?"

Sophia only shook her head. "Nothing . . . from you. . . ."

Mary grabbed Sophia and held her, eyes wild with tears. She spoke into Sophia's battered face once more: "What do you want God to do? Tell me, what is it you want of God?"

There were tears in Sophia's greying eyes. "Forgiveness . . . ," she breathed.

"Then it is yours," answered Mary. "Can you hear me, Sophia? It is yours . . . but you must forgive yourself."

Sophia's head shook against Mary's shoulder.

"Sophia, listen to me . . . what you seek is not outside of you; not in this church; not in the gospels; it is within. The Master . . . your God . . . does not dwell apart from you. . . ." Sophia looked into Mary's face; she heard the urgency in her voice, saw the compassion in her eyes. "You are God, Sophia . . . and God is you. . . ."

Sophia began to weep, and it hurt her to exert so much effort now.

"Nothing," insisted Mary, "absolutely nothing you could have done in your life, could change or diminish your divine nature. You were born as God."

"No," Sophia said weakly. "I'm a whore. God hates me. Hates my life." Her tears ran down her face. "Mary, look at me. . . . I'm a waste."

Mary stroked Sophia's face and blood-caked hair; she felt the dying woman's face turn into her scarred palm for comfort. "You made hard choices," Mary told her. "You endured much . . . endured things that obscured your vision of yourself. There is no blame. No hate. No loss . . . no loss yet. But your time is short. Sophia, believe my words, words you know to be true. Do not be afraid! See and love, Sophia! Love yourself again . . . love God again." She held Sophia's face firmly in her hand. "God does not exist beyond us, in another realm, apart from humanity. God is everything. Every tree is God! Every grain of sand! Every breath you inhale! And you, Sophia, like every other human being . . . you are God. Humanity is God."

Sophia stared deeply into Mary's eyes, wanting to believe.

"But you haven't much time left, Sophia. The Master has begun . . ."

227

Sophia swallowed painfully. "Begun?"

"Begun the gathering up," said Mary. "The gathering up of all the parts, all the aspects of Godhood that were shared with this planet. The tenure is over. The Master is reclaiming all that is recognizable; all that isn't lost. Please, Sophia . . . before you die . . . forgive yourself."

"Is . . . is that enough . . . ?"

"The most powerful force is love — and the most powerful expression of love is forgiveness. If it is bestowed with truth, it can alter the entirety of the universe in the beat of a heart. Believe."

"No . . . I can't. . . ."

"You can. You must. Forgive what was done to you and what you've done to yourself. Forgive with a pure heart and the Master will recognize you."

"Sounds so sim . . . ple . . . so . . . simple. . . ."

Mary choked back a sob: "It was never complicated — just a sharing on the Master's part and an observance on ours — try to see, Sophia, see past the scarring and bruising on your soul, past the injury, to what was injured. Find that and you have found yourself, God, the Master. All and one. The Master's genius is you, Sophia. See it." Sophia's eyes flickered and Mary spoke into them one last time: "Sophia, please . . . can you hear me? Sophia!" But there was no response. Mary placed her wet cheek upon Sophia's still face. "It's there. . . ."

"I found it. And I became — again. . . ."

The voice came from slightly above Mary's head, startling her. She looked up. Sitting in the pew was Sophia. Mary looked down at the lifeless form in her arms, and laid it tenderly in the aisle.

"How do you feel, Sophia?"

"New."

Mary smiled and let tears of joy spring to her eyes.

"I'm dead, aren't I?" asked Sophia, examining her smooth hands and arms.

"Yes."

Sophia looked around her. "Then why are we still in this church? And why," she asked with wonder, "am I naked? I thought I'd become spirit or something. . . ."

"The complete transformation is a gradual thing," explained Mary. "We are still here because we are waiting to be summoned; and you are not really naked, you are in a state of bodily semblance . . . no one alive can see you."

Sophia stood up and ran her hands over herself, over her semblance. Admired the renewed symmetry of her breasts, her belly, her hips. She smiled at the feel of her new texture, like dense water. She looked at her hands and admired the whiteness and grace of them, for her torn palms were once again smooth; so were her feet. The gash between her ribs was gone and her shoulder was mended; there was no longer any trace of blood or pain, and gone too was the anguish of emotional scarring. Her body and mind were clean. She was a child again.

She stepped out of the pew and past Mary, gliding her fingers through her hair, and suddenly she saw the bloodied corpse filling the centre of the aisle. She halted abruptly.

Mary watched her; watched her circle the battered body slowly, silently; watched her crouch low to examine it. The silence took on texture.

"Who is this poor woman?" asked Sophia softly.

There was a poignant sadness and a rapturous joy in the hearing of this small question; it tugged at Mary's soul. She reached down and took Sophia's hand. She knew she could never tell her the answer, for it would tarnish her renewed innocence with the pain of memory, the pain of confusion; the staining of humanity. She looked deeply into Sophia's wide eyes and smiled. "Come. Let's wait over here; this woman is no longer about us."

They walked to another pew, and sat talking and waiting for the summons. Mary was preparing Sophia for her ascension and reunion with the Master. "You see," she said, "the human soul is another aspect of the Master. What is different about this aspect is its mutability . . ."

"Mutability?" asked Sophia. "What's that?"

"Mutability means that something has the tendency to change or be changed . . . well, the soul, by its nature, is mutable."

"And that's not good?"

"It can be . . . if the change improves the soul; however, if the change alters it in a dark or hurtful manner, the soul becomes unrecognizable. Even to the Master."

Sophia folded her hands on her bare knees and stared at them long and hard while she thought. "So it's possible for God . . . I mean, the Master . . . to lose sight of what was left behind? To no longer be able to recover what was shared throughout the universe? To be unable to regather all the aspects that *make up the Master* . . . ?"

Mary nodded solemnly. "Much of what the Master shared in the creation of the universe is easily retrievable: the animals; the phenomena, terrestrial and celestial; plant life; the elements of earth, water, air, and fire; these aspects cannot change to the point of being unrecognizable. But. . . ."

Sophia saw Mary's mounting distress. "Please, tell me. . . ."

"Don't you see? The Master gave the greatest share of the aspects to the human soul. If too many souls become unrecognizable . . . and cannot be retrieved . . ."

Sophia said in a small voice, "The Master will be diminished. . . ."

Mary shook her head violently, her hands curled in claws of grief: "Not just diminished." She hid her face again, and spoke in a dead tone into her scarred hands: "If the Master cannot retrieve enough of the aspects that were cast out . . . the Master will no longer be."

"No longer be . . . ?"

"The Master will die."

The concept of God dying had a bewildering effect on Sophia; she sat stupefied while Mary wept quietly into her hands.

The two women sat together this way for a long time, until Sophia called out softly, "Mary . . . ? Mary. . . . What do you mean, the Master can die? I thought the Master was immortal."

"How can I put this?" said Mary. "It's all so" — she paused to find the right word — "so terrifying." She took a deep breath. "There was something . . . one thing the Master deliberately withheld and guarded from human knowledge: the possibility that enough of the aspects will not be regathered, that the whole kingdom will fall apart, become unravelled, like a loose tapestry . . . including the Master."

"So the Master isn't immortal or eternal. . . ."

Mary shook her head: "The Master once could have been immortal and eternal. In the beginning. However, in the creation of the universe and the distribution of the aspects — of the end of creation — the Master committed a glorious and potentially tragic act of will."

"What was it?"

"The Master assumed a sort of . . . conditional mortality."

Sophia's face registered horror. "What's so glorious about that?"

Mary spoke in slow, calculated phrases: "Try to imagine, Sophia, how the Master loved the human species, to give it aspects of such incredible beauty and complexity that they allowed the revelation of the self as divine. Although every aspect of the universe is the Master, they all existed without any awareness of that . . . except for humans. All the information and all the tools to interpret that information were available, but the truth had to be sought. Many people became despondent and quit the search, while most of those who persisted chose the wrong means — superstition, myth, philosophy, religion — but a few looked no farther than the poetry of their own flesh and soul, and through the reading of that verse came to interpret the profound kinship of all things. When one sees the similarities instead of the differences, the distinction between, say, a man and a flea is so minuscule that it's laughable. Because with enlightenment one comes to understand . . ."

"That in the end the difference between a man and a flea is no difference at all," said Sophia.

"Exactly," said Mary sadly. "No scientific probing, no intellectual acrobatics, no rhetoric can alter this truth. Glorious indeed, isn't it? A most glorious and loving gift; the opportunity to know."

Sophia nodded. "It really is a glorious thing. But I still don't understand why the Master imposed this . . . what was it? . . . conditional mortality? Isn't that the same as a death-wish?"

A single tear rolled down Mary's cheek. "Yes, it is. The Master gave up so much in the creation of the human animal, making it a suitable companion for eternity — hoping love would be returned for love. And the Master did all this to share the joy of Being. Understand: the Master did not need companionship. The Master existed in perfection before the creation and the sharing of the aspects." She paused momentarily, then concluded: "All acts of love are at risk of being received with indifference. It is this risk that gives the act value. The Master did not want to spend eternity surrounded by blind puppets — that could easily have been done. After the single greatest act of love ever performed, the Master willingly assumed the risk of extinction over an eternity of pain and loss."

"So the existence of the Almighty and the chore of eternal salvation depended upon us. Upon human souls." Sophia shook her head in confusion. "Seems like a pretty poor place for the Master to lay any hope."

"The Master believed it worth the risk."

"And what becomes of all the souls that were saved? What becomes of them if the Master can't complete the gathering?"

Mary lowered her eyes. "They too will cease to exist. They, along with the Master, will be nothing. As if it had all never happened. If at the end of the gathering enough of the aspects have not been recovered, the Master and everything else will just cease to be."

Sophia was still trying to grasp the infinity of the risk. So many questions arose in her mind that she didn't know where to start. "But why would the Master allow any human soul to become unrecognizable?" Immediately she felt a tinge of regret, fearing the question would anger Mary.

But Mary offered a weak smile and answered her: "The Master did not allow any human soul to become unrecognizable; that was the doing of the individual human will. When the Master created the soul and sent her into this world, she was virginal; but human tendencies often debased her, polluted her, and eventually transformed her."

"What do you mean, 'her'?"

"When the human soul was created, the Master gave it a gender," said Mary. "The human soul is feminine, Sophia. It even has what you might call a womb."

"Every human soul? Even men's?"

"Yes, even men's."

Sophia's eyes scanned to and fro as she thought. "But what would a soul need a womb for? And . . ."

Mary raised her hand to hold back the questions. "I am trying to explain how the soul becomes unrecognizable to the Master. When the womb of the soul becomes infected with contaminated seed, the very nature of the soul changes from its proper internal state to an external one, whereby the womb becomes exposed, vulnerable, and prone to more filth." Mary stopped and thought for a few moments. "Think of it this way, Sophia . . . when the womb of the soul alters, it turns outwards much like male genitalia." She looked solemnly to the floor, slowly nodding her head; then looked up and smiled, pleased with her analogy. "Yes, it's actually a lot like that. And after it becomes external the Master doesn't recognize it, for the soul is no longer in its proper form or adhering to its proper nature. A soul so polluted cannot be seen."

"I see," said Sophia quietly. She knit her brow, but all she could think to say was "Is that what happened to me?"

"Yes, and then you recovered — but it almost didn't happen," Mary chided her. "You came very close to being overlooked. Only your act of the will allowed for the renewal, a baptism that let your soul turn inward and become clean again, ready for the Master's seed to flourish within."

Sophia smiled in spite of the sadness between the two women. "Thank you," she said, with utter sincerity. Mary bowed in a regal manner. "And I'm sorry I doubted you," added Sophia. "I . . . I was so frightened . . . felt so alone . . . that I couldn't understand . . ."

"No apologies, Sophia," said Mary. "Doubt is part of the trial, part of the journey; without it, faith loses its lustre."

Sophia nodded; she clasped her hands together and brought them to her lips as she sat in thought. "Why were you here with me, Mary?" she asked. "How could you spend the time? The gathering is well under way, isn't it? But you've spent so much time here. What about all the other souls?"

Mary smiled and reached out to touch her cheek. "Beautiful Sophia . . . always concerned with others. Don't worry, the other souls are being tended to as well. Like all the other chosen immortals, I am scanning the planet, assisting the Master in the great gathering. At this very moment I am also in Peru, talking to a little boy dying of cancer; and in Utah with an ageing Presbyterian minister; and with an Inuit elder in the Canadian tundra; not to mention countless thousands of other places and people all over the planet."

Sophia exhaled softly in relief. "I was worried that I might have been singled out . . . that maybe others would suffer at my expense. I didn't realize." She lowered her head in a sudden rush of embarrassment. "Forgive my vanity . . . my foolishness. I — "

Mary bolted upright.

"What's the matter?" asked Sophia.

"The summons," answered Mary. "The summons has been issued. The Master is calling for you, Sophia."

"We're leaving now?"

"Yes. The time has come to rejoin the Master. Stand up." Sophia stood and faced Mary. "You are going to experience many splendid things in your ascension, Sophia. Are you ready?"

"I am."

Sophia felt Mary's gentle touch upon her eyelids. "Close your eyes." She felt Mary's hands holding her head and heard her whisper something unintelligible. There was a moment of silence, then Mary backed away from Sophia and took both her hands. When Sophia reopened her eyes she saw that Mary, like herself, was crying tears of joy.

"Are you coming with me?" asked Sophia.

"For part of the way. I'll take you before the Master."

Sophia was smiling in ecstasy when she suddenly felt a sharp cramp in her belly. She gasped and doubled over, then looked into Mary's face for an explanation, a reason for this disruption of a perfect moment. Finding no answer, she glanced down and realized what was happening. Between her feet were two tiny drops of blood; then a third. She looked at Mary with an expression of astonishment and awe.

"Beauty restored," said Mary. "Let us go."

Mary wrapped her arms around herself, clasping her own shoulders. Sophia did the same and closed her eyes. Immediately she had a sensation of detachment and weightlessness, as if she were gently spiralling, like the feathers on the shaft of an arrow in flight. All was peace and tranquillity. She felt something against her ankle, soft and airy; then fleetingly against her thighs, her hips, her arms and shoulders; it lifted her hair softly from her back and brushed against her cheeks and brow. It seemed to be gathering momentum and volume all around her.

Although she was not at all frightened, Sophia decided to open her eyes and see what was moving around her body. To her amazement she discovered that she was surrounded by a tremendous flock of pigeons and moths, thousands upon thousands of them; they extended beyond and behind her in a long, dense trail, guiding and even guarding her ascension.

She smiled and revelled in this winged escort; the magnificent sight was almost too much beauty for her to take. And through the screen of beating wings and flittering night-flyers she caught sight of Mary, who extended one arm above her head and pointed. Sophia looked past the pigeons and moths to a long, flat plain of light that had no beginning and no end; it stretched like an infinite ribbon through space. They rose past the edge of this plain — an edge of airy thinness — and stepped onto it while the pigeons and moths continued to fly higher and higher, until they disappeared out of sight into the blackness.

"They're waiting for you," said Mary.

"Who are?"

Mary nodded towards two small specks in the distance along the plain of light. Sophia could barely make them out, and she cast a questioning look at Mary.

Mary smiled and took Sophia's elbow to set her feet in motion. As they walked together Mary kept her eyes forward, keeping the pace brisk, saying nothing. Sophia realized that it would be futile to attempt any questioning now, so she tried to maintain stride alongside Mary.

The brightness emanating from the plain created enough hazy radiance to distort the two specks even as they grew closer, although they were gradually taking on humanoid appearance and stature. Sophia could at least make out that there was a great difference in their size: the taller was more than twice the height of the lesser. Then Mary stopped walking abruptly, and Sophia did the same. "What now?" she asked.

"They'll be here soon," said Mary.

"I told you I would wait. We have both been waiting for you, Sophia."

Sophia's eyes grew wide. "Mama . . . ?"

The smaller figure ran clumsily towards Sophia, arms outstretched, and Sophia fell to her knees to receive the warmth of her sister's touch. "Oh, Joelle!" She held her baby sister, feeling the memory of her skin in her hands and the cool softness of the round face against hers; smelling the summer sun in her hair. "Joelle . . . Joelle . . . Joelle. . . ." Sophia held the small child away to get a better look; she ran her fingers over Joelle's smooth face and through her fine, glossy baby hair: perfectly beautiful. There were no burn marks or scars, and the child's blue eyes betrayed no memory of the explosion; the little girl she held before her was the same one she had last seen by the grain-bins with a handful of wildflowers.

Then Medora approached her two daughters, and the three joined in a long embrace. No words were spoken between them; it was a purity of happiness that no language could have described. After a few minutes, Mary spoke up gently: "The Master awaits."

Medora nodded at Mary, took Joelle in her arms, then said to Sophia, "This dominion of retrieved souls — it is all so beautiful, taking on shape slowly." As they began walking, Medora's face became grave and she added unhappily, "We all hope it will survive the gathering."

Medora, Sophia, and Joelle walked along the plain of light, enjoying their reunion, until suddenly Sophia's feet stopped moving. She couldn't lift them; her soles held fast to the plain like steel to a magnet. Medora and Joelle stopped a few paces beyond, and Medora looked at her eldest daughter with an odd expression of pleading that Sophia could not understand. Joelle extended her little arm, opening and closing her fat fist, beseeching her sister to come. "Mama," Sophia called, "I can't move." Sophia turned to Mary, who was still standing motionless. "What's happening, Mary? What's holding me back?"

"Sophia, you are holding yourself back," said Mary.

Sophia stood there, perplexed. "Me? But, I'm n— I want to join with the Master!"

"And the Master wants to join with you."

"I don't understand."

"Search your soul, Sophia. There you will find something incomplete."

"Incomplete?"

"Something" — Mary paused, finding the right word — "unatoned."

Sophia looked again at her mother and sister, and heard Mary say, "Listen and it will speak to you."

She stood for a long time, slowly burrowing to the core of her soul to peel it away layer by layer, to find what it was she was hiding from herself. As she approached it, the mystery trembled and came to life to course through her body. It whispered to her mind in a familiar gruff voice: Sophia, I hurt.

She knew at that moment that her father was one of the lost, resurrected only long enough to make amends. Seizing the moment, her heart surged with longing to fill what was empty. In a voice squeezed thin and reedy with sorrow, she said, "Papa, I forgive you" — not knowing what benefit, if any, these small words might have upon the fate of Ezra Dépardieu.

Mary walked up behind her and put an arm round her shoulders. "Come on," she said softly, leading her to Medora and Joelle, while Sophia wept quietly.

Joelle reached out from Medora's arms to be held by her sister. Sophia took her little sister and was given a gentle kiss on her cheek.

"Was that painful?" asked Sophia. "For Papa, I mean."

Now Medora started to weep.

Mary sighed. "It's difficult to say with any certainty. . . ." She shook her head. "Only the Master would know. But I would imagine that that sort of resurrection, although brief, must bring a flood of emotions and regrets in your father's soul. Painful? I'm afraid it probably was. I'm sorry, Sophia."

Sophia was silent, then asked, "Do you think my forgiveness helped Papa? Wherever he is?"

"Again, Sophia, I cannot say for sure. But an expression of love can do no harm. I'd like to think you've made your father happier than he has been for a long, long time."

"I hope so," Sophia said softly, wiping her wet cheeks. Medora hugged her eldest daughter and kissed Joelle's head.

Sophia looked down the plain of light. "Is it much farther?"

Mary smiled and prompted mother and daughters onward. "Go on."

Sophia's face fell. "Will I ever see you again, Mary?"

"I hope so, Sophia. I truly hope we all see each other again. Goodbye, Sophia . . . Medora . . . Joelle. . . ." She turned quickly and walked away down the plain of light. Sophia watched her go, feeling a dull ache with each footstep the beautiful immortal took. She called out across the plain of light, "I love you, Mary."

Mary stopped. Without turning around she replied, "I love you too, Sophia."

Sophia looked at her mother, and then back at Mary, still standing with her back to them, and suddenly became aware of something beautiful, something extraordinary, filling her ears and soul; something that swirled and danced all around them. She stared into the blackness that had no boundary, to find its source, but it was everywhere. "Mary—? What's that? It's so beautiful. Is it music?"

"Not exactly. It's called the Song of Man."

The flat sharpness of Mary's words cut through the flowing silk of sound that swirled all about them. "Why do we hear it? What's it for?" asked Sophia.

Mary stood silent for a moment, then made a short sound that Sophia could not decipher as either a laugh or a sob. She turned to her mother, who returned the same worried look.

"For?" repeated Mary. "It's for understanding — for coming to know. It was always there. But in time it was drowned out. There was just . . . too much noise."

Sophia felt the swell of music around her, inside her. How could anything drown this out? "Mary . . . ?"

The shining black braids of Mary's head hung down and she raised her scarred hand abruptly. "The Master awaits."